The Silence of Souls

A Jessie Whyne Mystery

Danni Roan

Danni Roan Writes

The characters and events portrayed in this book are fictitious. Any similarity to real persons, living or dead, is coincidental and not intended by the author.

Contents

Chapter 1

A cool ocean breeze ruffled the waves, tugging at the straw hat on Jessie Whyne's head as she dug her bare toes into the warm sand.

Sunset wasn't far away, and she was enjoying the serenity of the silent shore. Jessie could see an old lounge chair at the far end of the private beach, bright red stripes fading in the coming darkness.

Tucking her knees under her hands, she rested her chin on them, gazing out across the soft waves. A seagull dove, breaking the quietness of the evening, and Jessie lifted her head to watch the bird chase a black puppy that was digging in the sand.

Jessie shook her head, wondering why anyone would let their dog run loose, even on a private beach in Savannah, Georgia. There were leash laws, after all.

As the puppy scurried into the weeds, long legs beating and ears flopping, Jessie rested her head on her knees once more.

The quiet scuff of feet on the sand made Jessie look up, a bright smile flickering across her face. "What are you doing here?"

"I'm on leave," a tall man with a shock of brown hair, standing in spiky splendor despite the humidity, looked down at her, a bright smile gracing his cheerful face. "My uncle may have mentioned you were here."

"It's good to see you, Buzz." Jessie smiled, taking in the man's long, pale legs sticking out of blue and white swim trunks, his flip-flops doing nothing to cover the oversized pasty feet. "Have a seat." Jessie patted the sand next to her. It had been months since she'd seen Theodore Benzelly, and though happy to see him, she felt awkward even as the man flopped down, dusting off his hands and giving her a goofy grin. "What brings you to Savannah?"

Buzz shook his head. "I have some time off." He looked at her. "I was hoping to see you in Macon, but Uncle Paul said you were away." He dropped his head. "I've been past your place a few times, but with work. . ." He shrugged as if that explained everything.

Jessie raised a brow. The words had been delivered in a flat tone as the man gazed out over the ocean, his expression pensive. "How about you? Uncle Paul said you were going on vacation. Did you take time off from the coffee shop?"

Jessie's smile was sad. Last year, Buzz had been her stalwart supporter as she struggled through issues back home, but once the mystery had been solved, she seldom saw the man. Then, turning her head and looking at him, her cheek still resting on her knees as the breeze fluttered her white skirt around her ankles, she shook her head. "I thought you were too busy to hang out with me." The breeze quickened, tugging at her hat, and she grabbed at it, holding it tight to her head.

"I see your mom finally got you to wear that hat." Buzz chuckled, his brown eyes on hers. "Your eyes are the color of the ocean, that blue-green of the sea." His comment fell between them, factual and jarring.

"What?" Jessie shook her head, wondering why he had changed the subject so abruptly. She had hoped Buzz would explain why he hadn't called or even dropped by to check on her. "It's just the light." Her eyes found the horizon, waiting to see what he would say next. The sun, setting behind them, had turned the clouds into a riot of reflected color. The waves glowed with the last rays of the sun, dark and mysterious, yet brilliant with a deeper shade of the sky.

For several minutes, the pair sat staring out at the water, both lost in thought. Jessie was confused by Buzz showing up after not hearing from him for months and his obvious avoidance of her question. She knew that his job as a policeman kept him busy, but hadn't they become friends?

"I'm sorry I haven't called." Buzz finally spoke. "I didn't know if you wanted me to hang around once we cleared up your little problem." He didn't look at her, keeping his eyes on the reflection of the sunset on the sea.

The sunlight glimmered, and Jessie tried to decide what she wanted to tell Buzz. She had been disappointed that once her mystery had been solved, the young man hadn't had time for her. She wouldn't call him a close friend, but he was a friend and had been someone she could talk to, at least for a time. Things changed. Jessie understood that too well. It had only been a month since Jessie's twenty-first birthday, a day that had changed everything.

"I've been put on disciplinary leave," Buzz said, his eyes still on the setting sun as he finally opened up. "It's not that I haven't wanted to see you," he hurried on. "I just didn't know if I was welcome."

"What?" Jessie sat up, turning to look at her friend. "What happened?" She glared, hurt and angry, shocked for a moment. "And we're friends, so of course, I want to see you."

Buzz folded in on himself as the sky went gold. "I almost hit a man we were arresting."

"Oh, my." Jessie studied his profile, seeing the turmoil on his face, and her anger evaporated. "That is not good." Her heart went out to the man. When they had spent time together, he had been serious about stopping crime, but his heart had been open, his smile bright and frequent, and his mind keen. Now he seemed a shadow of that man. She couldn't imagine Buzz hurting someone, and she wondered if there was another side to him that she had never seen. Was this why he hadn't been in touch? Had his job changed him?

"It was a domestic violence scene," Buzz continued, his troubles pouring out as if he hadn't heard her. "The man had bloodied his wife. He was belligerent, angry, and drunk." Buzz dropped his head further, lowering it almost between his legs. "Of course, he was shouting and threatening and resisted arrest." Buzz turned troubled eyes to Jessie, "He hit her again while I was standing there trying to get the cuffs on him. A hard backhand that tossed her to the ground."

Jessie rested a hand on his arm, her heart full of compassion as she met his eyes, but she didn't speak. She was sure Buzz had more to say, and while she wanted him to know she understood his anger and distress, she knew he needed to get this out in his own time.

"I raised my fist. Jessie, I wanted to pound his face to a pulp." Buzz turned, weary eyes on hers, and sorrow washed over her. He looked sad, distressed, and confused.

"But you didn't." Jessie's voice was soft. She knew she would have wanted to do the same thing if she had been in his shoes. Buzz was one of those good souls who only wanted to help. He was intelligent, funny, and willing to work hard, but this had pushed past that to something primal.

"The wife jumped me before I could." Buzz huffed, shaking his head in confusion. "He'd beat her bloody, and when I tried to step in, she jumped on me, scratching and flailing. Thankfully, my partner pulled her off of me. The man passed out. I got my cuffs on him, and we stuffed him in the back of the squad car." Buzz turned his head again, looking at the horizon, now painted in streaks of purple and rose. "I'm not sure I'm cut out for this job. It's amazing how people can be so cruel to each other."

Jessie didn't know what to say. Buzz had wanted to be a policeman his entire life. He had wanted to be like his uncle,

Paul Higgins, a well-known and well-respected police detective. She studied the young man who had helped her solve her own household mystery not long ago. His eyes were sad, troubled, and full of self-doubt. She wasn't used to the man looking discouraged like this. When he had helped her with her problem, he had always been smiling, his eyes bright with intrigue and curiosity.

Jessie turned back to watch the peaceful process of the oncoming darkness, her heart hurting for the loss of this man's sweet innocence. "I guess we're both questioning life at the moment." She sighed as the sky began to turn a deep midnight blue. "I've left my job," she spoke as the sea glowed gloriously. "I don't seem to know where I fit right now." She looked up, trying to capture Buzz's eyes. "I know it's not the same, but I understand about not knowing what to do."

Buzz raised his head, looking at her, a familiar sparkle of curiosity and concern in his eyes, but he didn't speak, which made Jessie offer a sad smile. Sitting with Buzz like this brought back a familiar feeling, and Jessie settled in, thankful for his friendship and hoping that it would become a consistent part of her life again.

"I turned twenty-one this summer." Jessie couldn't help but laugh as the man tipped his head like a confused dog. "Twenty-one," she repeated. "Coming of age is a big thing in the Whyne family. I've come into my trust fund." She blushed when Buzz raised his eyebrows, understanding. "Don't look at me like that." Jessie swatted his arm. "I know I'm a rich snob." Jessie shook her head. She had always been torn between being grateful for her family's wealth and being embarrassed by it. Jessie had finished college with two degrees in record time, and now as she'd officially become an adult, she was still no closer to knowing what she wanted to do with her life.

"I didn't say that." Buzz gave her a harsh look. The man didn't have an ounce of malice in him, at least he didn't when he and Jessie had been working together. "You're a good person, Jessie Whyne."

"Thanks." She shook her head. "I knew this was going to happen, so why was I unprepared? I don't seem to know what comes next." It felt good to share, and after Buzz had admitted his disciplinary leave, she felt a renewed connection with him, the old familiarity returning. "I grew up never worrying about where my next meal came from or how I would survive. My family is old money. Dad. . ." she swallowed, suddenly missing her deceased father. "Dad always taught us to do our own thing. To find something to do that we loved, and he made sure we'd have the means to do something with our lives, but I don't know what that is."

Jessie offered a wicked smile, garnering a matching one from Buzz as her spirits lifted. Moments ago, she had been alone, pondering her future. Now she had someone sitting next to her who understood. "I just don't know what I'm doing or who I'm supposed to be."

Buzz nodded, slumping again. "I get that." He looked up over the ocean waves, the setting sun reflected in glowing glory. "I knew forever what I wanted, but now. . ." He shrugged again. "I don't know." Wrapping an arm around Jessie's shoulders, he squeezed. "I thought you had two degrees?" Buzz looked puzzled. "Don't you want to do something with one of them?"

"I don't know." Jessie rested her chin on her knees again, fixing her eyes on the darkening waves. "Nothing seems to be right. I have no passion for anything I could do." She shrugged. "Teaching doesn't seem right, and my computer and business studies leave me feeling flat. That's why Cheryl and I came to the beach house here in Savannah. We both needed some time away from our everyday life." She smiled. "Cher is halfway through her master's degree and completely exhausted. She'll never admit it, but it's true."

The last rays of the sun flared, turning the clouds magenta, the last glow of reflected light dropping beneath the waves and taking with it the brightness of day.

"I guess you and I are in the same place." Buzz mused. "Different situation, but we're at a crossroads and don't know which way to turn." His broad shoulders heaved again. "Mom and Dad thought we could use my time off for a holiday." Buzz looked up as the first stars twinkled. "We rented a condo along the beach." He chuckled. "Your house in Macon looks great, by the way. The renovations and new exterior paint scheme really work. And yes, before you ask, I'm still living with my parents. Lame, I know," he raised his hand over his head in surrender, "but I don't have time to look for a place, and the rent I pay them makes extra stuff possible." He looked up, gazing at the darkening ocean. "Things like this." His head swiveled, and Jessie could see he was soaking in the beauty of the beach.

"You've been by?" Jessie gaped. "I haven't seen or heard from you in months." She shook her head, shocked that he had seen the house with its new look. A house he had been instrumental in helping her keep."

Buzz shrugged. "Too much happening." His eye stayed on the ocean, and Jessie could tell there was something he wasn't saying.

Cutting a worried glance his way, she decided to let the subject drop. "You need to come over sometime." Jessie patted his arm, releasing her grip as she pointed to a boxy house sitting on the beach, its white stucco walls a pale gray in the setting sun. "While you're in Savannah, you're welcome at the beach house any time. I'll talk Cheryl into cooking up something nice one night." She looked up, pinning him with her eyes. "And now that I know you do end up in my neighborhood occasionally, you can drop in there as well." She smiled. "I've missed you."

The sharp yip of a dog made them scan the beach, and Jessie sighed. "I'm starting to think someone has abandoned that dog."

"Where is it?" Buzz scanned the darkening beach. "We could call animal control to come to pick it up."

"They'll take it to the pound." Jessie twisted, meeting his gaze. "What if it belongs to some kid, and they've lost it?"

"You just said you thought it was abandoned."

"I guess I did." Jessie stood, reaching down and offering him her hand, smiling. Buzz clutched her hand, towering over her when he straightened to his full height.

"I think we're both at a crossroads." the man met her eyes, still holding her hand. "It's nice to have a friend here. I've felt kind of alone lately."

Jessie squeezed his hand, trying to offer empathy. The modern world was no easier on young people than in the past. It seemed that every person had to make their way through doubt and uncertainty.

"Hey, why don't you come out with Cheryl and me tonight?" Jessie smiled, a light in her eyes as the idea came to her. " I'm sure you could use a little fun."

"Fun?" Buzz gave her a skeptical look. "What kind of fun?"

" A Ghost tour." Jessie rolled her eyes. "Cher is still not willing to let it go that I saw a ghost, and she didn't. Even if it wasn't real." She chuckled. "Parlor tricks nearly made me lose my mind last year. A haunted house, my foot."

"You don't even believe in ghosts." Buzz grinned, a familiar spark flaring in his eyes. Jessie caught a glimpse of the man she knew, the grin making her smile as she dusted the sand from her white skirt.

"No. I don't." she grinned. "But these tours have a lot of history and mystery woven into them." She looked up, searching his face. "So, what do you say?" She squeezed his hand again, imploring.

"All right." Buzz shuffled his flip-flops, digging into the sand. A chuckle, cold and rusty, drifted from his lips, and he rested his other hand over the one she held. "Where and when?"

Jessie's smile widened as she glimpsed the fun-loving, inquisitive man she had known, peeking through his severe and craggy facade. Her heart swelled, and she thanked God that Buzz hadn't become so jaded by the cruelties of life that he wasn't still the man she had called friend. Turning, she tugged on the hand clasped in hers and began dragging him toward the lounge chair - now a shadow on the beach - where a tiny light flickered. The friendship she had felt for the man when they were working together, the trust swelled again, and she half-skipped as she led the way.

"Now," she laughed again. "I have to warn you. Cheryl is my oldest friend, she's two years older than me, but sometimes I think she was born too late." Jessie leaned in, her shoulder connecting with his. "She loves old fashion and prefers to buy her clothing at consignment or thrift shops. Today she's wearing an old bathing costume." Jessie bit her lip. "Please don't laugh." She looked up, trying to convey her stern thoughts to Buzz with her eyes.

"You're serious?"

"Yep."

"Okay. It's not as if I'm dressed to the nines as it is." He looked down, his eyes wandering over to Jessie's dress.

"What are you, ninety?" Jessie teased. "Who talks like that?" Her smile brightened. "Besides, you're fine," she said. "This is a beach vacation, after all." She grinned at his oversized button-up shirt and swim trunks. "I have a swimsuit under this." Jessie flipped her skirt, displaying bare ankles.

"My folks have been watching old movies," Buzz said, studying his feet as they strode through the sand, the beach chair growing clearer with each stride. Seagrass swayed in the wind as they approached their destination, and the darkness grew.

"Cheryl," Jessie called, stopping by the chair, her feet digging into the warm sand as the night cooled. "I found a friend."

"About time," a blonde woman in a nineteen-fifties one-piece black swimsuit with white piping turned her head, offering a smile. "Oh." She uncurled her legs, swinging to face them, her expression open, transparent, and cheerful in the light of a tiny clip-on reading lamp. "He's a tall one," she twisted, placing her feet on the ground. "I'd say he's legal, don't throw him back."

Jessie laughed as Buzz's eyes grew wide, and he turned to her, trying to understand, his feet fidgeting in the sand.

"Cher, this is Buzz. You remember, the policeman who helped me solve that little problem in my house last year." Jessie gave her friend a look trying to tell her to behave, but it was lost in the darkness around them.

"I knew he'd be cute." The slim woman stood, turning her little light on Buzz, studying him. "I was right." She wiggled her fingers in a fluttery wave. Her smile was wicked, and even in the minimal light from her portable reading lamp, her eyes were teasing.

Buzz shuffled under the scrutiny, and Jessie squeezed his hand, turning to give the tall man an apologetic look. "Buzz, this is my friend Cheryl." She smiled, shrugging. "She's a bit jarring when you first meet, but you'll get used to her. She's not nearly as dangerous as she appears." Her laugh fluttered, hoping Buzz would get the hint.

Buzz bit his lip, stretching out his hand as Jessie released him. "Nice to meet you." He shook the other woman's hand. "I hope you don't mind, but Jessie invited me along on your ghost tour." He looked awkward and uncertain, but Jessie could see he was determined to push through Cheryl's scrutiny. At least he still seemed to trust Jessie's judgment.

"Oh, goodie!" Cheryl pulled her hand back, clapping them together. "This is going to be so much fun." Her smile widened, visible as the stars came out. "Don't take me too seriously," she waved. "I'm giving Jessie a hard time about her dating status." She turned, looking at Jessie, who rolled her eyes.

Buzz looked at Jessie, eyes wide. "Don't worry," she laughed. "As I said, you'll get used to Cheryl. She's the artistic type." Jessie winked, hoping to put Buzz at ease, happy when he seemed to relax. She leaned in closer, feeling his warmth on her skin. "She's a terrible flirt, but Cheryl doesn't mean anything by it."

The trio chatted for a few more minutes before Jessie took Buzz with one arm and Cheryl with the other. "Come on then, you two. We'll go to the house and get ready for this tour." Her smile was bright, and her step was light.

"Whoo!" Buzz half-whistled. "Nice place." He looked up at the modern building. It was as much glass as it was stucco and blended perfectly with the surrounding shore. "Living rough, are you?"

Jessie placed her hands on her hips, giving him an angry scowl.

"You know this is my mother's place." She lifted her chin, eyes glinting, and Buzz bit back a laugh as Cheryl hurried inside, lights shimmering out onto the patio where Jessie glared up at him.

"I know." Buzz raised his hands in surrender. "I'm just teasing." He looked around, taking in the expanse of the beachfront, patio, driveway, and exterior. "Maybe I should be used to places like this," he shook his head, "but I'm just a simple man, and I'm not accustomed to..." he looked up at the small balcony above, "well, this."

"Lighten up, Buzz." Jessie grabbed his hand, dragging him toward the door.

"The beach house is nice." Her tone lightened. "Lots of views of the ocean and sunlight." She shrugged. "It's one of my family's houses." She met his eyes. "And you are always welcome in any of them."

"But?" Buzz looked down.

"It isn't cozy like my place." Jessie grinned.

Buzz was sure she was trying to make him feel comfortable, moving the conversation away from what might be an uncomfortable topic.

Jessie was one of those people who could be anyone's friend. She had once said that everyone was God's creation.

Buzz seemed to relax, letting her drag him inside to more white walls and tile floors. The whole building was sharp angles, open spaces, and bright light. "It's kind of stark," he said as they walked into a floor-to-ceiling entry. A set of chrome and glass stairs led upward, an art deco chandelier reflecting off the white tile. "You and Cheryl are enjoying it here?" Buzz peered around the room, stopping to wiggle the locks on the french doors. "Snug."

"We are." Jessie motioned for him to follow, entering a kitchen to their right that was all white tile and cabinets. The only splash of color was from a table with a chrome frame with a red inlay top. "This house was designed to let light in but keep heat out." Jessie smiled, shaking her head as he walked to a window, checking the latches. "It was the perfect place for two people who needed a break." She shrugged.

"Not what I would call cozy," Buzz turned from the window. "But it is airy." His eyes went to the catch on the window. "Seems secure."

"Leave it to a police officer to worry about that." She smiled, softening her tone, and Buzz relaxed a little more, the stiff tension of earlier ebbing like the tide. "It's a nice place to take the time to do some soul searching." Jessie turned, taking in the kitchen's lower ceiling. "The simplicity makes it easy to maintain, and the light and air keep it from having moisture issues."

Buzz shuffled his feet, turning and looking at the house. The entry was all glass above, taking up the full two stories, but the kitchen was low, allowing for rooms above. "It's nice." He turned, smiling at Jessie. "It's nice seeing you again, too."

"You say the sweetest things," Jessie laughed. She tipped her head, her expression growing serious for a moment. "I'm so happy you're here. Her smile stretched her face with delight.

Buzz ducked his head, hiding his eyes as Cheryl hurried down the chrome and glass stairway. She had changed into a green sundress with a soft white sweater draped over her slim shoulders.

"Ready?" the blonde woman grinned. "Let's go see some ghosts."

Jessie glanced back at Buzz, who looked up from under dark brows.

He offered a smile, falling into step with the two women.

"I guess we have to be."

"Where does this tour start?" Buzz said a short time later, his flip-flops slapping on the pavement as they walked toward town. He leaned toward Jessie, waiting for her reply. This time, Jessie held one of his arms and Cheryl the other. Jessie felt familiar, her hand light on his arm. He smiled, feeling like he'd won a prize as he led two lovely ladies into town. Buzz had called his parents, telling them he was going out with friends, and they had been thrilled that he was taking an interest in something other than work for a change. When he mentioned Jessie Whyne, he could hear the careful cheerfulness in their tone, but he chalked it up to the families being from two different worlds.

"It starts on Oglethorpe Square. They have some historian who will probably drone on forever about all the history of the city," she laughed, rolling her eyes, obviously still delighted. Cheryl replied, giving a little skip. "I love this stuff." Her smile was bright and her enthusiasm contagious. "Oh, and I hope you don't mind being up late, because I've added the additional tour down river to Tybee Island."

Buzz grinned, looking at Jessie. "She's lively," he whispered.

"Now, that's the Buzz I remember." Jessie smiled, squeezing his arm. "You should always be smiling."

Buzz studied Jessie's face as she turned away, a pretty face familiar to him from their time investigating her household mystery and the photos he had taken of a memorable night out. Buzz kept the smile on his face, watching Jessie examine the street. She was pretty, vibrant, and someone he could call a friend.

They walked under the streetlights three abreast, an easy rhythm to their steps as Buzz led, shortening his stride to accommodate his companions. Downtown was still busy, bars and nightclubs hopping as they made their way toward the quieter square, passing darkened shops with eclectic window displays.

"There's our group now," Cheryl pointed to a gathering of people assembled around the bell tower of a Spanish-style building. "The stories from this tour range from the 1700s through the Civil War."

"That's a lot of history." Buzz grinned. "Do they include crimes from those times?" He turned, interested as he looked at Cheryl who offered a winning smile.

"I think so." Cheryl swayed beside him, effervescent. The clothes she had decided to wear only added to the theme. Buzz smiled, understanding why Jessie liked this woman. Cheryl came across as eccentric but caring, and any friend of Jessie Whyne's could be a friend to him.

"Some of the stories are spooky and gruesome," Jessie leaned around Buzz, her skirt brushing his calf and tickling as they stopped with the crowd. It had been months since he's seen her, yet he was feeling that familiar ease with her once more as her hand warmed his arm. "Others are tales of tragic love," Jessie said, giving Cheryl a wink and making the woman sigh with longing.

"So. . . fiction." Buzz chuckled, ducking when both women released him, smacking him with the floppy hats they still wore. He felt refreshed. His laughter was natural, and his worries nearly forgotten. Perhaps his parents were right, and this time off was what he needed. He looked down, still smiling as the girls took possession of him once more. Perhaps what he needed was a friend like Jessie. His eyes brushed over the young woman, watching as the sea breeze whipped her hair around her shoulders. They had worked well together in Macon; maybe they could help each other work through the problems they faced now. Jessie squeezed his arm again, and his heart swelled, thankful for a friend.

"This is the best vacation." Jessie held onto Buzz, Cheryl mirroring her action. He smiled, flexing his biceps and making them laugh. It seemed like forever since he had simply been with two people he could enjoy. For the first time in weeks, Buzz felt like he was welcome and accepted for who he was.

"Tonight should be a fun diversion from all of our worries." Jessie looked at Buzz with a hint of worry in her eyes, and he nodded, understanding. "It's made all the better because you two are here."

"I'm glad I happened to see you at the beach," Buzz winked, his smile brightening.

"You mean, you're glad your Uncle Paul told you where to find me." Jessie raised a brow. "Paul has a knack."

Buzz shrugged, trying to disguise a glimmer of guilt. He had wanted to see Jessie, and that desire had - in no small way - affected the family vacation plans. "There is only so much swimming and watching TV a guy can do." He ducked his head, still grinning. "Mom and Dad are watching reruns of Perry Mason. I think they are hoping it inspires me." He shook his head, gazing at his shoes in mock shame.

Jessie's laugh was bright, and he watched as she shook her head, her chestnut-colored hair cascading down her back in silken waves.

"Good evening." A man's deep, methodical voice rose above the crowd's chatter. "I'm Dr. Ivan Crumm," he offered, scanning the crowd as if addressing a classroom. "I'll be your guide tonight."

"He's not very inspiring," Cheryl whispered as she rolled her eyes. "I hope this isn't going to be a waste of money."

Buzz studied the man. The guide was average. That was the best word to describe him. Not short, not tall, slightly balding, with wire-rimmed glasses, with a very 'professor boring' vibe. "He must be okay. Otherwise, they wouldn't pay him," Buzz said, trying to encourage them to stay. He didn't want to go back to the condo only to be alone with his thoughts. He had been over the events of the night that had led to his disciplinary leave a million times. He hadn't hit the man, but he wondered if he would have if he hadn't been stopped. Buzz had never questioned his choice of careers before, but the anger that flooded him every time he thought of that night was unfamiliar and uncomfortable.

"Hey," You still with us?" Jessie tugged at his arm, pulling him back to the present.

"Sorry," Buzz smiled, turning his attention back to the man explaining the tour and making sure everyone had a brochure and map of the route.

"Come on," Cheryl dragged him to the back of the group as they started off down a path behind the building, slipping into deep shadows and spotty street lamp illumination. "It's going to be great!"

Buzz chuckled, leaning toward Jessie again. "She's enthusiastic." His eyes scanned the crowd, his arms tense under the grip of Jessie and Cheryl as he tried to see into the semi-darkness of the trail.

"That's Cheryl," Jessie giggled. "She's all in, all the time."

Buzz felt his instinct kick in as the tour twisted behind old buildings and under the deeper darkness of live oaks. His ears were tuned to the narrator but also aware of night sounds and the chatter of the crowd. They trundled along streets, stopping at historical sites where hair-raising tales of death and deception were told, making the crowd shift nervously as liberal libations and imagination took their toll. Nervous giggles and tense whispers filled the night after the tour guide paused at an ancient tavern's back door. The group grew hushed as a light flickered, making shadows jump.

"A highwayman was hanged here," Dr. Crumm said, his glasses glinting like empty eye sockets when a street light flickered. "It's said he rides past each full moon looking for the innkeeper's daughter he had loved." The soft sound of hoofbeats made everyone turn, and Buzz could feel the girls clinging to his arms. A burst of laughter filled the night as a horse-drawn carriage rolled by, the horse placidly walking streets long familiar.

"I think they planned that." Jessie's grip relaxed. "Clever."

Buzz nodded, grinning as the group turned, following the guide as the grassy path carried them down toward the harbor.

The professor was thorough but not especially exciting. However, the guests, many sipping from tall drink glasses, made up for it with enthusiastic additions to the tales.

"It's all so tragic," Cheryl commented dramatically. "Gruesome even."

Buzz smiled at the woman's turn of phrase. She was obviously enjoying the drama, and her face was full of excitement each time he caught a glimpse of her in the harbor lights.

"Some weren't so bad," Jessie leaned around Buzz, her shoulder brushing his as she met Cheryl's eyes. "The one with the star-crossed lovers was almost sweet."

Buzz glanced down, offering a smile. He shook his head, thinking that the tale she spoke of had been explicitly added to spark romantic notions among some. His eyes flickered to Jessie, then back to the small tour boat, they were approaching.

Dr. Crumm turned everyone's attention to the water lapping quietly at the shore. "For those who bought the extended tour, our ride awaits." The man smiled, gesturing at the open barge-like boat. The crowd quieted, some stepping onto the boat, others breaking off and heading back into the city.

Cheryl hurried to a seat at the front of the boat, Jessie and Buzz slipping onto the bench next to her as Crumm continued to speak.

"Our last tale tonight," the guide began, "is a tale of the sea. Savannah has always been a shelter for shipwrecks." The guests settled and the tour operator set the boat in motion, slipping into the Savannah and heading for the sea. "But the currents, the Gulf Stream slip, and the varying depths of the coastline have been known to hide many mysteries still to be uncovered." The older man smiled, which created a dark, foreboding look in the shadows. "Add to that lighthouse point, and you have a ready-made disaster."

The tour boat picked up speed on the empty river and soon they were at the mouth of the water, hugging the shore of Tybee Island. A bright beam of light illuminated the waves, picking out white water crashing on hidden dangers beneath. A foghorn blew across the expanse, wisps of white covering the waves as the cloud bank rolled in over the water.

Several tourists titered as the warm, dank air coalesced into a thick fog, making oohing and aahing sounds as the guide continued.

"The AnnaSwift, a ship laden with treasure from the south, and a cavalcade of many wealthy passengers. . ."

Buzz leaned in, listening as the man's voice continued the tale. The foghorn called again, and everyone tried to peer through the heavy fog.

"What's that?" a woman's voice quivered as green light glowed through the fog.

"It's a ghost ship!" another person cried as an eerie light danced over the sea.

Buzz swiveled his gaze toward the speaker, following as others broke in.

Excitement bubbled through the crowd. Cheryl's hand tightened on Buzz's arm, and he grinned, feeling lighter than he had in days. This had been a good diversion. A fun trip through the past with just a hint of danger to make it exciting. His eyes scanned the crowd again. Everyone seemed to be enjoying the spooky feeling of the tour, but he wondered if some of them would even remember the tour in the morning.

"It's just the running lights of a ship," Buzz whispered. He felt Jessie give his arm a pinch. "Ouch!" He turned, glaring at her.

"Don't spoil the fun." Her eyes sparkled. "It's a ghost ship." She scowled until he nodded.

"That's it," a man spoke, his eyes trying to focus on the eerie glow. "The AnnaSwift has returned for her revenge."

Jessie and Cheryl gave a mock shiver, and Buzz lifted his arms, draping one around each girl, offering protection. His grin grew wide as he took in the theater of the night, and he caught the softest titter from Jessie.

The guide smiled, watching the crowd point and comment. "The Annaswift went down just off this shore. It disappeared on a night like this one. As the ship sailed out of port, a fog bank rolled in, and the ship vanished, never to be seen again." Dr. Crumm smiled again, taking his glasses off, wiping them with a handkerchief from his blazer pocket. "It's said that on a foggy night, she sails again. So the crew and travelers are doomed to neither arrive at their destination, nor return home, but to wander the sea for eternity." The man tried to make his voice spooky, but for the sober, it sounded strained and unnatural.

The evening ended as the foghorn blasted again, the eerie glow disappearing in a wink as the tour boat turned, chugging up the river in a wash of chatter and delight. When they returned to the harbor, the professor dismissed the crowd.

"I hope you all had a wonderful time on the tour," the man smiled as the sounds of Savannah filled the void the foghorn had left. "Please remember that tips are welcome, and you can add them through your app." He smiled as people began wandering off toward bars, restaurants, or hotels. A few even walked down to the ocean, settling in the sand to watch the waves. "Join us again soon."

For several moments the trio stood gazing out at the shrouded sea. Buzz grinned, his arms still draped around Cheryl and Jessie as the crowd wandered off in different directions, Dr. Crumm hurrying away, presumably to wherever he lived.

"I'll walk you two home." Buzz looked around as the group dispersed. "I wouldn't want anything to happen to you." He chuckled, but his jaw was tense as he turned them toward the beach and the long walk back.

"Come in for a coffee when we get there," Jessie insisted as they walked the three miles to the beach house. "It's been a long night, and you still have to walk home in those." Her eyes peered down at his oversized flip-flops.

Buzz looked up at the sky. The fog had rolled in, filling the beach with a deep mist, but between the fast-moving clouds, he could catch a glimpse of the stars in a midnight sky. "It's getting late. The tour was more than an hour."

"We're on vacation." Cheryl smiled, her feet making a soft sound in the sand. She leaned around Buzz, giving Jessie a bright grin.

Buzz sighed, dropping his gaze as he surrendered, following the path along the shore. "All right." He tipped his head, looking at Jessie. "One drink."

"It'll be like old times," Jessie said, wrapping both hands around his arm as they all strolled toward home.

Buzz settled at the small chrome and red enamel table in a bright white kitchen as Jessie pulled out juice bottles and the makings for other drinks. She wobbled a bottle of sparkling water in front of him.

"Or would you rather have coffee?

He smiled. "Coffee."

Jessie turned, fiddling with a fancy coffee machine before pulling cups from the cupboard. She had a similar machine in her Arts and Crafts home back in Macon, and the familiarity set him at ease.

"Thanks," he said as she placed a steaming cup in front of him while Cheryl dug out a tin of shortbread cookies. "This place is nothing like the plantation house." He gazed out the bank of huge windows on three sides of the room.

"You've been to The Estonia?" Cheryl asked, slipping into a chair.

"Yeah." Buzz lifted his cup, looking at her over the rim. "My uncle lives there." His eyes flickered to Jessie. "We had a few pow-wows there when Jessie had that unpleasantness at her house." His eyes grew dark, his face serious. "I can understand why Uncle Paul wanted you to go to the estate. The plantation is huge, but you have so many people at the elder-care facility who care about you. Between the staff and the residents, no stranger would have gotten in."

Jessie rolled her eyes. "Yes, but then the miscreant would have gotten away with it." She looked between Cheryl and Buzz, her eyes lingering on his. "As for this house, I think that was the idea." Jessie grinned, placing two more cups on the table. "It was supposed to be something different. My grandparents are the ones who built this place when they were first married, but mom had it renovated when she and Dad wed." She giggled. "Apparently, it is a perfect honeymoon spot."

"Your mom's taste is fantastic." Cheryl shifted on her chair at the end of the table while Buzz sat across from Jessie, his long legs tucked under his chair to keep from stepping on her toes.

"I'm confused about something," Buzz sipped from his mug, accepting a cookie when Cheryl passed the tin to him.

"What's that?" Both girls answered simultaneously, giggling at the act.

"If your mom has this place, why did she spend a month in Florida this fall?" He looked around, taking in the white cabinets, pale teal walls, and modern appliances. "I mean, if she was looking for a beach escape, what could be better, and there is plenty of room for your little brother."

"Jessie grinned." They wanted to spend a couple of days at Disney." She lifted her mug, holding it in front of her as the steam wafted toward the ceiling. "Joey wasn't quite ready for that, but they tried. They stayed in the park for two days, but it was exhausting, so they moved to the house in St. Pete instead."

"Your little brother is so sweet," Cheryl laughed. "I miss going over and playing with him." She shook her head. "That's the only problem with trying to do my studies so fast. I have no time."

Buzz smiled. He was the youngest member of his extended family. An only child born to the youngest daughter of the Higgins clan. His parents had always seemed old to him, and though he had many cousins, he'd seldom been around toddlers. Other than Uncle Paul and his mother, most of the Higgins family was scattered to the four winds. He rarely saw them aside from family reunions, which he had missed for the past two years due to his job.

"You know you're always welcome to drop in." Jessie turned concerned eyes on her friend as Buzz sipped his coffee. He didn't know Cheryl well enough to comment, but Buzz could see the weariness in the young woman for the first time. Her smile slipped, and a hint of shadow filled her eyes.

'I have no time." Cheryl sagged, clutching her cup, her eyes down. "I love what I'm doing, but it's a lot to handle."

Jessie reached out, taking her friend's hand, and Buzz could see the compassion in her eyes.

"That's why we came here." Jessie smiled, encouraging. "Why don't you finish your drink and head to bed. You can sleep in tomorrow."

Buzz gazed down at his mug, hiding his sad smile. Jessie was a good friend. He could see how she cared for Cheryl, and his heart softened. He didn't have many friends outside of work, and hanging out with other young officers always led him down the same path - drinking or talking about work. Jessie was the only female friend he had outside of the department, and her kindness and warm nature were a breath of fresh air to his weary soul.

Cheryl nodded, gulping her beverage. "Thanks, Jess. I needed this." The blonde woman looked up, taking in the house and her companions. She smiled, her brown eyes sparkling. "This was a good night." Her smile brightened, and that sense of enthusiasm returned. "Do you think the tour made that green glow on the water for our entertainment?"

"It was probably just a ship with its lights on." Buzz considered the idea. "Or maybe they do it with mirrors." He grinned, his tone teasing. He chuckled, stepping out of swatting distance and watching as the girls offered a fake glare.

"Ugh." Jessie groaned, but her smile was bright. "Only a cop would say something like that. I can tell you're torn between finding a rational explanation and some deeper plot. Maybe you've been reading too many detective stories."

Cheryl laughed, drained her mug, and shook her head. "I'm going to bed. I can tell you two are going to pick this night apart. So I'm out. Why can't you just accept the spooky?" Her smile was tired as she looked between Buzz and Jessie. "We're on vacation, not solving crimes. Suspend your disbelief for a minute or two, copper." Standing, Cheryl put her mug in the sink and headed up the open staircase to the floor above.

"Good night," she called, her voice drifting back as she paused, ducking low to give them a grin. "Sweet dreams," she added as she disappeared.

Buzz shook his head. "She is rather dramatic, isn't she?"

"A little." Jessie laughed. "She's always coming up with fun things to do."

Silence filled the house for a few moments as they finished their coffee.

"I'd better go, too." Buzz twisted his mug in his hands, not meeting Jessie's eyes. "It's late." Finally, he looked up, meeting Jessie's gaze. She seemed relaxed but somewhat pensive. "Hey, don't worry. You'll figure out what comes next."

Jessie nodded. "You, too."

Buzz stood, knowing it was time to go. "Maybe I'll see you around?"

Jessie stood, her brow wrinkled. "Are you leaving Savannah?"

"No." Buzz shook his head, feeling awkward. Confused emotions tugged at him, and he moved toward the door. "I'm sure you're busy."

Jessie followed him to the door, reaching out and touching his arm. "Hey, don't go running off on me again. You disappeared after our last little adventure, and. . ." she smiled, "I missed you. I'm glad Paul told you to look me up." She wrinkled her nose. "You don't want to spend your time off watching old cop shows, do you?"

Buzz chuckled. "No." He shifted, his flip-flops slipping. "Are you sure you want me around?"

"Yes." Jessie placed their hands on her hips, her blue-green eyes blazing. "You are my friend." The anger on her face evaporated, and her smile flashed. "Besides, I need a buffer with Cheryl. She'll have us chasing moonbeams next."

Buzz laughed, his heart feeling light again. "Okay. We'll make a plan." He looked at Jessie. "Do you still have my number?"

"Yes."

"Good." Buzz kept his tone flat. He had wondered why she hadn't called but then thought she might be thinking the same thing. "Give me a call tomorrow." He brushed a lock of hair from her face as she opened the door. "Good night."

Jessie smiled, stepping onto the patio, a motion-detecting light flashing to life as she tipped her head, listening. "What was that?

"What?" Buzz stiffened, peering into the night, alert as he felt his blood pumping in his veins. "Did you hear something?"

"Yes." The smell of the ocean and cool, damp air filled his lungs. Buzz moved to stand behind her, protective and ready to defend.

"There." Jessie pointed. "The sound is there."

Before he could stop her, Jessie rushed out onto the patio, running barefoot toward the beach.

Instinct kicked in as adrenaline surged. Buzz kicked off his flip-flops, running after Jessie, his fear spiking as he ran toward the unknown.

"Jessie, stop!" His legs pumped as Jessie dropped over a rise in the sand. Dread surged through him, and Buzz leapt, landing behind her, alert for any danger. Adrenaline and instinct clashed as his feet sank into the sand.

"He's hurt," Jessie looked up at Buzz.

"What?" His eyes dropped to the girl, her hands on a small, dark form that whined pitifully, and he let out a breath of relief.

"The puppy." Jessie looked up, her eyes sad. "He's hurt. Help me."

Buzz closed his eyes, letting his breathing return to normal, then bent, lifting the little dog who whimpered but didn't struggle. The burden was light, its skinny body shivering in the cool night air. It seemed to sense that they were there to help. "Jessie, you can't just run out into the night like that," he admonished as Jessie stood. "It can be dangerous, as you well know." The puppy whined pitifully as Buzz cradled him, turning to follow Jessie back to the house.

Jessie stopped, turning to blink at him. "I heard the puppy and was scared for it. I didn't think." She paused, looking at the man, holding the wounded dog. "I'm sorry if I worried you. I thought you could hear it, too."

Buzz nodded. Once again, Jessie's big heart had led her to act rather than think. She was a smart person, not prone to putting herself in danger unless instinct overcame intellect. He smiled, remembering the trouble this had caused when her anger at strange disturbances in the night had gotten her hospitalized in Macon a few months ago. Perhaps youth made her bold, but he could see that her nature would always lead her to action rather than fear.

"I understand," his eyes were serious. "But do try not to do it again." He smiled, knowing that Jessie's generosity came from her soul.

Jessie nodded, dropping her hand. "Come on."

Buzz fell into step once more. "Man, he stinks." the man sniffed as he carried the dog into the house. Jessie closed the doors behind them.

"Bring him into the bathroom." Jessie led the way.

"What are you going to do?"

"I'll see if I can help." Jessie looked up, her azure eyes filled with pity. "Then I'll see if we can find his owner."

Buzz placed the puppy on a white rug, cringing when blood dripped onto the pristine fabric.

"Maybe he was hit by a car?"

Jessie grabbed a cloth, ran it under warm water, and dabbed the puppy's wound on the dog's right shoulder. "I think he's been attacked." She cleaned the laceration, and the little animal looked at her with trusting eyes.

"It doesn't look too deep," Buzz said, leaning over her shoulder as she worked.

"He also has sand burs in his paw." Jessie flinched. "I need to get them out."

Buzz looked up, his eyes meeting hers and seeing the concern in her eyes. "I'll hold him."

It was one in the morning before Buzz left Jessie. They had patched up the puppy, and he had promised to come by in the morning to check on it or possibly help Jessie take it to the vet.

"You'll be okay walking home?" Jessie had asked, making him smile.

"This coming from the girl who kept sticking her nose into trouble last year?" He grinned, softening the rebuke. "I'll walk to the road and call an Uber." His eyes lingered on her for a moment as he pulled his phone, which was sealed in a waterproof bag, from his pocket.

Jessie smiled, not arguing the point. "Be careful." She turned back, looking at the dog.

Buzz had carried the creature - rug and all - into the living room, laying it next to a fireplace insert.

"Thanks," Jessie grinned. "I'll sleep down here on the couch."

"You might want to change first." Buzz looked at her white dress, streaked with sand, blood, and grime. "I'm afraid that is going to be ruined." He looked up. Perhaps she was a grimy, smelly mess, but she still looked good.

Jessie looked at the dress and sighed. "Mom got a whole 'beach wardrobe' for me before I left Macon." She tugged at the dress. "I can't say I'm sad. I'd rather be in jeans."

"Lock up behind me," Buzz said as Jessie walked him to the door. "I'll see you tomorrow."

"I will," Jessie laughed at his reminder. "Good night."

Buzz stood on the stoop a moment longer, looking back through the door as Jessie locked it behind him. "Be safe," he whispered, turning for the road, his thoughts full of the night and the girl he hadn't seen in months.

Looking up at the sky, the night air cool and welcome, Buzz ambled down the beach, heading toward the tourist area of Savannah and the condo his parents had rented. His eyes took in the reflection of the water on the dark beach as he shoved his hands in his pockets, thinking of his night out. He had told Jessie he would call for an Uber, but his mind was as foggy as the ocean air, and the walk would do him good. It was nice seeing Jessie again, but the feelings he had crammed into a corner of his heart threatened to break free, and he didn't know if he could deal with that right now. His life was upside down. The path he had chosen was broken by doubt and fear. Was there room for Jessie in this troubled time?

Chapter 2

Warm sunlight splashed through the high window on the top floor, falling on Jessie where she sprawled on the couch. A soft whimper drew her attention, and a wet nose bumped her hand.

Blinking, Jessie stirred, sitting up and rubbing her eyes.

"You're feeling better," she grinned, reaching down to stroke the puppy's head. She had been up every two hours taking the animal out to relieve himself and now felt groggy.

"Good morning!" Cheryl's voice bounced down the back stairs, her feet clattering on the glass steps. "Jessie!" the cheery tone changed to disgust, "What is that?" Still a few steps up, the young woman paused, leaning over the chrome railing.

Jessie stood, stretching. "That, dear friend, is a puppy."

"You can't keep that thing." Cheryl grimaced then walked the rest of the way down the stairs leaning over the sofa as the puppy whined. "Look at that thing. Ew!"

"Only until he's better and we find his owner." Jessie laughed, seeing the expression of horror on her friend's face.

"He smells." Cheryl wrinkled her nose. "Oh. He's hurt." Cheryl leaned further over the square back of the couch, her brown eyes examining the dog with care. “Has that thing been here all night? He’s ruined your mom’s rug.”

Jessie bit back a smile, her eyes looking at the once-white rug, covered mainly by the black puppy. “Buzz helped me patch him up last night.” She reached down, stroking the mutt’s head. The poor thing was on the beach and injured. I think he was kicked, or maybe the seagulls overwhelmed him.”

“By the smell of him, I’d say he was in the trash and competing for food against the flying rats’ food.”

Jessie smiled. “I’ll get him to a vet today and hopefully cleaned up a bit as well.” She wrinkled her nose, sniffing. “He does smell.” Her tone softened as she looked at the dog, her smile growing when his tail thumped against the floor. “He’s a good boy,” she said, scratching the puppy’s ears.

“I guess he’s kind of cute.” Cheryl’s expression softened, but her tone was reserved. “For a mutt. Just keep him away from me. You know dogs want to crawl all over me for some reason. I hate being licked.” She turned, walking behind the couch and heading for the kitchen. Jessie could hear the coffee machine coming to life.

Jessie rubbed the dog’s head again. “Come on, you.” She headed for the back door, letting the puppy hobble along behind her. The living room area on the west side of the house was still shadowed, as was the small grassy backyard. The high white walls, rough with stucco work, held the coolness of the night before as Jessie opened the double glass doors. “ We’ll take you outside and then get some breakfast.” She paused, looking at the puppy, realizing she didn’t have any food for him, and wondered if she could order some from a local store.

The dog limped out the door and onto the stone patio, gazing up at her with loving eyes. The little brute was filthy, and Jessie couldn’t deny that he smelled of old garbage and dirty dog. His long black coat was matted. Long feathers of hair stuck together with burs and grime.

Jessie leaned down, petting the dog's head, and was rewarded with an enthusiastic wag. "Come on." She walked the dog out into the small back garden. A high wall surrounded the back area, much taller than the six-foot wall around the front, and a lovely square patch of grass - carefully groomed by a caretaker - beckoned the pup.

Jessie watched the dog sniff around the yard, his right front paw raised as he limped to a corner filled with dew-drenched grass. For the first time, Jessie realized that the animal had white on his front paws and a white ruff down his chest that was nearly obscured by dirt.

"You are kind of cute." She mused, watching the dog explore.

"Good morning," Jessie wheeled, smiling when she saw Buzz. He was dressed much like he had been the day before, in shorts, a lightweight print button-up, and flip-flops.

"Hey." Jessie's smile was bright. "I take it Cheryl let you in and told you where I was?"

"With a promise of coffee and breakfast. I don't know what she's making, but it smells better than the corn flakes I had at five a.m." He stepped out onto the stone lanai, ducking his head under the door. "I brought something for the mutt." Buzz lifted a bag of puppy food and a leash with a collar already attached. The goofy grin was shy, and Jessie hurried to thank him.

"You didn't need to get up early to do this." She looked at the leash in his hands, gazing into tired eyes. "You didn't get much sleep either, huh?"

Buzz shook his head, watching the puppy approach.

The puppy trotted up to them, sniffing at Buzz's flip-flops. The man stooped, fastening the collar around the dog's neck as the pup shifted his attention to the bag of dog food Buzz had placed on the stone pavers at his feet.

"Wow! This was sweet." Jessie looked at the puppy, trying to bite through the bag. "You didn't need to."

Buzz shrugged his eyes on the dog. "We didn't rescue the mutt to let him starve." His shoulders rolled as if his kind gesture was nothing, and his humility touched Jessie's heart.

"Thanks." Jessie squeezed his arm, making him look at her. She was happy to see that he hadn't lost his kindness, despite his troubles. Smiling, Jessie released the man. "Come on," she said, taking the leash from Buzz. "I think we are almost ready for breakfast. After your generous donations, I think you deserve more than corn flakes."

Buzz grinned, tipping his head as Jessie walked into the house. Picking up the dog food, he tucked it under his arm as they made their way to the kitchen. "I figured you'd need it. Do you still plan on heading to the vet?" The man's words followed her through the shaded living area and into the bright kitchen filled with the morning sun.

"Yes." Jessie looked over her shoulder, offering a smile. "But first, food. I'm starving."

They entered the kitchen, Cheryl casting them a glance as she pulled something out of the oven. The smell of bacon or ham wafted toward them, and Jessie's stomach growled.

"Buzz, why don't you wash up while I get this critter fixed up. What are we having, Cher?"

Jessie watched her tall friend slip past the front stairs, then she bent, digging in a lower cupboard to find a bowl before dumping some of the dog food into it. She smiled, setting the puppy chow before the mutt, happy when the dog dug in.

"I think I'm going to change," she added with chagrin, looking down at the baggy sweats she still wore. "Be right back." Her eyes met Cheryl's as she reached the stairs. Was she changing because Buzz was here or because her mother would have been disappointed? Jessie couldn't tell, but by the look on her friend's face, Cher must have thought it was because of Buzz.

Cheryl winked, making Jessie shake her head as she trotted up the stairs headed for her room.

Half an hour later, Buzz helped Jessie get the puppy into his car. As Jessie climbed into the passenger seat of his old sedan, Buzz looked back at the block-like structure he had just left. The house was a cube within a cube with all four corners primarily made of glass. A matching white stucco wall surrounded the house, rising high like a cresting wave at the back yard and slowly dropping to a height of five or six feet at the front. Wide black iron gates sat open, leaving a winding path to the front door. Smiling contentedly as they headed toward a veterinarian clinic down the road, Buzz cataloged the house and surrounding area. An instinct he often didn't even notice anymore.

"Nice digs," he said, slipping behind the wheel. "It's like a box with a flat Z floor plan."

"It's Art Deco." Jessie smiled. "I love the light, though."

"It's nice." Buzz grinned. "Kinda sank, I guess you could say." He started the car listening to Jessie's laugh.

"You and your old-fashioned words." The girl shook her head.

"I blame Uncle Paul and old movies." Buzz felt oddly at ease. His shoulders relaxed as he glanced back at the house. It was strange how quickly he could adapt to Jessie's more opulent accommodations. He was used to simple. His family was primarily blue or white-collar workers, and he might have felt out of place if not for Miss Whyne. Instead, he offered a bright smile as his eyes slipped over Jessie, who seemed perfectly at ease in his old car. She was special. A friend he didn't know he needed.

"The condo we rented has one window facing onto a dingy balcony with views of the sea." He shrugged, starting the car. "It's okay, but nothing like this. Your beach house is simple, but it seems big because it is so open and bright."

Jessie's eyes were troubled as she looked at him. "You aren't unhappy where you are, are you? We have two more bedrooms upstairs if you need to stay somewhere else."

"No." Buzz chuckled. "We're comfortable, and it's only for another week." He sighed, thinking about returning to Macon while still on administrative leave.

"Buzz, are you okay?" Jessie's voice was kind.

"Yeah." He looked at her for a second, letting the car roll down the circular drive. "Now and then, my troubles back home catch up with me." He smiled, pushing the thoughts away. "Right now, though, we have a puppy to look after."

The sun shone, filling the car with warmth, and Jessie rolled down her window, letting the sea breeze ruffle her hair. She could tell that Buzz was worried about what would happen when he returned to Macon. She hated seeing him like this. Last year, when they had worked together, he had been bright, full of hope, and always optimistic. But, unfortunately, the dark cloud hanging over his head could change the man forever.

Stealing a glance at Buzz as he drove, hands at ten and two, eyes focused on the road. Jessie studied his profile. He had a strong jaw, but not too square. His face was open, his profile slightly long, softening the angular lines of a straight nose and broad brow. Looking at him objectively, Jessie would have to admit that Theo Benzelly was handsome, if not rugged.

Pushing the thoughts away, she focused on their mission, scanning the buildings for the sign she sought.

"There's the place," she pointed at the sign that read, "Pet Clinic." The building was typical of a low, square, and squat beach town but with big windows and a deep overhang above the door to soften the harsh sun.

Buzz parked, climbing out of the car and lifting the puppy in strong arms.

Once inside, they hurried to a counter where an older woman in a bright green smock greeted them, looking at the puppy.

"You must be Jessie?" the woman smiled. She was plump and motherly, making them feel at ease. "I'm Alice. We spoke on the phone." She lifted a clipboard, handing Jessie a pen. "If you'll fill this out, please?" She smiled down at the puppy, her blue eyes compassionate in a round face. "Aw, poor thing. What happened?"

"We don't know." Jessie began filling out the paperwork. "We found him last night." She scowled, looking at the paper. "Do I have to give a name? We don't know it."

"We need it to create a file." Alice pointed for Buzz to put the puppy on the counter. "We can always just give him a number." She looked between them. "I always think that's so cold, though. Don't you? I mean, he deserves a name." She stroked the puppy's head with an index finger.

Jessie looked up at Buzz, his hand steadying the pup that was sitting and panting on the countertop. "He looks like a mutt to me." The young man shrugged.

A slow smile spread across Jessie's face, and she scribbled on the page.

"Muttley?" Buzz leaned over her shoulder, reading before looking back at the dog.

"At least for now." Jessie finished filling out the paperwork and handed it back to the clerk.

"Dr. Aries will see you in a few minutes. Please bring Muttley into the examination room." She led them through a door on the far wall and down a long corridor toward a room.

The puppy whined, and Buzz made soothing sounds as they walked into the stark examining room.

Buzz placed the puppy on the stainless steel table, turning to Jessie when the animal whimpered, shivering in fear.

Jessie draped an arm around the little mutt, and he leaned against her, looking up with longing eyes as the clerk walked out, closing the door behind her.

"It's okay, Muttley." Jessie scratched under his chin. "You'll be fine, even if you do smell like an old garbage truck." She looked up, smiling at Buzz, who stood close by.

"He does stink." Buzz agreed. "Do you think the vet will care?"

"I'm sure he's used to this kind of thing. Animals don't always smell pretty." She rested her hand on the mutt's neck, watching the minutes tick by as they waited.

Only fifteen minutes had passed before the door opened again, and a man in a white smock stepped inside.

"Now, who do we have here?" He offered his hand to Buzz and then Jessie, making introductions. "I'm Dr. Aries. Oh, a stray." The light reflected off wire-rimmed glasses, his dark hair was slicked back, and his face was pleasant.

"Yes. We found him last night." Jessie patted the puppy as the vet palpated him, looking for any other potential problems.

"It looks like he tangled with the seagulls. They can be fierce." The vet shook his head as he began tending the dog, "I'm going to give him a shot and a sedative. He doesn't seem to have any major issues, but he'll need a few stitches, and I'd recommend you let our resident groomer, Missy, have him after I'm done. She's excellent, and the dogs love her." He stroked the pup's head, then looked up with a smile. "Even the strays."

Jessie glanced at Buzz then nodded, flinching when the puppy yelped at the prick of a needle.

She stroked Muttley's head as he grew sleepy and finally stretched out on the table.

"You can leave him with us." He looked down at the puppy, "Come back in a couple of hours."

"Okay." Jessie gave the puppy another soft stroke, meeting the doctor's eyes. "You're sure he'll be alright?"

"He'll be fine." The doctor's smile put her at ease. "We deal with this sort of thing all the time. But unfortunately, lost or abandoned dogs often end up here. This little guy is skinny but other than these cuts, he'll be fine."

Jessie nodded, giving the dog one last stroke, then turned as Buzz opened the door, escorting her out. As they made their way to the car, she looked up at her friend again.

"Do you have time for all of this?" She paused at the car, looking at Buzz over the hood. "I'm sure you'd rather be doing something other than escorting a stray dog and me to the local vet."

"I have nothing better to do." Buzz's familiar grin shone, and Jessie relaxed. "Besides, it's nice to catch up." He shrugged. "Life has been too busy."

"I appreciate it. I've never had a dog, and I'm not sure what I'm doing." She shook her head, pulling the car door open. "I don't even know how long you are staying here in Savannah. Sorry."

Buzz opened his car door, nodding for her to get in. "My folks booked the condo for two weeks." He smiled. "I have plenty of time." He slipped behind the wheel, closing his door and turning to look at Jessie as she buckled her seat belt. "Carting a puppy to the vet is better than spending all day worrying and getting stuck in my own head." He tapped his skull with an index finger before starting the engine, his eyes still on Jessie.

"So now what do we do while we wait?" Jessie asked. "The vet said a few hours."

Buzz looked down at Jessie's t-shirt, smudged with grime. "You might want to get cleaned up. I can drive you back to your house."

"Ugh." Jessie looked at her shirt, pulling it up and sniffing it. "Good plan. We can check in with Cheryl as well."

Buzz shifted the car into gear, turning back toward the beach house as Jessie looked out the window. The ride back was quiet but comfortable.

A few minutes later, he was making the turn down the long drive, his eyes scanning the pristine beach before him. Stopping in front of the house, he parked the car, turning to look at Jessie.

"Coming in?" she asked, offering an en" Don't " "ouraging smile.

"Give me a minute. I'll be right in." Buzz climbed out of the car as Jessie opened her door and headed toward the house.

The house was quiet as Jessie unlocked the door. "Cher?" She called, but only silence replied. Then, turning to see what had happened to Buzz, Jessie caught a glimpse of the man, his bare back rippling with muscle as he pulled a clean t-shirt over his head. She smiled, wondering if it was a cop thing to keep a change of clothes in the car.

Jessie moved away from the window as the man turned, pulling the shirt over tight abs as he trotted to the house.

Opening the door, Jessie let Buzz in. "No one's home." She said, avoiding looking at him. "Cheryl must be out."

Buzz turned back, squinting into the bright sunlight and looking back at the sea. "Maybe she's down at the beach."

Jessie looked up, forcing her eyes to meet his instead of lingering on how his shirt clung to his torso. "I'll change," she said, offering a half-smile. "Then we'll go check."

Buzz studied the white stucco and glass house as Jessie hurried upstairs, her sandals clicking on the glass steps.

It was a pretty house, but it seemed cold and empty compared to the home Jessie had recently purchased and renovated. A place that was filled with what the girl loved and reflected her personality and kind heart. This building was all hard angles and cool surfaces. The entryway was a simple yet solid french door with an expanse of thick white stucco above. It was topped by a huge window that allowed the afternoon light to pour in. The whole place reminded him of something he had seen in an old movie. The nouveau movement of architecture had swept the world in the 1920s. Though the structure seemed basic, Buzz knew that the simplistic look was costly and opulent.

Buzz could hear the ocean waves crashing through the wide-open french doors, and he turned, walking through the kitchen, past the peninsula countertop and table to the open plan of the living area. The house was basically a square box stacked to make a two-story home. Buzz looked up the stairs of this room that ran up the opposite side of the house from the stairs at the entranceway. Overall, it was a pleasant, almost cool-looking home. This place had been designed to be simple, full of light and sea breezes. Even the furniture was light with shades of sand-beige, pale blues, teals, and greens, matching the dunes and waters surrounding it.

Buzz walked to the white stone fireplace, its sharp lines matching the rest of the house. He rested an elbow on the mantle. Looking up, he studied a large watercolor painting of the surrounding landscape. The artist had captured the sway of the seagrass as if a breeze were blowing by.

Jessie trotted back down the stairs a few minutes later, wearing dark blue shorts and a white blouse. She looked bright and cheerful, and the scent of strawberries tickled his nose as she approached, making Buzz smile. "Now you're looking more like you're on vacation." He gazed down at his own shorts and t-shirt.

Jessie ruffled her damp hair, gathering it together and twisting it into a messy knot as she fastened it with a clip. "I hope I didn't take too long." She looked up, her eyes on his dark shirt. "I wanted to wash the smell away."

Buzz grinned, sniffing. "I think you succeeded."

Jessie laughed. " I guess we're ready then. Shall we?" she took his arm, snatching the straw bonnet from the highboy as she led him out of the room, back through the kitchen to the front door.

The warm air wrapped around the pair as they stepped out onto the sand, heading for the lawn chair by the water. The sea was a soft green, the waves crashing in rhythmic time as they walked toward the shore.

"The water is calm today," Buzz offered as they walked. "It would be a good day for a swim."

"Do you swim much?" Jessie looked up, still holding his arm.

"I have been doing a lot of it since we got here." He shrugged. Not being into the nightclub scene, Buzz had spent his time at the gym, running or swimming to burn off his nervousness and distract him from worry.

"How about you?" He looked down, seeing Jessie's sunkissed skin that practically glowed.

"Some." She smiled. "We mostly swim in the pool, though. It's always calm."

"Pool?" Buzz blinked. "I didn't see a pool."

"It's tucked around the corner behind the trees. I'll show you sometime." Her eyes landed on her friend stretched out in a canvas chair, pulling her attention from the conversation.

"There you are." Cheryl waved, looking up from her book. Today she was wearing a yellow swimsuit that looked more like an extremely short sundress than a bathing costume. Black and white embroidered butterflies graced the left shoulder and right hem of the suit, giving it a whimsical look. "Where's the mutt?" she turned, sitting up as she looked between Buzz and Jessie.

"He's still at the vet's. He needed stitches, and the doc suggested that he get a good grooming while he's there." Jessie smiled. "We'll pick him up in a couple of hours."

Cheryl looked up, smiling at Buzz, her eyes assessing him and he ducked his head at the scrutiny. "What have you been up to?" he asked, his eyes drifting out over the ocean. He knew Cheryl was Jessie's friend, but she still made him feel a little awkward.

"Reading!" Cheryl waved her book enthusiastically. "I'm reading about all of the ghosts of Savannah. I walked down to that little book shop in town while you were gone. This is a doozy." She waved the book again, almost hitting Jessie in the stomach.

Buzz reached down, grasping the book in her hand, stopping the wild flailing. "This doesn't look thick enough to hold all of those stories." He grinned, releasing Cheryl's hand.

"This is only about the ghost ships." Cheryl laughed. "Pull up a chair. I'll tell you all about the good ones."

Jessie looked at the empty beach. "I'll grab some chairs. She turned, starting back toward the house but veering toward a small shed surrounded by waving grass.

"I'll help," Buzz called. Are the chairs in there?" Buzz asked, catching up with her.

"Yes." Jessie opened the door, and he ducked inside, pulling out matching canvas folding chairs. The chairs weren't the modern plastic or steel versions, but old teak wood that folded out, creating a comfortable canvas sling to sit in.

"Blue or yellow?" Buzz asked, holding one chair in each hand, as he bent over to fit inside the shed.

"Yellow." Jessie reached for a chair, but Buzz tucked them under his arms, ducking out the door into the sunlight. "I'll get the door," she yelled as he headed back to the strip of beach where Cheryl reclined.

Opening the chairs, Buzz pushed them into the sand until they were stable, waiting for Jessie to join them. A moment later, they settled in the chairs, legs outstretched and soaking up the sun as the cry of sea birds punctuated the soft swoosh of waves.

"What that professor said was true," Cheryl began, snuggling down into her chair, her legs curled under her. "Hundreds of ships have either sunk or been washed up into the trenches of this shoreline." The woman jumped right in, her nose buried in the book.

Buzz closed his eyes, settling in for a lecture and relaxing as the morning breeze kissed his skin.

Jessie elbowed him, forcing him to look at her as Cheryl continued.

"I have a feeling we're going to need refreshments for this."

"What?" Cheryl looked up, glancing between them. "Good plan." She nodded. "I'll wait."

"Give me a minute." Jessie dashed to the house, leaving Buzz and Cheryl to enjoy the sun and surf as they both sat staring at" " " "the waves.

Buzz leaned back in the chair, resting his head against the backrest, the sun brushing his face with warmth and soaking in. He sighed, relaxing as the beach vibe finally reached him.

"This is nice," Cheryl said. He smiled, hearing her flipping through her books. "We all need a break sometimes. Jessie is the best, letting me come out here and chill. Don't get me wrong. I love learning and my job, but it is exhausting. I took a month off of summer school, and decided to just indulge my whimsy." Her voice was light, and Buzz cracked one eye, turning to look at her as she adjusted a flopping yellow hat over her head.

Closing his eyes once more, he didn't comment. He got the impression that much of Cheryl was whimsy. Her eclectic attire, vibrant personality, and vivid imagination seemed a jarring contrast to the hardworking impression he had gotten from her in other ways. Could people really separate work and daily life so easily?

Silence filled the moments as they ticked by, the sun creeping higher in the sky.

"Okay," Jessie's voice made Buzz look up, watching as she hurried back, a heavy-looking tray in her hands. Taking in the scene, a flash of guilt filled his chest. He jumped up, taking the folding table the girl had tucked under her arm and setting it in front of the chairs. He should have offered to help.

"Thanks." Jessie settled the tray of iced drinks on the table, sighing with relief when Buzz adjusted the table to ensure it could hold the load. "I brought iced tea and fruit." She poured everyone a drink, adding chunks of sweet fruit, then took a glass and slipped into her chair. "Now, about these ghost ships, Cher." She winked at Buzz, and he spluttered on his drink. Everyone knew that Jessie Whyne didn't believe in ghosts.

"It's estimated that over twelve-hundred ships have sunk out there." Cheryl waved toward the ocean, with her book. Absently taking a drink from the table as she jumped right in. "The currents, shoals, and trenches all added to the loss of vessels ranging from the Revolutionary War to WWII." She looked up over her sunglasses, placed her drink back on the tray and held the book up for everyone to see. "This chart shows where all the ones that have been discovered rest." She looked back at the book, concentrating. "The AnnaSwift left Savannah at the end of the Civil War, carrying wealthy landowners and their treasures. It was heading to the Caribbean where they believed they could start again and not lose their family wealth and privilege to the invading North."

"And it vanished?" Jessie sat up, pushing her floppy hat back on her head.

"Yes." Cheryl nodded. "The ship barely got away before soldiers arrived. "The port had been blockaded since 1862, but profiteers were active and could slip out of the harbor with smaller boats."

Jessie opened her mouth to ask a question, but Cheryl waggled her finger, stopping her.

"The AnnaSwift was thirty feet long and had three masts." Cheryl smiled, "In other words, it was fast." She frowned, returning her gaze to the page. "The thing is, no one heard any attack on the ship. She slipped out of her mooring, disappeared into the fog, and was never seen again."

"Spooky," Jessie teased, looking at Buzz. "So, now it haunts the shore on foggy nights?"

Buzz grinned. It was obvious that Jessie didn't believe in ghost stories and was humoring her friend. Of course, they had seen something the night before, and he couldn't help but wonder if the tour organizers had rigged something up to tantalize tourists. He shifted, looking out at the placid waves and sipped his drink, his mind turning the story over as he listened.

"That's what the story says," Cheryl looked up and giggled. "It's all good fun. Who knows?" Her smile grew wicked, "maybe that was the ghost ship out there the other night. Whoo-waaw," she finished making an eerie foghorn sound.

Jessie looked over at Buzz, biting her lip. "We don't believe in ghosts or ghost ships. My personal haunting last year proved that there is always a logical explanation." She shook her head looking back at Cher.

Cheryl sat up, her feet plopping onto the sand as she looked at Jessie and then Buzz. "Yes, but what if there's more to this story than meets the eye? The ship was real. So where did it go? What happened to it?

"Cheryl, you are looking for adventure. You really need to learn to relax. This is a vacation." Jessie stretched, patting her friend's knee.

Cheryl rolled her eyes, sighing dramatically. "Well, it's fun reading this stuff." Her eyes flickered to the sea. "So much history." Looking back at her book, she flipped a few pages. "They have a whole community of treasure seekers. It's not what it used to be, though." Cheryl shook her head. "Did you know that whatever you discover, you have to share with the state? Even offshore finds have to be reported, and often a salvage crew barely breaks even on their investment." Cheryl spun back onto her chair, tucking her legs up, and gazing at the book.

"Then why do they do it?" Buzz asked, sipping his tea, his eyes still closed against the glare of the sun. "If it isn't profitable, why bother?"

"Adventure!" Cheryl squealed, sitting up straight again, grabbing her hat as the breeze stiffened. "Can you imagine finding sunken treasure? It has to be exciting, and even if you are barely making a living at it, you get to do something amazing."

Buzz peeked at the girls, watching as Jessie reached over, squeezing her friend's wrist and offering a sweet smile. "We are not here for adventure. We are here for a long rest." She flicked her eyes to Buzz, her gaze pleading for support.

"Maybe everyone thinks we 'young folks'," he put air quotes around the words, "have endless energy, but we don't. The world keeps changing around us. Some days it feels like we're walking on a bridge that is crumbling with each step." He sat up, straddling the chair and resting his elbows on his thighs. He looked out at the slowly rolling waves. "We keep working hard to make a difference, but the rules change, and we're left tired and confused." A touch of bitterness filled his voice, and he cleared his throat, willing it away.

"That's why we're all here." Jessie glanced between Cheryl and Buzz, his eyes following her. "To rest and recuperate." A smile slid across her face, her full lips bright from the kiss of the sun. "How about we go out tonight? My treat." She turned, looking at Buzz.

Buzz gazed out at the ocean again. It was getting warm now, and he considered suggesting they go back inside.

"What do you say, Theo?" Jessie asked. The use of his real name snapped the man's head around, and he sighed, seeing Jessie's teasing smile.

"Sounds good. Who gets to pick the place?" He shook his head, wondering if Cheryl knew his real name was Theodore. He much preferred his nickname, but what could he do? Uncle Paul had let the cat out of the bag months ago.

Jessie opened her mouth, ready to reply when her phone rang, and she pulled it from her back pocket. "Hello?" She looked up at her companions. "Oh, yes. I understand. Can we stop by and see him before you close?" Silence echoed. "Thank you. Please let me know what else I can do." Jessie hung up, and Buzz could see that her eyes were sad. "That was the vet. Muttley has an infection in his right paw, and they want to keep him overnight."

"I'm sorry." Buzz lifted a hand toward her, then dropped it into his lap. "Will he be okay?" Buzz asked, trying to hide the concern in his eyes. His instinct had been to reach out. To comfort Jessie, but he had no right.

"Yes, he needs a course of antibiotics, and since he's undernourished and has the cut on his shoulder, they'll want to keep him on an IV drip." The young woman looked up, trying to smile, but he could see the worry in her expression.

"I'm sorry," Cheryl wrinkled her nose. "I know I'm not a dog person but. . . that poor puppy." Her eyes grew pensive, and she grabbed Jessie's hand. "I wonder where he came from? Who would just abandon a helpless dog?"

Jessie nodded. "I hope he's just lost and we can find his owner." She looked at Buzz. " He's "I'll ""I keep thinking about some kid who has lost their dog and is worried sick. Once he's healthy, we'll put up flyers and try to find an owner."

"I wish people were more responsible with animals." Buzz looked between the girls. He smiled, encouraging. "I'll help.- He's a mutt, but he deserves love as much as anyone."

Jessie turned bright, hopeful eyes to him, and the gaze touched his heart. He would do whatever he could to help for as long as he could.

The waves crashed on the shore, seagulls cried, diving and ducking for fish. A warm breeze whispered in the seagrass, and the trio leaned back into their chairs, lost in their own thoughts as they relaxed, seeking to regain strength and inspiration.

Chapter 3

"You're all set," a woman in a pair of puppy-print scrubs handed Muttley's leash to Jessie, glancing up at Buzz standing behind her as she collected him. "He's sweet." The woman offered a bright smile, her blue eyes twinkling. "He's a little scared, but he'll get over it."

"Thank you." Jessie peered at the name tag on the woman's shirt. "Missy. You must be the groomer."

"Yes. I volunteer here once a week." she scratched the puppy's ears, and he leaned into her. "He's not in bad shape for a stray. I've seen dogs with loving homes in worse condition." Then, digging into her pocket, the short, pretty woman in her fifties dug out a card. "If you need a groomer again, this is me."

Jessie took the card, reading the elegant scrawl. "I'm afraid I won't be keeping him. We'll try to find his owner before I head home to Macon." She looked up at Buzz, hoping he would agree to help.

"Oh. That's sweet." Another bright smile. "I hope you find them." Blue eyes looked down to study the pup. "He's going to be big, you know. Just look at the size of those paws. He's probably a cross between a Black Lab and an Irish Setter, by my guess. He'll be loyal if a tad hyper."

"Another reason why we need to find his people." Jessie smiled. "He needs time and dedication. Thank you again." Jessie looked down at Muttley. "I'll take good care of him while he's with me." She stroked the dog's head. "How big?" Her eyes returned to the groomer, curiosity getting the best of her.

Missy placed her hand a little over hip-high. She wasn't an overly tall woman, perhaps five foot five, but that was still a significant height. "They're both smart breeds, so if you work with him, he'll be easy to train. Won't you?" She cupped the puppy's head in her hands, making smoochy faces at him. "Who's a smart boy?" The tail thumped on the table, making Jessie smile.

"You know you have plenty of room for a dog," Buzz said, making Jessie turn to look at him, askance. "Do you want me to carry him to the car?" The man continued before she could remind him that she wasn't keeping the dog. Together they looked back at the pup who wiggled happily on the table. "We need to get back, Cheryl's making lunch, and I'd hate to see what she has to say if we're late." The man's smile grew, making Jessie laugh.

"Thanks again." Jessie shook the older woman's hand, stepping out of the way while Buzz lifted the puppy and headed toward the front of the office.

"Don't let him get used to that," Missy called after them. "He's got four feet. You only have two."

Jessie followed Buzz to the front desk, noting that Buzz still held the dog in strong arms.

"He looks so much better." Alice turned from a file cabinet, handing a paper and a bottle of liquid antibiotics to Jessie. "He even looks happy."

Jessie laughed. "I think he's already getting spoiled," she said as she paid the bill for Muttley's care. Then, turning to Buzz she cocked a hip and raised a brow. "I think you can put him down now."

Buzz bent, placing the dog carefully on the floor, cringing when the puppy whimpered.

"You can walk," Jessie said, wagging a finger at the dog and ignoring his pleading look. "You're a big boy, and you'll be bigger very soon." she bent, scratching under his chin. "We'll go slow, but even on three feet," her eyes scanned the bandaged paw, "you're still faster than we are." Jessie looked up at Buzz. "Don't you give in and pick him up, either." She smiled, seeing the kindness she had been so accustomed to on the man's face.

"But those eyes," Buzz teased, turning and heading for the door as Jessie put the medicine in her bag and tugged on Muttley's leash. She stopped, watching her friend hold the door for a man who walked in carrying a pet caddy that hissed and spat at the puppy, making him cower in fear.

A warm breeze wrapped around them as Buzz held the door, the smell of salty air filled Jessie's nostrils, and the puppy crowded close, wary eyes scanning the surroundings. The parking lot was fairly quiet, but a few people were bringing animals in for treatment.

"He's still scared." Buzz walked beside them to the car, hefting the dog into the back seat. "He sure smells better now." the man grinned.

"And looks better, too. His coat is a little shorter, but all of the burs and matting are gone. He should be more comfortable with this new look, too, especially in this heat." Jessie slipped into the front seat as Buzz got behind the wheel. It was nice having his help, but she was worried about him. He wasn't the same man from a few months ago. She looked back at the puppy, knowing he was a good distraction for her friend. As Buzz started the car, pulling out of the parking lot, she thought about what she knew of him.

Buzz had known his entire life what he wanted to do and be. If he was questioning his life choices, how could she make up her mind what to do?

"I hope you're enjoying your vacation." Jessie looked along the road, the sea to her right as they pulled into traffic.

"I am." Buzz said, but his voice was flat. "At least when you and Cheryl keep me busy." His grin flashed.

"And what of your problem?" Jessie asked, trying to sound cheerful. "Any news?"

Buzz shook his head. "No. I don't know what is going to happen. Mostly these things work themselves out, but that's not really the issue." They followed the road a while until Buzz could make a U-turn and head back toward the beach house.

"You feel lost." Jessie stated, understanding.

"I feel uncertain." Buzz let out a sigh, and Jessie turned, studying his profile. "I want to serve and protect, but all I do is paper work or deal with the dregs of society." He flinched as if someone had hit him. "Listen to me. When did I start thinking of people like that?"

Jessie reached out, touching his arm, trying to offer comfort. She knew what confusion felt like.

"Hey." She offered a smile. "You'll figure it out. I'll pray for you."

Buzz cut his gaze to hers, holding it for a full three seconds before turning back to the road. He looked confused and unsettled by her comment.

"Thanks." He smiled. "Now, I think it's almost lunch time." He chuckled, but there was no warmth in the sound.

Jessie let the subject drop. She was sick of overthinking her own life choices, how much more so was Buzz, especially when someone else held the power to decide for him.

"Yes." She forced the thoughts away, filling her voice with as much cheerfulness as possible. "We'll make the pup comfy and then figure out what we want to do for the day." Jessie's smile brightened as she left her worried thoughts behind. "We all need a good dose of fun."

She, Buzz, and Cheryl had spent the evening together, and Jessie had been pleased when Buzz offered to take her back to the vet this morning to pick up the dog. She was sure she could have managed, but Buzz was bigger and stronger, making lifting the puppy into the car far easier on both of them.

"What are you doing today?" Buzz guided the car with ease as they headed back toward the private beach and house.His smile was back, and Jessie could see that he, too, had forced the troublesome thoughts away.

Jessie chuckled. "I'm sure Cheryl has a plan. She usually does. If you don't have anything going on today, there's always room for one more."

Buzz shook his head, serious eyes on the road ahead. "All I've done since getting here - other than our adventures yesterday - is wander the beach, swim, and watch old movies with my folks. I'd love a change of pace."

"You'll have to be brave," Jessie laughed. "You never know what will happen when you're with Cher." Jessie felt a kinship with Buzz, a new-found closeness. They were both at loose ends, uncertain of what they would do next.

"Cheryl is a dynamo, isn't she?" Buzz smiled but didn't take his eyes off of the road.

"You have no clue." Jessie turned, looking over the back of the seat as the puppy whined, soulful eyes darting between them as if following the conversation.

"Cheryl is interested in everything. She loves discovering new things. She would be out every night if I let her." Jessie giggled, reaching out to pat the dog's head. "I met Cheryl at school. She is so smart, but she is easily distracted, too. She was a couple years older than me, but we hit it off."

"So, she likes to party?" A wrinkle appeared on the man's brow.

"Not party, exactly. More like explore. She wants to be out doing something all the time." Jessie grinned. "Cheryl is spontaneous, insightful, and full of life. She's so much fun and can always find a good distraction just when I need it. Don't get me wrong. She's super serious about her job and studies. I don't know what that brain of hers does, but she seems to be able to juggle ten things at once."

"Doesn't that get exhausting?" Buzz chanced a glance in her direction.

"No." Jessie shook her head. "I guess it could if we both didn't have other things to do, but we always found balance. When we were roommates, Cher would drag me out to do something fun, like one of those escape rooms or just dinner and music when I got too serious."

"If she could go out every night, where would she go?" Buzz glanced her way again.

"Well, for instance, tonight she wants to go to the maritime museum. Since last night's excursion, she's obsessed with ghost ships." Jessie's laugh was light. "I know she's just having fun, but Cher does not know how to do things halfway. She's all in, all the time."

"No wonder she's tired." Buzz turned into the drive, rolling past sand dunes and down a long lane that ended in a circular drive at the front of the house. "I was exhausted at the Academy, and I was only focusing on one career."

Jessie sat looking at him for a moment. "Cheryl will fixate on something for a while but then when she understands it, she's ready to move on to something different. Come on. Let's see what she's come up with for lunch." Jessie grabbed the door handle as Buzz switched off the old sedan. Stepping out into the blazing sunlight, Jessie opened the back door of the car, the puppy staring at her with troubled eyes as he gazed at the pavement below. "Out you get," Jessie said, waiting until the pup moved to the floor then stepped gingerly onto the pavement. Snatching up his leash, she led him up a curving sidewalk lined with low growing plants to the door, Buzz on her heels.

"It was nice of you to get Cheryl away from her routine for a while." Buzz grabbed the door, pulling it open, letting the cool interior air wash over them as Jessie and Muttley stepped inside. "We all need a break sometimes."

"How about you?" Jessie turned with her back to the stairs and looked up into his eyes, the feeling sunlight from the window above on her skin. "Do you need a break? Will this vacation be enough to make you feel like you're on the right path again?"

Buzz offered a wry grin. "My bosses seemed to think so." He shook his head, dropping his gaze. "For me it goes deeper. To be honest, I'm sick of thinking about it." He sighed, avoiding her eyes as weariness, sorrow, and a hint of anger flashed across his face.

"Hey," Jessie touched his arm. "It will all work out. You just have to believe."

Buzz raised an eyebrow but didn't speak, doubt filling the depths of his brown eyes. "Have a little faith," she urged.

"There you are!" Cheryl called from the top of the stairs. She was wearing a blue denim jumpsuit belted with a white scarf, her hair in a long ponytail that swayed as she took the first step. The puppy, sitting between Jessie and Buzz, gave a happy yip as she started toward them. "Lunch is almost ready."

"Something smells great," Buzz's familiar smile returned. "I might get spoiled hanging out with you ladies."

"That's the idea." Cheryl skipped down the stairs, grabbing his arm and turning him toward the kitchen. "Lunch in ten." She looked down at the dog, skeptically. "Maybe he should go outside." She sniffed. "At least he smells better."

Jessie followed Buzz as Cher dragged him to the table, seeing that he was happy to focus on anything but his worries, and she let it go. Sometimes she needed to remember that they were all young and had time to figure out this thing called life.

Jessie bit back a laugh. "I'll leave him in the yard for a bit, but he can't stay out there all day. It's too hot." She started toward the living room, happy to let Cheryl drag them all along in her wake for the day.

"Speaking of hot, wait until you taste this dish." Cheryl waggled her perfectly penciled brows. "It's delish." Jessie shook her head, as her friend busied herself in the kitchen, indicating for Buzz to sit at the table.

"Be right back," Jessie winked at Buzz as she walked Muttley through the kitchen toward the back door, drawing a goofy grin as she walked the puppy to the back yard. Someone had placed a bowl of cold water on the stone patio along with a bowl of kibble, and the puppy tugged at the leash, heading for it. Jessie let the dog go, following him to the bowl where he lapped thirstily. Unsnapping the leash, she stroked the puppy. He looked and felt much better, barely flinching when her hand strayed close to his stitches.

"I feel ya, Muttley." she said, remembering the stitches she had needed last fall after getting hit on the head. "They'll heal." She smiled at the bowls on the stone patio. Cheryl was not a dog person, this was true, but she was a kind soul, and Jessie knew it had been her who had made a special space for Muttley. Overhead, a seagull called, and Muttley cowered. "Don't worry, boy. You're safe." Jessie cuddled the dog for a moment, feeling him relax before letting him return to his food. "I'll be back soon." She stood, letting her eyes take in the familiar space. It was a large square of white wall, a long patio of white stone sprawled before the door, and lush plants filled the border and corners. A table sat in a corner under a wisteria tree, and a gate on the far side of the wall led to the pool deck. Overall, Jessie thought it was the perfect place for the puppy to stay.

"There you are," Cheryl chided as Jessie walked back into the kitchen. "Get washed up. Lunch is served." The blonde woman gestured at the table laden with crackers, cheese, meat, and fruit. "I just need to get the main attraction from the fridge."

Jessie smiled, giving Buzz a wicked grin. "Bossy, isn't she?" she whispered as she headed for the bathroom, scrubbing up before coming back into the kitchen. "And what is the main surprise?" she asked, looking between Buzz and Cheryl. "I'm starving, so I hope it isn't one of those new skinny experiments you've been making."

"Buffalo chicken salad." Cheryl placed a large bowl of a somewhat pink-looking mess on the table, and Jessie looked at Buzz, a question in her eye.

Buzz grinned. "Trendy food," he chuckled. Pausing as Jessie bowed her head and sitting quietly when Cheryl did the same.

"Well, dig in." Cher said, before filling her plate. "It's spicy," she added as Buzz grabbed a cracker, added a dollop of the chicken salad to it and popped it in his mouth.

"Mmm," He hummed. "Good." His eyes got wide, and he grabbed for the glass of iced tea by his plate. "Hot!"

Cheryl laughed. "I warned you. I used every pepper sauce I know of in this mess." She leaned on the table, her blue jump-suit accentuating her pale complexion. "I like spicy food."

Jessie hurriedly prepared a cracker, her actions covering her grin at Buzz's discomfort. Jessie nibbled a cracker, tasting the tangy heat of the chicken salad while her friend handed Buzz a celery stick drenched in ranch dressing to cool his tongue.

"It's good." Jessie agreed, after her first bite. "Do you really think we need spicy food in the middle of summer, though?" Her eyes flicked to Buzz who was wiping tears from his eyes as he guzzled his iced tea.

"Yes." Cheryl, grinned. "It's good for you, and after the heat, you feel cooler."

"I thought that was what air conditioning was for." Buzz croaked. "You two must have asbestos tongues."

"You'll get used to it, if you hang out with us for long." Cheryl laughed, making a salad of the greens and adding chicken salad and crumbled crackers to the plate drowning it all in creamy ranch dressing.

"Next time you tell me something is spicy, I'll heed the warning." Buzz chuckled, lifting his glass. "Can I get a refill and some more of that dressing?

The rest of the lunch was wonderful with everyone carefully measuring the amount of chicken salad they put on crackers or salad. The fruit, cheese, and other veggies were a perfect complement to the hot dish. Liberal amounts of ranch dressing moderated the heat, and overall it was a pleasant meal.

"So, are we all going out tonight?" Cheryl looked between Jessie and Buzz. "Are you sticking around?" she offered Buzz a bright smile. "I have a fun evening planned."

"Cher, you always have a plan, so just spill it." Jessie turned, glaring at her friend as she dug into her food. "I already told Buzz he can come along." She looked at Buzz who nodded. "I think you said something about the Maritime Museum."

"Goodie!" Cheryl clapped her hands with delight, her face breaking into a happy grin. " The more the merrier, I always say. I've got everything figured out. This afternoon, we'll go to the museum and see what we can find out about the AnnaSwift." She waved a hand around, her bright red nails flashing in the sun. "I want to find out about buried treasure and if anything has ever been found of the ship." She scowled. "Imagine all of those people lost at sea." She shook her head, the serious moment disappearing with the action.

Jessie turned, giving Buzz a grin. "What did I tell you?"

Buzz chuckled, looking down at his plate.

"What have you been telling him?" Cheryl sat up, one brow raised in question as she rested an elbow on the table and leaned on her hand.

"Only that when you find something interesting, you jump in with both feet." Jessie smirked, looking at Buzz who nodded again.

"Oh." Cher waved the comment away with a grin. "I can't argue that point. I love learning." She looked between Buzz and Jessie. "So, are we all doing this?"

"Sure." Buzz agreed, his eyes turned to Jessie, and she could see that anything that kept him from worrying over his job was welcome. "I haven't seen much of Savanna, yet, and what better way to do it than in the company of two lovely ladies?" He chuckled, wiggling his eyebrows and making the girls laugh.

"How about we do dinner on the wharf?" Jessie suggested. The collection of food items were quickly disappearing as the three of them enjoyed the meal. "I hear there's a great seafood place there. After the museum, we can watch the ships go by."

"Perfect!" Cheryl enthused as they finished lunch.

"Are you sure?" Buzz asked. "We ate out last night." He shifted on his chair before looking at his friend.

"We're on vacation." Jessie gave the man a hard look. "We're supposed to indulge a little." She shrugged. "Besides, I've budgeted for everything." She watched Buzz battle with himself before he relaxed, his familiar grin returning.

"I'll clean up." Cheryl offered, seeing that everyone seemed to be finished. "You get ready or figure out what to do with that dog." She gave Buzz a wink, and Jessie saw his cheeks flush.

"I am ready." Jessie protested, looking down at her shorts and white top. "I will go check on Muttley, though." She looked at Buzz. "You might want to come along," she hissed. "You don't want to be underfoot when Cher is loading a dishwasher."

"Thanks for lunch." Buzz said, standing as Cheryl started collecting plates.

Jessie walked through the living room, past the second staircase, and to the double french doors, Buzz on her heels. Opening the door, she stepped out onto the grassy lawn, seeing the puppy sniffing in the flower beds. "Do you think he'll be okay while we're gone?" She asked. "What if he eats something bad for him?"

"He'll be all right here." Buzz stooped as the puppy trotted to him, still favoring his injured paw. "Won't you buddy?" He looked up at Jessie. "He's been on his own for a while, and has been fine until he tangled with seagulls."

The dog yipped, tail wagging as Buzz scratched his ears.

"You think so?"

"Sure." Buzz stood, stretching before walking toward a small table in the shade of a wisteria tree.

Jessie followed him, smiling when the puppy hurried after Buzz.

"The place is secure." The man raised a hand, looking up at the tall solid walls surrounding the garden. "He has food and water, and we'll be back before he gets too lonely." He pulled out a chair at an ornate white wrought iron table, taking a seat. The glass of sweet tea still in his hand beaded with sweat as Buzz stretched out his long legs and sighed with contentment. "I'd be comfortable here."

Jessie slipped into a white metal chair, the puppy walking under the table to flop at her feet.

"Okay." She smiled. "If I get worried we'll make it an early night. There's no one around to call in to check on him. We're pretty isolated here."

Buzz gazed around the garden. "That's what's nice about it." He looked at the garden. "It's crazy busy where I'm staying." He looked under the table, smiling at the pup. "What will you do if no one comes for the dog?"

Silence echoed in the garden, with only the sounds of birds and the sea. Jessie fidgetted, guilt at the idea of dropping the puppy at a pet adoption place battling with her confusion about her life.

"Oh." Jessie finally spoke. "You don't think he belongs to anyone?" She looked up, hoping Buzz would reassure her that they could find the dog's owner.

Buzz shrugged, drawing Jessie's eyes to his broad shoulders. "It's a possibility. But he's a mutt." The man looked up, taking in the house and stucco wall. "I can't see many people who own places out this way wanting a mutt."

Jessie opened her mouth to protest then closed it again. He was right. Many people who could afford a property on a private beach like this one would only want purebred dogs of high quality.

Jessie sagged. She didn't have time for a dog, did she? "Yeah, you're probably right." Jessie turned the thought over, unsure of what she would do if no one claimed the dog. "If someone in this area lost a dog it wouldn't be a true mutt but a designer dog."

Buzz turned, his dark eyes meeting her azure blue gaze. "So what is your solution?" He held her eyes steady, forcing her to answer.

Jessie looked down at the puppy sleeping at her feet, and her heart twisted. The little beast was alone in the world but lay there trusting her with his life.

"She'll keep it," Cheryl called, walking out of the house through the sliding doors. The wide bell bottoms of her denim jumpsuit swayed as she carried a tray of iced tea and cookies to the table.

"What?" Jessie protested, sitting up straighter. "I didn't say that."

"If no one claims that puppy, you'll keep it." Cheryl smiled. "You have that nice house and big property. It would be perfect for a dog." The blonde woman smiled. "Now that you have the yard and garden in order, and some of the folks from Estonia have insisted on keeping it up, the pup would love it at your house." Cher placed the tray on the table, giving Jessie a knowing look. "Besides, you'd never be able to abandon it."

"Plus, it would be a bit of extra personal protection." Buzz grinned. "The groomer said he would be big, and he would be a great guard dog," His eyes sparkled, and Jessie knew he was thinking about her problems last year.

"I can't." Jessi shook her head. "I'd have to train him, and what about work?" She shook her head. "It's too much. I don't even know what I'll be doing when I get back to Macon." A hint of panic filled her voice, and a paw landed on her foot. Jessie looked under the table, meeting sad brown eyes.

"Uhm, you aren't working right now." Cheryl sat, crossing her arms and giving her friend a hard look. "You have plenty of room, and," she glared, "you can always have him trained."

Jessie sighed, looking up at Cheryl and Buzz who stared at her. "We will see." She replied, stubbornly. "I'm still going to try to find his owner." Jessie gave them a determined glare. "He's so cute. Someone must own him." The puppy whined, and she reached under the table to stroke his head. "I think this conversation is upsetting, Muttley." She reached for a glass, letting Cher fill it with tea as she tried to end the discussion.

Cheryl turned, looking at Buzz, a knowing gleam in her eye, making Jessie run a hand over her face as she groaned.

"I'm not keeping him." Jessie blustered, one last time.

"Sure." Buzz and Cheryl replied. "We believe you." They both wore matching grins that Jessie wanted to wipe from their faces.

Jessie rolled her eyes, but then looked down at the puppy who had closed his eyes, chin on her foot. He was peaceful in sleep, his head resting on his paws. Could she give him up if she had to? There were already so many questions to be answered in her life. She looked up at Buzz. He seemed to like the dog. The thought that he could adopt the pup flashed through her mind, but she pushed it away. He already had enough happening, and she was worried about him. He had been so sure of what he wanted in his life, and now... now he wasn't sure he had made the right choice. What if she made the wrong choices and ruined everything?

Cheryl refilled glasses, playing the part of the perfect hostess as they relaxed in the shade. It was good to see her friend rested and interested in something new. Letting go of her concerns about the puppy, Jessie breathed in the smell of fresh blooms, sea air, and warmth as she relaxed, sipping tea in companionable silence.

"We'll head over to the museum around three," Cheryl broke the silence, her eyes on the sky. "It shouldn't be crowded then, and we can head right to the display we're interested in."

"You're interested in it." Jessie corrected, smiling over her glass at Buzz. "Buzz and I are just along for moral support."

Buzz lifted his glass in mock salute, his eyes sparkling with laughter.

"It'll be fun." Cheryl insisted, still serious. "You wait and see. We'll have all sorts of tales to tell after this excursion." She leaned forward, eyes bright. "Maybe we'll see the ghost ship again tonight."

"Cher, that was not a ghost ship." Jessie shook her head.

"You keep your negativity to yourself." Cheryl leaned back in the chair, flipping her ponytail over her back. "I'm having fun."

The interior of the Maritime Museum was cool and quiet after the heat of the later afternoon sun and the long walk along the beach. Buzz held the door while Jessie stepped through after Cheryl.

"It feels good in here," the man said as he stepped inside, moving against a wall as his eyes adjusted to the light. He brushed the sweat from his face, soaking in the cool air blowing from vents in the ceiling. "You'd think more people would be escaping the heat."

"Everyone is doing tours," Cheryl said, leading them through the quiet building. "The most popular are the plantation tours, but that's old school to us." She grinned, looking at Jessie who groaned.

"Not all plantations are like ours." Jessie looked at Buzz. "The places around here are gorgeous and the history rich."

"I thought The Estonia was full of history." He grinned, a wicked gleam in his eye. "All those old people have history."

"Buzz!" Jessie chided, smacking his arm.

"Just kidding. That place is amazing." He shrugged. "Uncle Paul sure likes living there." He looked around the museum. "Maybe we'll do a plantation tour one day." He stepped out, his soft soled shoes quiet as he followed Cheryl. The woman seemed to know where she was going, so he was content to let her lead the way. "I think my folks are doing some sort of bus tour that goes around to different plantations." He shrugged, "that is not for me."

"What, you don't like crowds?" Jessie asked as they moved into a separate area of the museum.

Buzz shivered dramatically. "Being crowded into a small space, my knees crammed up to my chin while I wait on someone else to tell me what to do? No thanks." Buzz ducked his head, leaning forward to whisper in Jessie's ear. "Besides, the tour is for retired folks."

He grinned when Jessie laughed, and once again regretted not keeping their friendship up after last year's adventure. His eyes fell on Jessie, her chestnut hair was twisted into a messy knot and held in place with a clip. Her smile was bright, and she still laughed often. The girl was pretty, but on the one night he had accompanied her to a dinner theater, she had amazed him with her elegance and beauty. He still had treasured photos from that night that no one else had seen.

Jessie Whyne was smart, funny, curious, and brave. She was also the daughter of one of the wealthiest women in Georgia and came from a very different world than Buzz. At times she was easy to be around, and at others she seemed a world away; someone out of reach who moved in circles he couldn't hope to fit in.

"Here it is!" Cheryl's voice was bright as she pointed at a painting of a two-masted sailing vessel. "This is the AnnaSwift."

Buzz stepped up behind the two women, hooking his hands behind his back as he peered over their heads at the painting. "It's pretty." The image was sketchy but spoke of motion, and he could almost imagine the boat slipping through open water.

"Yes, it is." Cheryl shook her head, her tone serious. "It was an old ship by the time they left the harbor on that fateful night. From what I've read on the internet, the ship was reported to be in good shape, though. No one seems to think it sank because of damage or neglect."

Buzz continued to look at the painting while Jessie turned scanning the room.

"Then what happened to it?" Buzz asked, curiosity getting the better of him. He glanced down at Cheryl. "You seem to know a great deal about this."

"Some believe the ship was overburdened with people and goods." A man's voice echoed in the quiet, interrupting their conversation. The trio turned as Dr. Crumm appeared, wiping his glasses with his handkerchief.

Buzz wheeled, surprised he hadn't heard the man approach. He scanned him. An innocuous man with a kind smile and grandfatherly eyes.

"The people on that boat were fleeing the northern army. Many believe that they packed every valuable they owned, including a hoard of gold." The man shook his balding head, gleaming in the overhead lights. "All nonsense, of course. The ship was probably captured further out to sea by the Union ships blockading the harbor. They could have taken possession and delivered the AnnaSwift to another port, claiming the prize as salvage."

Buzz glanced at Jessie who had been looking at other displays but turned now, giving her attention to the historian.

"Your tour the other night inspired me." Cheryl smiled at the man. "I've been digging into the history of the legend ever since." She shuffled her feet, nervous energy and excitement evident in every fidget. "I love history."

Dr. Crumb smiled, stepping up close to Cheryl. "It's all just a fairytale, my dear. It was a bit of fun for the tourists. After all, it was a ghost tour." He shook his head. "There's nothing to the tale. People love to make up stories about these little mysteries." He put his glasses back on, folding his hands behind his back and gazing at the picture.

"Aren't you giving away trade secrets?" Buzz asked, watching the man.

Dr. Crumm turned, giving Buzz his full attention. "Young man, very few people actually research these things. Most are content to trundle through the streets of the city, indulging in the spookiness of the stories and then forgetting them by morning's light." He smiled, turning to look at each member of the group. "I can see that the three of you are interested in true history."

"It is rather fascinating," Cheryl turned from the man, looking at the painting. "Did you know that they didn't even file a manifest with the harbormaster before setting sail?"

"So I've heard." Dr. Crumm adjusted his glasses, looking at the painting. "I wouldn't expect anything else, though. After all, they were escaping the incoming army." He paused, offering a sad smile. "It's sad that they don't make ships like that anymore. Impractical, I know, but they were amazingly beautiful and sophisticated for their time."

"Wooden boats are still considered classy," Buzz mused. "A lot more work than fiberglass. If this ship still existed, it would be a landmark."

"You sail?" Dr. Crumm asked, curiosity written in his gaze.

"I had an uncle who was in the navy. When he came back he got a sailboat and trolled around the south. I went out with him a few times when he was in the area." He shrugged. "It was fun. Being on the water can be relaxing."

"A peaceful pastime," Crumm smiled. "I'm no good out on the water, myself. I get dreadfully sea sick on the calmest of days. No, I'll stick to studying them, and let others do the sailing."

"Have you worked at the museum for a long?" Jessie asked, turning away from the picture, her eyes steady on the man.

"Yes. I was a history teacher at a community college nearby, but I've always been fascinated by shipwrecks in the area. When I retired, I decided that working here part-time might be fun. The tours are a lark. A little extra money for frivolity's sake." He chuckled softly. "It keeps me out of trouble."

"You must know a great deal about the salvage operations in the area." Cheryl turned her attention to the man. "The laws of salvage are so complex and convoluted." The young woman's gaze was intense and Buzz was glad she wasn't questioning him.

"I'm not really interested in that side of things." Dr. Crumm smiled. " Treasure hunting is a very tedious and often dangerous operation." His tone was placid, his smile kind. "Of course, if you are curious about salvage, we have some amazing finds right here in this building. Come along. I'll show you." He turned, not waiting for a reply, and the three visitors fell in behind him.

Buzz took one more look at the painting, his eyes scanning the room and cataloging old ships logs, additional paintings and schematic, as well as a model of the ship. He had never been fascinated with boats or sailing, but he could understand the appeal of both. Hurrying to catch up, he fell in behind the girls, listening while the professor continued to expound on the delights the museum had in store. The older man seemed pleased to have a captive audience as he droned on.

"This is a 1700s cannon ball," the man pointed at a glass case. "It's in remarkable condition for its age. The ship carrying it was in a battle with a Spanish frigate and sadly came out the worse for wear."

"What about treasure?" Cheryl asked, eyes bright as she stared at the case. "Gold, silver, all of those things. Didn't the Spanish ship tons of it back home from the new world?"

Buzz grinned, enjoying Cheryl's enthusiasm. For the most part, treasure was something best left to the movies. He turned, looking at Jessie who was listening as she moved around the room.

"Oh my, yes." Crumm grinned. "We have a few bits from that era." He led the way further through the building, stopping at a display of sparkling gold coins, melded by pressure and age. "We're very proud of our collection."

"It's a lump." Cheryl said looking at the small collection of vaguely coin-like items.

Crumm chuckled, shaking his head. "Yes, but you can clearly see the Spanish imperial seal. These coins were from that era. Most people respond as you did." He continued. "They think treasure is like what you see in films - shiny coins, sparkling jewels, and strings of pearls - but the sea takes its toll on anything left in her grasp."

"It must be very rare to find things like this." Jessie finally spoke as she examined old bottles, pottery, and debris from the wreck. "I imagine someone could make a fortune diving for wrecks."

"More like lose their shirt." Dr. Crumm turned, light glinting off his glasses as he spoke. "Between the cost of finding a wreck and the odds of anything valuable actually being onboard, and then the regulations from state and federal agencies, only a tiny percentage of salvage crews ever make a profit." The man smiled again, tipping his head so his eyes shone. "Of course, there is the prestige of finding treasure. Sadly, that doesn't usually equal income."

"It's complicated, then?" Buzz asked, curiosity about the range of maritime salvage laws sparking his interest. Up until now, he had been enjoying the quiet and ambiance of the museum. He had always enjoyed history, but he wasn't planning on becoming a diver in search of sunken gold.

"Yes. There is a great deal to consider before anyone decides to dive for sunken ships. The balance between preservation and ownership can be tempestuous at the best of times. You also have other governments who often want their cut." Crumm pointed at the display case. "This was contested for years before we could display it."

"Thank you." Cheryl, smiled at the man. "You're very knowledgeable."

"That's my job." Crumm nodded. "If you young folks have any other questions, please feel free to stop by my office." He pointed up at a bank of windows overlooking the floor. "Enjoy your visit." He turned, his gray tweed blazer swaying slightly as he walked away, his shoes making soft clicking sounds on the wooden floor.

"Bye." The trio waved, turning back to the display then moving through the room and slipping between glass cases and trying to take everything in at once.

Buzz watched the girls hurry to see as much as they could as the sky outside began to reflect the ending of the day.

"I think it's almost closing time," Cheryl sighed, turning from a huge model of a paddle wheel boat. "We'd better go." She gave one last glance at the area, then grabbed Jessie's arm, pulling her toward the door.

"Besides," Jessie grinned, slipping an arm around her friend. "I'm getting hungry." She looked up at Buzz expectantly.

"You know me. I'm always hungry." Buzz laughed, looking at his watch. It's almost seven already." Turning, he led the way back toward the front door and the darkening sky. He released the door as the girls stepped through, still arm-in-arm. A hand grasped his arm, and he smiled at Jessie who looked happy and content. It felt nice to wander through Savannah with Jessie and Cheryl. For the first time in weeks, he felt some of the weight and worry slip from his shoulders, and he realized he was starting to enjoy his unplanned leave.

CHAPTER 4

The restaurant was a two-story timber structure covered in clapboard siding, the top deck open to the air and a perfect place to watch the waves. Darkness had descended during the drive to the eatery, but lights along the beach sparkled on the water.

The trio made their way to a table on the deck, letting the cool breeze off the Atlantic wash over them as they ordered. Live music played at the back of the balcony, and everyone settled in for a relaxing evening.

"That was very enlightening," Cheryl said, steepling her hands as she rested her elbows on the table and stared over the railing. "The museum. . .all those ships."

Jessie looked, smiling at Buzz. She knew that Cheryl wouldn't let this go until her curiosity was satisfied. She was now fixated on shipwrecks and buried treasure. Not that there was much to be found anymore. Most wrecks had been well explored, and with submarines, sonar, and other means of tracking the ocean floor, more ships had been found in recent years. Still, as much as Cher was enjoying the idea of ghost ships, Jessie knew that there was only a hint of truth to the myths.

"Cheryl, we are not here to investigate shipwrecks, legends, or myths. We are on vacation and are supposed to be resting." Jessie looked to Buzz for support, and he nodded.

"R&R." Buzz grinned. "Rest and relaxation." His smile grew. "I think we're all ready for that."

"I know," Cheryl agreed, sagging a little, her eyes losing a little of their sparkle. "I just found it interesting."

"Cher, you find everything interesting." Jessie laughed, patting her friend's hand. "You do enough research in your studies, you need to lighten up and have fun."

"Oh fun!. We could go dancing!" Cheryl's spark returned, and Jessie shook her head.

"See? I told you. Cher is into everything." A wicked gleam entered Jessie's eyes, and she hooked her gaze on Buzz. "Buzz is a fantastic dancer," she said. "He seems to know all the old steps and most of the new"

"I'd have to see it to believe it." Cheryl challenged, raising her brows as she looked at Buzz. "A long, tall drink of water like you. You must have two left feet."

Buzz took a step back, eyes wide. "Now wait a minute." His eyes darted to Jessie. "No one said anything about dancing." He looked at Cheryl. "And I don't have two left feet."

"Cher." Jessie growled. "I told you Buzz can dance. We had a great evening last fall, tripping the two-step and all of that." she waved a hand as if that explained their night out as she took Buzz by the right arm as he dropped his head in defeat.

"Yes," Cheryl looked at her friend, giving Jessie a questioning look. Buzz, the subject of the discussion, was all but forgotten, standing at Jessie's side examining his shoes. "But I didn't see it." she nodded toward the band. "After we eat, you two can show me."

Buzz looked between the two women, a startled expression in his eyes, and Jessie took pity on him, patting his arm. "He isn't here for your entertainment, Cher. Isn't that right Buzz?"

Both women turned, pinning him with their eyes.

"What?" he stuttered. The man lifted his head, gaping, eyes wide like a deer in the headlights.

"Who had the tuna?" A server arrived, a heavy tray in hand and a welcoming smile on her face.

Jessie laughed, seeing Buzz's relief as the meals were distributed, and he escaped any further scrutiny as they dug into the piping hot food which was as good as the reviews said..

As everyone concentrated on their meals, Jessie contemplated the night she and Buzz had been dancing during the course of their investigation. She had been surprised at his skill on the dance floor. Her mother had insisted that all of her children learn to dance. She had them instructed in everything from a simple waltz to the watusi. The Whyne family had been part of many charity galas and events and were often required to step onto the floor. But Buzz. . .he had been a surprise.

"So, how come you can dance?" Cheryl piped up as she popped a bite of cheddar biscuit in her mouth. She clearly had not been distracted from the subject for long by the arrival of the meal.

Buzz looked at Jessie, his ears going red as he ducked his head and grinned with embarrassment. "I was clumsy." his voice cracked, and he cleared his throat.

Cheryl looked at Jessie then back at Buzz, making Jessie hide a giggle behind her napkin.

"What does being clumsy have to do with dancing?" Cheryl leaned on the table, and Jessie considered saving Buzz from her but decided to see how he handled her flamboyant friend.

"I've always been tall," Buzz began. "I grew fast and was all feet and gangly legs. By the time I was fifteen, I was already six-foot-two. Everyone thought I was made for basketball." His cheeks flushed as he continued, and he pushed a scallop around on his plate, sliding it through shimmering garlic butter. "Dad didn't know what to do to help, so mom made me take dance lessons, hoping I'd gain some coordination."

Jessie smiled, trying to imagine Buzz as an awkward teen. He was tall, fit, and confident now, if easily embarrassed and a little shy.

"Oh." Cheryl sat up, offering Jessie a grin. "You have a smart mom."

"I do," Buzz agreed. "Sadly, I learned to dance but got no better on the court." He shrugged, his eyes flicking to Jessie. "I didn't really like basketball, anyway. And though I tried out for a few other sports, none of them really caught my interest. I had a plan for after high school, and they didn't involve getting busted up playing games."

"I still need to see it to believe it." Cheryl grinned, her eyes straying to the tiny dance floor. "Go on Jess, dance with Buzz."

"Me?" Jessie gaped. "You're the one who is curious." She shook her head. She was sure Cher would pull something like this and though dancing with Buzz was fun, did she want people assuming they were a couple?

"Yes, but I'm not risking my toes to those clod-hoppers. Besides, you said he danced well, so go for it."

Jessie turned pleading eyes to Buzz, offering a silent apology for her friend.

Buzz folded his napkin, placed it on the table, and offered his hand with a welcoming grin.

"What?" Jessie laughed. "You, too?"

"We might as well put an end to this now." Buzz laughed. "At least I know you are skilled on the dance floor and that all of my toes will be intact tomorrow."

Jessie gave Cheryl an exasperated look but slipped her hand into Buzz's, standing and letting him lead her toward the floor. His hand was strong, warm, and familiar, and in moments they had both slipped into the stream of dancers. Even after months of not seeing him, Jessie felt confident and safe moving through the steps with Buzz, and she enjoyed the feeling of moving as one around the floor.

"This is familiar," Buzz grinned, his hand on her waist as they twisted to a quick tune.

Jessie laughed, following his lead and giving in to the music. "I can't believe Cher did this," she said, noting the gleam in her partner's eye. "Tell the truth, you're having fun."

"It is fun." Buzz laughed. "Aren't you here to enjoy yourself?" His eyes grew serious for a moment. And Jessie felt sorry for dampening his enthusiasm.

"I guess so." Jessie chuckled, spinning as he twirled her with perfect control. "Okay, yes. I'm having fun. You really are a great dancer."' She leaned into him, letting her worries drift away as she enjoyed the closeness and comradery.

"Jessie!" Cheryl's voice broke over the dance floor, pulling them to a stop as the band missed a note. "It's back!"

Buzz squinted at Jessie, his hand still in hers. Giving a tug, he dragged her through the crowded restaurant to where Cheryl leaned half-over the railing, others joining as she pointed out to sea.

"What in the world?" Jessie grumbled, squeezing in next to her friend.

"The ghost ship!" Cheryl bounced on her shiny sandals. "It's back."

Jessie turned, following her friend's arm to the green glow on the sea. The hushed whispers of diners became a subtle backdrop to the image that appeared as more people crowded the rail. Drifting across the water, shrouded in thin wisps of fog, a ghostly galleon sailed. A tall, double masted ship, a mere flicker of outline on the inky water.

Jessie shivered, the night air flitting across her skin like icy fingers. She knew it was a hoax, and she kicked herself for not asking Dr. Crumm more about the tour. Still, the silence of the vessel had a foreboding look that struck at her soul.

"It's a gag," Buzz leaned over Jessie's shoulder, the warmth of his body battling with the frightening chill the image evoked. "You know, for the tour."

"The tour doesn't start for another twenty minutes," Cheryl twisted, looking up and giving him a glare. "That is something else." Her slender arm pointed out to see, her index finger tracking the ship.

The other patrons whispered and giggled as they watched the ship go by, but Jessie barely heard them.

"I don't know what it is," Jessie said, wrapping her arms around herself against the sudden chill. "But something strange is happening in Savannah." She looked up at Buzz, and he stepped a little closer, his warmth a comfort as her mind began picking at the puzzle.

The green glow flickered, the glowing outline of the ship evaporating into thin air as the moon broke the horizon.

"That is not a ship with it's running lights on in the fog." Cheryl, placed a hand on her hip, looking at Buzz with defiance. "You could even see the sails and shape of the ship."

Jessie turned, crammed between Buzz and the railing as she looked up, meeting his eyes. He leaned close, protective and strong. "Now I'm curious. I think there is more to this than a ghost tour putting on a show." she said, meeting his dark eyes. " Aren't you?"

Jessie watched as Buzz dropped his head, taking a step back, then looking up at her from under his spiky brown hair.- "What do we do?" His smile spread, and Jessie grabbed his hand. Reaching for Cheryl with her other hand, she headed back to the table.

Jessie curled her arms around her knees, gazing out at the quiet ocean below. A breeze ruffled the hem of her night gown as she snuggled on the narrow balcony at the front of her room. She was tired, but her mind was spinning from her night out with Buzz and Cheryl.

Images, ideas, and feelings tangled in her heart, and as the moon glowed over softly lapping waves, she tried to sort them out. The evening had started as something fun, but now thoughts of a ghost ship plagued her mind. There was something odd going on, and though her mind told her it was all some elaborate publicity stunt, her instincts couldn't agree. Resting her chin on her knees, Jessie sighed. She didn't believe in ghosts, unless you could count the Holy one. Jessie's lips tugged into a grin until the memory of dancing with Buzz pushed other things away.

Being with Buzz again had lifted her spirits. The thought zipped through her mind, making Jessie laugh. She hadn't meant her thoughts to go this direction.

Spinning around the dance floor in Buzz's arms had brought back memories of their adventure together last year. Buzz was a fantastic dancer, better than the majority of men she had danced with at events. She smiled again, her heart pinching as she remembered dancing with her father. She missed him and his inquisitive mind. Carl Whyne had died several years earlier from a massive heart attack, taking with him a piece of her soul.

Jessie loved her stepfather, Brand. The man had come into her mother's life unexpectedly, but he had made Audrey happy, filling her life with love and giving them all Joey. The surprise baby was a new blessing to everyone.

Thoughts of her family made Jessie smile. She loved them and knew that they would always love and accept her. The problem was, she didn't know where her place in the world was or where she fit in her family. How had things gotten so muddled?

Her mind twisted back to dancing with Buzz. The feeling of being in his arms was light and fun. She wished that life could be like that; someone else leading the steps as the days rushed by.

Looking up, Jessie studied the moon, a broad crescent sparkling on the dark water below. The world was beautiful. Nature worked in sync as one season rolled into the other. There was an order, but why wasn't there order in her life?

"God," Jessie whispered, looking at the stars. "What am I doing? What am I supposed to do with my life?"

She propped her elbows on her knees, resting her chin in her hands. A ship's horn blared, and she straightened, peering over the low rail toward the dark water. Cheryl was obsessed with the ghost ship after the tour. The AnnaSwift, surely nothing more than a myth, had captured Cher's attention, and she was determined to follow any trail until she knew the truth about the ship. Jessie had to admit she, too, was curious about how the tour operators made the ship seem to appear and disappear in a moment. The sea breeze pricked her skin, her mind rolling over what she knew. Would a tour give away so much by putting on such a display? If one tour paid for the effect of a ghost ship, couldn't others monopolize on it as well? Wasn't part of the appeal of a ghost tour triggering a person's imagination and letting it fill in the blanks? What you couldn't see or explain was far spookier than green ghost lights that could be explained away.

Jessie shook off the tingle of the unknown, smiling as she thought about how happy the idea of a ghost ship had mady Cheryl. What harm could come from poking around and discovering the spooky secrets of a fake ship?

Resting her head on her knees, Jessie sank into thought once more. A wet nose bumped her elbow, and she looked down at the puppy who had wandered outside to join her. "Hey, Mutt." Jessie rubbed his ears. "Do you need to go out?" The dog rolled over, exposing his tummy covered with white and black speckled fur.

The puppy squirmed with delight, tail thumping as his long ears flopped on the floor. The dog's pink tongue lolled out of the side of his mouth in a canine grin.

Jessie laughed, scratching the puppy's tummy again. "You sure are cute. Tomorrow I'll take pictures of you, so I can make flyers. If you have an owner, we need to find them."

The puppy whined softly, rolling over and dropping his face on Jessie's leg. She rubbed his ears and relaxed as he closed his eyes. As the puppy fell asleep, Jessie considered her next steps. Cheryl wanted the full story of the AnnaSwift, and Jessie had to admit that investigating the fake ghost ship might be a good distraction from her concerns. Sitting and worrying over her life choices didn't seem to be helping. Maybe if she focused on something else, life would fall into place.

"Come on." She shook the puppy gently. Standing, she headed back into her room, the moon streaming through the wall-sized window facing the ocean. The puppy trotted through the door, skidding on the tile floor as he trotted to the bed. "Oh, no you don't." Jessie wagged a finger at the dog. "You sleep in your bed." she pointed to the plush bed she had purchased at a shop on the way back from dinner. The puppy sat down, looking up at her with pleading eyes, but she shook her head.

The little dog dropped his head, reminding Jessie of how Buzz did the same thing when embarrassed or thinking. A moment later Muttley turned three times on his bed, then dropped down, resting his head on his paws.

"Good boy," Jessie said. Hoping that tonight she wouldn't be up every couple of hours to take him outside.

Climbing into the cool sheets of the bird's eye maple bed, Jessie closed her eyes, once more thinking about Buzz. He had only gotten a couple of hours of sleep last night, but he hadn't hesitated to spend the day with her and Cheryl. He had helped her with the puppy, returning to check on him after dinner.

Jessie smiled then yawned, rolling over and hugging her pillow. She knew that Buzz was used to different shifts and long hours, but he had looked weary when he left an hour ago. It seemed that she and Buzz were both at a crossroads in their life. His would be decided by a group of officers determining his fate; and she was left to figure it out on her own. A verse, one of her mother's favorites, came to mind, and Jessie relaxed.

"A man determines his plans, but God directs his path." Jessie whispered the sound into the night. Letting her mind and body relax, Jessie determined to get a good night's sleep. She would indulge Cheryl's whim and keep Buzz from brooding over his suspension.

A breeze ruffled the sheer curtains covering the open door, and the puppy barked, trotting to the balcony to peer over the stucco wall.

"Mutt?" Jessie called. Climbing out of bed and hurrying through the door. "Muttley, what are you doing?" The pup had his front paws on the wall but turned, looking at her before giving another yip.

Jessie hurried toward him, dropping her hand on Muttley's head and looking out at the beach. A shadowy figure walked along the private beach. The silhouette was masculine, broad shouldered, and lean.

"He shouldn't be there." Jessie looked down at the dog who yipped softly. "This is a private beach. Invitation only." Jessie bit her bottom lip, wondering if she should call the police. Was the man watching them or was he just out for a stroll? Her family had never had any worries about the beach house being burgled, but things changed, and a house sitting alone like this would be a prime target. Slowly, she shook her head. Perhaps the man on the beach needed the silence afforded by the narrow strip of land to think. She refused to let life color her attitude to the point that she saw danger everywhere.

She was all too familiar with the need for silence. The past few months of her life had been quiet. Filled with family events, work, and then her birthday. Jessie pushed the thought away, watching the figure turn and stroll back down the beach toward the town. They hadn't come near the house or seemed suspicious. Silently, she whispered a prayer for the stranger. Everyone needed grace, and she was suddenly starting to understand what that meant.

The puppy nudged her hand, and Jessie smiled, leading him back into the bedroom and pointing to his bed. The dog settled in and Jessie did the same. Climbing into bed, the sound of the waves lapping at the shore lulling her to sleep.

Buzz looked up at the white house. The big box of glass and stucco was secure, and the silence of the night wrapped around his troubled heart. It had been fun going out with Cheryl and Jessie for the night. It had been a perfect distraction from his worries. Even Cheryl's enthusiastic determination to learn the secret of the disappearance of the AnnaSwift was a fun puzzle to dig into.

They had discussed it over dessert, though Buzz had found himself thinking about other things, and needed to refocus as the coffee was served.

Jessie had winked at Buzz as Cheryl sketched out a plan of investigation, and he knew she was only enjoying the distraction in the same way he was. There was no real mystery, just a fanciful story about a missing ship.

Glancing at the house once more, he thought he heard the puppy yip, but the sound disappeared on the seabreeze. Turning, he shoved his hands in the pockets of his shorts and headed back down the beach.

Tomorrow would come early. He chuckled. He was used to long nights and late hours behind a desk. Trying to fit his workout, morning run, and work routine into a day had been a challenge, so he had gotten used to little sleep. Tonight, instead of feeling exhausted, he felt relaxed, his mind torn between his suspension and the task of finding a suitable answer for Cheryl's quest.

His toes squished in the cool sand, the soft feel of the waves tickling his feet. The rhythmic swish and sush of the water easing the fear and uncertainty of his mind.

A smile pulled at his lips as he ambled down the beach, soaking in the sound of peace. A fog horn mourned into the night, and he looked up, seeing the green glow on the water.

There was no silhouette of a sailing ship now, just the eerie iridescent glowing on the water.

Buzz turned, trying to see what was moving through the water. There was no reason the ghost tours should be putting on a show tonight. Some of the bars in town were still open, but most of the town was closed for the night as town folks and tourists sought their beds.

Maybe Cheryl's little mystery would turn out to be more than a little fun, and he could regain some of the confidence he had been losing as the days dragged on. His head had been so tangled with doubt he hadn't been able to enjoy his life. His parents had seen it and had worried over it. Even as a grown man, he appreciated the love and acceptance they offered.

Once again, Uncle Paul had been right; he had needed to look up Jessie. Her friendship was just what he needed. He dropped his head, digging his toes into the sand. A friend. Just a friend.

CHAPTER 5

"Jessie!" Cheryl's voice echoing through her door woke Jessie from confused dreams. "Get up. We have to go to the harbor."***

Jessie sat up, rubbing the sleep from her eyes, feeling something heavy on her legs. "Mutt," She scolded as brown eyes lifted to hers, and the dog's tail thumped on the comforter. "Bad dog."

A soft whine told Jessie that the puppy understood.

"Jessie!"

"I'm coming." Jessie pushed the puppy off the bed as she threw off her blankets. "Give me a minute." She stopped halfway to the private bathroom. "Wait. What do you mean we have to go to the harbor?" Jessie was used to Cheryl's unannounced activities, but that didn't mean she couldn't be surprised. With seemingly boundless energy, Cher was always up early, and Jessie never counted on sleeping late when they were together. She smiled. Working at the college coffee shop had kept her flexible with her sleep schedule, anyway.

"I'll explain over breakfast. Now hurry up."

Jessie could hear Cheryl trotting down the hall. She shrugged, looking at the puppy who gave her soulful eyes. "I guess we'll find out." She shook her head and hurried into the bathroom, took a quick shower, brushed out her hair, dressed in casual summer wear, and applied a touch of make up.

"Come on, Mutt." Jessie called the dog as she opened the door and headed for the stairs that led to the living room and back door. The puppy rushed down the stairs, still favoring his right front paw slightly as he ran through the double doors and out into the yard.

Jessie laughed. The dog was quickly adapting to life in this house. He hadn't had an accident, yet, as she had consistently taken the animal out every couple of hours to answer nature's call. Last night, he had even whined, waking her when he had to go. "Be good," she called as they ran down the stairs, the dog galloping out into the back yard.

Heading to the kitchen, Jessie suppressed a yawn, sniffing as the smell of pancakes tickled her nose.

"So, what's going on?" She asked, walking into the kitchen and scanning the mess Cheryl had made. Bowls, mixer, and batter seemed to cover the counter.

"Set the table." Cheryl looked over her shoulder from where she stood at the stove flipping pancakes on the gas griddle. "Buzz will be here soon, and I'll explain." Cher flashed Jessie a bright smile. "Hurry up now. Set the table. Breakfast is almost ready. You don't want the string bean to have to wait do you?"

Jessie couldn't help but laugh. Cheryl's enthusiasm for everything was contagious, and her flamboyant personality attracted others into her atmosphere like a planetary pull. "I like the outfit," Jessie giggled.

"This?" Cher looked down at her blue, wide-legged crop pants and striped crew neck shirt. "I feel so eighties today." She laughed, tossing her hair as she turned back to the grill.

"I take it we have a sailor theme today?" Jessie grinned, heading to the cupboard for dishes. "Is Buzz eating with us?"

"Really?" Cheryl scoffed. "Have you seen the man? He needs to be fed."

A laugh broke from Jessie's lips as she placed dishes on the table. "He does seem to be able to eat," she agreed. She paused, growing serious for a moment. "I wonder if part of that is the hours he keeps. I mean, I know he works long hours at the station, and now on vacation he's up early, and I swear he was out walking on our beach last night."

He looked tired yesterday." Jessie shrugged, grabbing plates and doing as she had been instructed by setting the table.

"He's my age," Cheryl tsked then offered a bright smile, her flaming red lipstick a perfect contrast to her outfit of the day. "He can handle late nights." She shook her mane of golden hair. "We're young, Jess. Don't forget," she added as she flipped another pancake.

Jessie gave Cheryl a skeptical glance. "Because burning the candle at both ends doesn't leave people worn out and grouchy."

Cheryl's shoulders lifted in a shrug. "What can I say, life is interesting. Who wants to miss it sleeping?"

A car rolled into the driveway as Jessie placed silverware and napkins on the table. Peering out the window, she saw Buzz climbing out of his old blue sedan, his lean body unfolding as he slipped from behind the wheel. She watched as he stood, stretching and rolling his shoulders under a white button-up shirt covered with a muted green print. She smiled, imagining the clumsy teen under the confident facade of the well- built man.

"Oh, Buzz is here!" Cheryl enthused, standing on tiptoes to look out the window. "Better get the coffee. Well, move it." She added looking at her friend and making Jessie laugh.

"Aye, aye, skipper," Jessie teased as she pulled mugs from the cupboard, placing them on the table before filling a shiny silver carafe and adding it to the collection of dishes. Being here with Cheryl was just what she needed, and now that Buzz had joined them, she felt like she wasn't completely mired in decision making. The distractions, though frivolous, were fun. Buzz knocked on the door. A streak of black zipped past Jessie as the puppy skidded across the tile floor, and she headed for the door.

"Muttley," she scolded, as the puppy danced by the front door, offering a friendly bark. "Sit."

The puppy pranced, tongue lolling as his whole body wagged along with his tail. "Just a second," Jessie shouted through the door, grabbing the dog's leash from the wall and clipping it onto his collar. Holding the leash firmly in one hand, she unlocked the door, letting Buzz in.

"Good morning," Buzz greeted as the dog lunged at him, bouncing around him in joy, making Jessie stagger a step toward him.

"Good morning." Jessie smiled brightly, trying to pull the dog off her friend. "Someone is happy to see you."

Buzz stooped, petting the dog. "He looks much better. I hope he's not the only one happy to see me," he added with a goofy grin.

"He is feeling better." Jessie pulled the dog back, opening the door wider so Buzz could come inside. "We're all happy to see you."

"What are we doing today?" Buzz leaned in, whispering as his eyes found Cheryl placing a massive stack of pancakes on the table. "I got a text telling me to be here by nine." He shrugged, waiting.

"I have no idea." Jessie shut the door, releasing the dog who followed Buzz into the kitchen. "Based on the attire, though, I suspect boats might be involved. Note the nautical theme."

Buzz looked up, taking in Cheryl's slim form and nodded. "I see what you mean."

"Finally." Cheryl said dramatically. "Sit. Eat. I'll explain everything." She smiled as sunlight splashed across the room. "We have to be at the harbor by ten, so eat up." She untied the white apron, hanging it on a peg and smoothing her blue and white striped crew-neck shirt.

Jessie shrugged, taking a seat while Buzz did the same. Moments later, a platter of bacon joined the pancakes, and

Cheryl began to explain as she pushed the platter to Buzz who began filling his plate.

"I did some research last night," she said, pouring syrup on her pancakes. "They have a shipwreck tour that takes you out into the harbor and tells you all about the different dive sites. I booked three places." She smiled, taking a big bite of pancakes.

"Cher, you should have asked." Jessie looked at Buzz, her eyes apologetic. "What if Buzz has something else to do?"

"Do you?" Cheryl leaned on an elbow, looking at Buzz.

Buzz shook his head, his mouth full of pancakes.

"See? We're good." Cheryl waved Jessie's concerns away. "I checked, and you can even bring the mutt. So, you can't claim you need to stay home with him." She glared at the dog who looked longingly at Buzz's food from his seat on the floor. "So, it will be a great adventure."

"You don't mind?" Jessie asked, looking at Buzz as she toyed with her food. She didn't want to impose on Buzz. He had helped her before, but maybe now he would rather fill his time doing something else. He had already ferried her and the mutt to the vet and had been with them most of the past three days.

"No. It sounds fun." Buzz, looked at her, eyes shining as he broke off a piece of bacon, dropping his eyes to the puppy. "Sit." he said, waiting for the dog to plop his haunches on the tile floor before giving the animal a bit of crisp bacon.

"He already ate," Jessie said, looking between the two of them. "You'll spoil him."

"He's a dog. He'll always be willing to eat more." Buzz offered a bright grin. "At least he's smart. You'll have him trained in no time." He dropped his hand, petting the puppy. "I wouldn't normally feed him something at the table, but you said you weren't keeping him."

"I'm not keeping him." Jessie protested, stiffening. "I need to take pictures today and get them up on lost pet sites." She pushed a piece of pancake around on her plate, soaking up some of the syrup. "I don't have time for a dog."

Buzz looked between the puppy and Jessie, a half-smile on his face, making Jessie sigh. "I can see you, like Cheryl, think I'm keeping him, but I'm not."

"Whatever," Cheryl giggled. "Just eat. We need to go."

By nine-thirty the trio was headed for the marina, the puppy following, securly leashed and happy to be back on the beach.

"It's a nice day for a walk," Buzz said as they made their way around the bend of shore leading to the harbor and an array of boats bobbing in their slips. The boats were lined up, shimmering in the sun as they floated on the still water. Long quays led to each slip, wooden walkways floating on large plastic barrels that allowed them to rise and fall with the tide.

"It's beautiful." Jessie sighed. "Like one of those puzzles with the ships sparkling harbors. I love the water." She looked up, shading her face from the sun and wishing she had grabbed her silly bonnet. "We used to come down here when I was a kid. Dad knew how to sail and took us out sometimes."

"Not as far to go as town, either," Cheryl agreed, her rope-soled boat shoes silent on the sand. She was the only one not wearing shorts, but she looked completely comfortable in the loose fitting navy pants, a big canvas bag over one shoulder. "It's nice to walk places around here instead of having to drive everywhere."

Buzz nodded. "Macon is a little different. Spread out yet chunky, so unless you're downtown or in your neighborhood," he smiled at Jessie, "you pretty much need to drive." He stopped, breathing deeply of the salt air. "I've been running this beach each morning before sun-up, and it is amazing. I get to race the sunrise home."

Jessie looked at her friend, scanning his slim body, wide shoulders, and long legs. "I hate to run."

"No wonder you're in such good shape." Cheryl grinned, patting a rock hard shoulder. "Now hurry up, that's our boat." She clomped onto the boardwalk, hurrying toward a sailboat, her wide pant legs flapping as she moved.

Jessie looked up, seeing a large white catamaran rocking in the wake of a speed boat that was leaving the bay. She looked down at her shoes, glad she had good deck shoes. Buzz would have to remove his flip flops while on board, not only was it boat protocol, but it would prevent rubber marks from maring the fiberglass. "So, what is the schedule?" she asked, glancing at her friend.

"You'll see." Cheryl gave a little skip, hurrying forward to greet a lean, well-muscled man with sandy hair. He stood on the dock, holding a thick rope line in his hand as he unwound it from the hulyard attached to the dock.

"This is going to be interesting, isn't it?" Buzz asked, walking at Jessie's side as Cheryl hurried ahead and waving at a sailor.

"Always." Jessie laughed. "Always." She walked slowly down the floating dock, her feet holding firmly to the decking as a boat passed, making the whole structure rock.

"Good morning!" the man talking to Cheryl looked up, offering them a grin. "I see we're all here." His New Zealand accent was crisp but easy to understand. "I'm Allen, and I'll be your guide today." He had one foot on the deck of the boat, the other firmly on the dock, as he twisted the heavy rope, securing it. "I hope you all like the water." He tossed his head, sending his shaggy bangs out of his eyes.

"Thanks." Jessie stepped forward. "I was told we could bring the dog." She looked up, catching a glimpse of Cheryl. "I hope that's all right. He's only a puppy."

"Yeah." The man grinned down at the puppy as he finished securing the line and stepped onto the boat. "Maybe your boyfriend can carry him on board. Some dogs take a bit to adjust."

Jessie's eyes went wide. "Boyfriend?" Jessie looked between the sailor and Buzz, embarrassed that the assumption had been made. She knew they had been spending a good bit of time together, but couldn't a boy and a girl be friends?

"We're just friends." Buzz ducked his head, hiding his expression as he picked up the dog, his tone flat. "I can carry Mutt."

"Let me help you." Allen's smile widened as his eyes ran over Jessie's slim, sun-bronzed legs. Jessie was used to walking that fine line between friendly and flirtation with people at the coffee shop and thought nothing of the man's actions. When he offered his hand, helping her hop from the boardwalk to the deck to join Cheryl, she offered a smile. "Thank you. I see my friend is making her self at home." She shook here head looking at Cher who was already lounging on the front nets that spanned between the two independent hulls.

"This is perfect." Cheryl placed her hands behind her head, looking up at the tall mast, "almost like a giant hammock."

Feet firmly on the deck, Jessie looked over her shoulder as Buzz jumped easily aboard, cradling Muttly tightly as the boat swayed with his added weight. As soon as his feet hit the deck, he kicked off his flip flops, tucking them under a tarp. "Nice boat."

"Thanks, mate." Allen nodded at the partially hidden footwear. "A lot of people don't know that foot wear for boats is very specific." He tossed the rope onto the deck as Buzz set the puppy on the solid fiberglass. The tall man took a firm grip on the leash as the dog began sniffing curiously at the boat. "If everyone is ready, we'll get started." The boat captain and guid, coiled the rope, releasing another from the pier. Still smiling he slipped under the cover of the cabin, starting the engine and guiding the boat out of the dock.

The low hum of the boat motors made the dog tip his head curiously, but Muttley stuck close to Buzz, not making a fuss.

Buzz found a spot on the deck, sitting and stretching his long legs as Muttley crowded in close. The dog swayed, looking at the deck, confused but interested, a hint of fear making him quiver.

"It's okay, boy." Buzz stroked the dog's head. His hand ran the length of the dog's body, soothing until Mutt relaxed.

"Is he scared?" Jessie asked, slipping onto the deck next to them, her hip pressed against the puppy between them. She smiled, happy to see that Buzz wasn't impatient with the dog.

"This is new," Buzz smiled looking around the boat. "He'll adjust." His brown eyes flicked to Jessie. "Like I said, he's smart. The perfect match for you."

Jessie smacked the man's peck with the back of her hand, then flinched at the contact. "I told you, I'm not keeping him." She chuckled, giving him a grin.

"We'll see." Buzz's eyes had returned to the harbor, and he seemed to relax as Allen guided the boat out of the slip and toward open water.

"You really don't think he belongs to anyone, do you?" Jessie looked down, stroking the dog's head, and his tail slapped her hip hard.

"I don't." Buzz shrugged. "I guess we'll have to see what happens."

Jessie sighed, looking up as they broke the shelter of the harbor and headed into deep water. The boat took the first few incoming waves straight on, skipping over them and falling into the trough. The double hulled boat was more stable than a regular sail boat, and the actions were smooth, less choppy than other boats she had ben on. The engines died, and Allen walked forward, unfurling the main sail.

"We should have smooth sailing today." The blonde man spoke. "The water is calm." He smiled, setting the sail as he introduced them to the day's activities. "Our first stop is a boat that went down in the fifties," he said as wind caught the sail, and they drifted silently toward a yellow buoy in the distance. "It was a private yacht that hit a shoal and went down in a storm. No lives lost, fortunately."

Cheryl, twisted from where she sprawled, on the netting, a breeze ruffled her hair. "That's good to know. I've heard that a lot of ships have been lost out here."

"Too true," Allen replied.

Jessie, rested her back agains the fore deck, looking up at the sail. "How often do these tours run?" Her voice was peaceful as she soaked up the sea and the sun. Her hand rested on the puppy relaxed, falling asleep between her and Buzz.

"Three days a week." Allen smiled, moving along the narrow walk way to the helm. Slipping into the captain's seat, he took the wheel, shouting over the wind. "My main focus is salvage." He leaned around the helm, offering a smile. "I do this on the side. Since I dive on these sites all the time, I know them well and can take tours or scuba groups out in between the money work."

Cheryl stood, walking toward the cabin cover where Allen guided the cat. "So, are you familiar with the legend of the AnnaSwift?" she asked, giving him a bright smile that would have melted many a heart.

The man rolled his eyes, shaking his head. "That old myth." Allen chuckled. "That's just a tale the tours spin to get people excited and sell them trinkets."

"So, you don't believe the ship ever existed?" Cheryl slipped onto a bench seat under the shade.

Allen shrugged, his eyes forward. "I believe the ship was real, but the story around it gets bigger and more outlandish every year. I've had tours who came here looking for the wreck and the mythical treasure. It's a good story, and it's good for business, but it's just that - a story." The man's accent was smooth and his words seemed full of knowledge and authority

"What about the ghost ship that everyone has seen out here?" Buzz spoke, and Jessie's ears perked up. "We saw it again last night, full sails and all."

Jessie twisted looking back at their guide who grinned, shaking his head. "It's all hocus pocus. None of it is real. A trick. They project it from somewhere on shore." Allen laughed. "Like I said, good for business." He patted this helm before him. "This boat was a salvage I took when it went down in a storm. She was pretty busted up, but fixable. The problem was that the insurance company found it cheaper to write it off than have it pulled up and refitted. I never could have afforded a slip like this. Fortunately my mates and me could do the work. Now it's my tour boat." He smiled, his eyes bright with delight as he guided the boat toward the buoy. "We've made the money back taking people on wreck dives or for cruises."

"How long have you been a diver?" Jessie asked. She studied the man's face, but his eyes were focused on their destination. It seemed odd that he would take the time salvaging a boat that had been written off by others.

"Ages now." Allen's eyes flicked back to her and he smiled again. "I trained as an underwater welder, back in New Zealand. The money is amazing, but the risks are high. After almost losing a leg in an accident," he flinched, "I decided to do something I was passionate about instead of working for the money."

"People should try to do what they love," Cheryl grinned.She smiled at the handsome man. Her eyes traced his legs, them moved up to his handsome face.

"It's not always that easy," Jessie sighed. "Some people aren't sure what they're good at."

Buzz dropped his hand on her shoulder, giving it a pat. "And others seem to know exactly what they want until they get it."

Jessie nodded, her heart going out to Buzz. His whole life was on hold and she knew how that felt. She thought of what he had told her when he found her on the beach. She couldn't imagine Buzz angry. His warm, goofy grin came to mind. He didn't have a mean bone in his body.

A solemn atmosphere dropped over the group, and they settled into silence until the boat reached the first marker. Sun dazzled on the water, as Allen set the wheel and moved along the deck. Using a hook, he attached the boat lines to the buoy. As he dropped the sail a feeling of excitement filled the others and they rose moving to look over the rail. ,

"This wreck is a good one to dive," the guide said, his lilting tone making the story come to life. "It's largely intact, and because the boat is big, over sixty feet, you can dive in and out of it. Much of the interior is still beautiful. The fact that it isn't too deep makes it a favorite for experienced or inexperienced divers." He handed them each a tube with a viewing port, and they peered into the water, watching a shape come into focus beneath the murky depths.

"If you dive, we could set up another tour."

"Cool." Jessie said.

"Very cool." Cheryl agreed. :"I know Jess and I have never been diving. How about you Buzz?"

Buzz shook his head.

"No worries," Allen grinned you can always learn."

"You can see that the yacht settled bottom down." Allen moved around the group. "That makes it easy to move through. "Of course the huge hole in the hull isn't so inviting."

The trio chuckled, studying the wreck in the murky depths.

By lunch time, they had seen three wrecks and learned a great deal about the water off the Savannah shore. An old city with such history and depth didn't disappoint, and when they anchored off the shore of Hilton Head Island for lunch, Jessie was feeling intrigued. It was easy to understand why dive and ghost tours would used legends of lost ships to entice tourists. The rich history and sometimes seedy past of the port fueled the imagination. She had visited Savannah many times with her family but they had usually stuck to shore. Sometimes they would take the old sailboat out on a calm day, but her mother had sold that when her father passed. Now, the only boat the Whyne's owned was a small woodcraft speed boat from the fifties. A collector's item that was maintained at the marina.

As Jessie gazed at the shore line, chatting with her friends. Their guide and host for the day, moved about in the galley.

"Lunch!" Allen stepped out of the main salon, a large tray in his arms. "Your friend asked for our best."

Buzz moved from the rail, his dark eyes meeting Jessie's as they walked aft, to the covered deck where a table and bench seating made a comfortable change from the heat of the sun.

He smiled, placing the array of sandwiches, fruit, and veggies on the table in the shade. "Drinks?"

Jessie shook her head. "No cocktails, thanks." her eyes scanned the table. "This looks great."

Allen gave her a bright smile and quick wink before returning to the galley. A moment later he returned with a cooler full of sodas, juice, sparkling and spring water.

Cheryl, still sitting on the benchseat, began preparing a plate, and Jessie slipped into the booth, scooting to the middle of the table to make room for her long-legged companion.

"I'm getting spoiled hanging with the two of you," Buzz commented, placing two sandwiches on his plate.

Muttley snuggled at Jessie's feet, his head raised as he sniffed the air. He had adjusted to the sway of the boat and was now interested in the smell of the food.

Allen fixed a plate, returning to the captains seat as everyone, filled their plates. The food was refreshing. Cool eats on a hot day.

As the crew nibbled, the conversation turned to what other wrecks they would see and where it was possible to do scuba lessons in the area. Allen was a wealth of knowledge. He was friendly, informative, and full of lighthearted factoids that made everyone laugh.

A breeze blew across the boat, and Jessie found herself relaxing, the light rocking sway of the catamaran settling muscles she didn't know were tense. Beside her, Buzz listened to Allen's tales, making quick work of the stacked meat and veggies, between slices of sour-dough bread.

"You look like you're enjoying yourself," Buzz said while Cheryl picked Allen's brain for more information on the AnnaSwift.

"I am." Jessie sighed. "Cheryl is having fun. Being on the water is relaxing, and even the dog is happy." She grinned, leaning in, her shoulder pressing his. "I think Cher is flirting with our guide."

Buzz smiled, flicking his eyes between Cheryl and Allen. He had figured out quickly that Jessie's oldest friend was prone to flirt.

Cheryl gave them both a quick glare before turning back to Allen. "Have you ever tried to find the shipwreck?" Cheryl asked the sailor as she rummaged in her bag.

Jessie tried to catch the man's reply but a crunching sound met her ears. The sound was coming from under the table. Giving Buzz a startled glance, she peered under the table only to find the puppy gnawing on a rawhide bone. She looked up, glaring art Cher, who shrugged, her attention once more on Allen.

"And she says she doesn't like dogs." Jessie whispered, making Buzz grin. She shook her head, returning to her meal. "Are you having a good time?" Jessie looked up, meeting Buzz's brown eyes. "I can see that Cher is."

"Yeah." He nodded, his smile relaxed as he stretched his legs and extended one arm behind him on the bench. Buzz lifted a bottle of soda, sipping. "I like boats." His smile grew. "I'm enjoying this wild goose chase as well." The man shrugged. "It's nice to be involved in a mystery that can come to nothing. A fun story we can track to its source. That's the thing about legends. No one has to get hurt."

Jessie studied him for a moment, popping a strawberry in her mouth, as she considered his words. The idea of a ghost ship was fun, but being here with friends and finding the time to unwind was better.

"What's out there?" Cheryl pointed around the edge of a slip of rock, making everyone look.

Allen lifted his head, peering in the direction she indicated.

"That's lighthouse point. It is not a place I care to go." He shook his head.

Jessie sat up, squinting along the water. Following the curve of the shore she could make out a smaller island, the outline of a lighthouse visible. The water off the point was choppy, indicating rocks, or reefs below.

"That's Tybee Light. It's the oldest and tallest lighthouse in Georgia," Allen continued. "The water in that area is treacherous. The Savannah River pours in at that point, and unless you know the water well, it's too dangerous to sail. There is a narrow trench leading to the river but if you stray into other areas disaster is likely to strike."

"Isn't that the direction the ghost ship comes from?" Buzz asked. "I mean, last night at the restaurant the boat sailed from the point to open water before it disappeared."

Allen shrugged, lifting a sparkling glass and sipping. "Special effects can only do so much." He chuckled. "I hope I'm not ruining all of your fun while you're in the area?"

Jessie listened, turning over the facts. Allen seemed to know the area well. The fact that he was quick to dismiss the ghost ship as a hoax only added to her own belief.

"Not at all." Cheryl smiled. "That's why I booked this tour. I want to learn everything I can about AnnaSwift and what happened to it. I know special affects can be used in odd settings and since I don't think any of us believes in ghosts, you can't ruin our fun."

Jessie turned, biting back a laugh as she looked at their guide. "She gets fixated on something and runs with it. It won't last."

"Will, too." Cheryl lifted her chin, pushing her blonde hair over one shoulder and letting the breeze cool her neck, not taking her eyes from the point far down the coast. "I know. Tomorrow, we'll visit the lighthouse." Cherly grinned. "Besides, we might as well see everything while we're here."

Jessie grinned, turning to Buzz. "I hope you are open to traipsing all over Savannah. I'm pretty sure you're included in this adventure."

Buzz grinned, scooping up a piece of fruit. "I don't have anything better to do."

Allen looked between the two women and shrugged. "If you do, make sure you look up my friend, Lars. He's an old diver and sea dog who knows the history of this area better than anyone I know."

"We'll try." Jessie nodded.

"Since you know this area so well and you already do salvage. Why not look for the treasure yourself?" Buzz asked, his eyes on the same point where Cheryl was focused. "I mean, just to see if it could be real."

Jessie looked at her friend, surprised by his question. Buzz didn't believe in all of this. He had made that clear.

"Nah." Allen shook his head, standing and gathering the dishes. "It's just a story. Even if a ship like that went down, the odds of finding it are next to nil. I'll stick to pulling rich men's boats from the shoals and cashing in on the cost of the job. Besides, that happened so long ago there can't be much left of the boat." The man stacked everything back on the tray, hefting it and turning toward the galley. "Besides, it doesn't pay, digging up treasure. The state and government get most of your take."

They set sail again, each enjoying the stories and vision along the ride. The water was soothing, and by the time they returned to the boat's slip, everyone was laughing and ready for dinner. The all-day tour had been well worth the time and money, leaving the trio happy to be together in Savanna.

Jessie tipped Allen, thanking him for the tour and information and telling him she would recommend his tour to family and friends as she stepped out onto the dock. Buzz carried the puppy, walking beside Cheryl who was planning the trip to the lighthouse in the morning.

"She's obsessed," Allen said, nodding toward Cheryl as she sashayed over the wooden dock. ***

"It will pass." Jessie laughed. "Cher always needs a project. When we get home to Macon, she'll forget all about it."

"You all be careful, now. There are those even in this fine place who will take this sort of thing seriously. Many have searched for the AnnaSwift, and I'll tell you, the treasure hunting business can be dangerous."

Jessie turned, studying the man, but his smile returned, and she shook her head. "But good for business?" She laughed. "We're not interested in treasure. Cheryl is having fun and letting her imagination run wild. It's all in good fun."

"Good on you." The man gave her a mock salute, hopping back onto his boat and disappearing below.

"How about dinner?" Jessie called, catching up with her friends. "My treat."

Buzz opened his mouth to protest, but she shook her head. "My treat," she repeated, giving him a warm smile. "I should enjoy all of my ill-gotten gains, after all."

As they reached the shore, Buzz put the dog down and they all paused, adjusting to the feel of solid ground.

Setting off again, Jessie looked up at the sky, noting the progression of the sun as the day waned.

Buzz chuckled. "I take it you are speaking of that little windfall you received at the end of your house renovations?"

Jessie rubbed the back of her head, but nodded, remembering the troubles her so-called windfall had created. "You were a big part of putting an end to that disturbance." She smiled. "You know I sold almost everything we found. Of course I kept a few things as keepsakes." Jessie slipped he arm in his. "Now. What do you say?"

Jessie looked at Buzz and he dropped his head in surrender.

"Fine." He offered a grin, and Jessie smiled, Muttley trotting at her heels.

"Not me." Cheryl scowled, looking at the bright sun moving toward the horizon. "I'm going home." She raised one finger. "One, I want to do some research on the lighthouse." She glared at Jessie when she rolled her eyes. "Two, I have a book to read that has been sitting on my ereader for months." She yawned dramatically. “Besides, I’m tired after our day on the water, I’m ready for a hot bath and good sleep. You two go have dinner, and have fun.” She wiggled her fingers, puling her phone from her bag.

“We’ll walk you home.” Buzz said, offering her his other arm.

“That’s a long walk home,” Cheryl protested, shaking her head

“The exercise will do us good.” Jessie laughed. “Besides, I’m going to put Mutt in the backyard. He’s had a big day.”

Cheryl looked down at the dog, raising a brow. “I don’t have to look after him, do I?”

“No,” Jessie laughed. Cheryl had always been funny about dogs. “He’ll be fine in the backyard.” She gazed at the sky. “It’s already cooling off, and he can have his dinner out there.” She looked down at the puppy who was sniffing at the path. “He’s already pretty good around the house.”

They chatted about their day of sailing as they walked home, and Jessie was relieved to walk into the house, letting the cool air conditioning wash over her. “Do you mind if I clean up real quick?” she asked, turning to Buzz.

“No, go ahead.” He took the puppy’s leash. “I’ll get him settled out back while I wait.” He looked at his loose fitting shirt, then up at the girl.

Jessie grinned. “You’re fine.” She looked down at the dog then back up to Buzz who smiled. “Are you sure you don’t mind dealing with the dog? He isn’t your responsibility.”

“Go.” Buzz chuckled, the sound filling the foyer as they stepped inside. “I think I can handle one little puppy. Then, when you’re ready, we can take my car.”

“Thanks.” Jessie dashed up the stairs, catching a glimpse of Buzz walking the puppy through the house to the back yard.

Buzz followed Jessie’s directions without complaint to the restaurant she had chosen. She had changed into a summer dress and sandals and looked refreshed as she sat in the car gazing at the scenery outside. Huge old oaks lined the road, and he glanced at his casual shorts and shirt, wondering if he should have gone home to change instead of playing with the puppy while Jessie freshened up.

"Don't worry," Jessie said, looking at him. "You're fine. I checked on the dress code before I made the reservation."

Buzz tugged at the collar of his shirt. "Just needing a reservation makes me nervous." He offered an awkward smile. He and Jessie, though friends, were from totally different worlds. Her easy manner with money and the finer things in life were a jarring contrast to her down-to-earth and friendly nature. He knew that Jessie had worked while in college when she could have coasted on her family's money, but now, being with her again brought all of the differences back.

"Buzz," Jessie spoke again, and he flicked his eyes toward her. "You don't seem as comfortable with me tonight. Is something wrong?"

Buzz opened his mouth to speak, then closed it again.- "Have I done something wrong?" Jessie didn't turn away from the window.

Buzz shook his head, finally speaking. "No, I just don't know about anything anymore. I feel completely out of sync with life. You might not know what you want to do yet, but you have time and the resources to figure it out."

"I see." Jessie's words were soft, and she finally turned to look at him as they pulled into a parking lot. "Maybe I'm different from you," she spoke. "But I am your friend, and I hope you feel the same." She met his gaze as he pulled into a parking space and turned off the engine. "I know my family is rich, but I hope you don't hold that against me. I know some people do, but our blessings have been hard-earned and have cost us much. I don't know why God gives one thing to some people and something different to others, but I didn't ask for this." she dropped her gaze, looking weary. "I'm trying to figure out how to use what I have for God and to help others. I just don't know what that is, yet."

Buzz felt his heart stutter, and his shoulders drooped. He hadn't meant to make Jessie feel strange about her money or who she was. She was wonderful the way she was, and he finally let go of his pride. Reaching across the car he grasped Jessie's shoulders, turning her to look at him. "I'm sorry." He offered a lame smile. "Sometimes I just don't get why you'd be my friend." He tugged, pulling her into his arms and giving her what he hoped was a friendly hug.

Jessie's arms wrapped around his waist as her face pressed into his chest. "You are worthy of being a friend," she finally said. "And I've missed you."

Buzz chuckled. The young woman felt good in his arms, and his heart rate quickened. "Thanks. I missed you too. I'll try not to be a jerk." He released her, and she smiled, bright eyes flickering up, meeting his. Friendship and acceptance beamed from Jessie. Perhaps she was no closer to knowing what direction she wanted to go but being a friend to him, meant the world. Over the past few years, Buzz had let his life be taken over by his job. First, his studies at the police academy. Then his focus on learning to be the best cop he could be. Jessie had dropped into his life, unexpectedly and he didn't know how to balance her friendship with the rest of his life.

"Good," Jessie added. "Besides, now we have to put this AnnaSwift thing to rest before I leave Savannah, or Cher will drive me crazy."

Buzz laughed, opening the door. "I'm in. Now come on. I'm starving."

Jessie laughed. The sound was light and happy, filling Buzz with joy. "You're always hungry."

"Hey," Buzz protested, slapping his flat stomach as they walked toward the beach front restaurant. "This fine physique requires a lot of fuel."

Jessie chuckled shaking her head as the reached the door an Buzz pulled it open.

"So, do you think there really is a mystery here? You know this whole ghost ship and treasure thing?" Jessie asked, as a hostess seated them.

"A make-believe one, yes." Buzz agreed, looking up as a waiter arrived. They ordered and settled in to wait for their meals. "Savannah is one of those cities that thrives on history, and tales of mystery. It makes it a grea place to visit, but I would think that none of these treasure tales are real. Usually, there is a simple explanation to all of it. Like Dr. Crumm explained."

Their meals arrived and they grew quiet for a moment, savoring the smell of the dishes.

"I know Cheryl is having fun and frankly, the distraction has been great," Buzz said as he cut into his steak, hunger making his mouth water. "The fact is that we all have to return to reality once we go home." He waved his fork around, holding his steak knife in his other hand. "That's what vacation is all about. Disconnecting from our regular life."

He looked down at the succulent steak. When ordering, Buzz had studiously ignored the prices listed, forcing himself to take Jessie at her word. It wasn't easy to accept Jessie's treat, but if he was indeed her friend, his pride shouldn't get in the way. "I think it's a great diversion for Cheryl and everything she organizes will give us both time to figure out what comes next in our lives."

"You don't think they'll fire you, do you?" Jessie looked up from her surf and turf platter, her eyes serious.

A wave of worry hit, Buzz but he forced it away. He would not let his problem ruin the night. "I doubt it will come to that." Buzz shook his head. "I think they just want to give me some time to cool off and think about my actions." He shrugged, stabbing a bite of steak with his fork. "I'm not even sure if that is what bothers me the most." He paused, lifting his fork and meeting Jessie's eyes. "What if the job is changing me? Can I live with that?" He shook his head again. "I've been over this again and again. No matter how I look at it I can't decide." Popping the bite of steak into his mouth, he sighed with delight. The food was delicious. "Let's talk about the AnnaSwift." He said after finishing the bit. "At least that isn't going to change my life."

Jessie nodded as Buzz imagined spending the next week following Cheryl from one place to another. He was content to spend his time with Jessie and if traipsing after a fake mystery kept everyone happy he was all in.

Chapter 6

Buzz slept better than he had in weeks that night, and with the sun barely cresting the waves, he pulled into the circular driveway at the beach house. The sunrise painted the glass of the french door a shimmering pink. Stopping at the front of the house, he glanced back at the dawning of a new day then knocked.

Cheryl had insisted he be there by six am, and since he usually got his run in early, it had been easy to comply. He smiled as a soft whimper from the other side of the door caught his ear. Apparently, the little mutt was up and ready to greet him.

From the corner of his eye, Buzz caught movement near the kitchen window. He leaned to the right, trying to see who was there, but a moment later, Jessie opened the door, a bright smile on her sleepy face.

Buzz grinned, surprised that she was fully dressed, if barely awake. She had pulled her hair back with a scrunchy, her attire casual and bright.

"Come on in," she said, waving him through the door. She had a firm grip on the puppy's leash as he bounced around Buzz's feet. "I hope you slept. We need our driver to be awake, at least." Tugging on the leash, she pulled the dog close to her, making room for Buzz to walk by.

"Good morning." Buzz greeted Jessie then the puppy who followed them into the kitchen. "Where's the boss?" His teasing tone was light, and Jessie chuckled as she walked to the coffee pot, drawing two cups of cappuccino.

"She's getting dressed." She looked down at her own attire then up to Buzz as if wondering if what she wore was suitable for their adventure.

"You look good," Buzz said carefully, stepping around Muttley and taking the cup Jessie offered. She was wearing knee-length shorts, a striped shirt, and tennis shoes. "At least that looks like a practical outfit for visiting a lighthouse." He glanced down at his usual shorts and pale blue buttoned-up. "I wore regular shoes today instead of flip flops in case Cheryl has us racing up and down stairs." He wiggled his feet, his toes thumping on the tile floor.

Jessie chuckled. "Here comes the director now." She peered at the stairs as Cheryl began her regal descent. "Oh, my goodness!" Jessie gasped, making Buzz spin to look. "Cher, what are you wearing? You look like Minnie Mouse."

Cheryl grasped the chrome railing, sauntering down the stairs. "This is an authentic 1950s sundress," she said, pointing her nose toward the bright window at the top of the house. "And I'm wearing sensible shoes, so don't complain."

Buzz felt his eyebrows rise as he took in the outfit, feeling under dressed as Chery furled the wide red skirt, covered in white polka dots. "See?" Cheryl splayed her feet, showing red, rope-soled, wedge sandals. Her feet came to rest on the floor as everyone gazed at the shoes. "You know, Chery continued, "your mother would love it if you paid more attention to your own attire."

Jessie gaped, turning to look at Buzz who hurriedly lifted his cup, slurping the hot brew as he refused to comment.

"Smart man." Cheryl patted his arm as she passed, making him splutter. "It's not like I expect people to have my fashion sense." Buzz watched over the rim of his mug as Cher gave Jessie a faux scathing look. "After all, I'm eccentric." She laughed. "Seriously. I'm good. These are the best shoes, and you can take pictures of me at the lighthouse."

Buzz looked between the two women, amused by their banter. Cheryl definitely had an eccentric sense of style, but he liked Jessie's down to earth attire and practical attitude. Besides, he had seen Jessie in formal attire. Her poise and elegance would put most women to shame.

"Oh." Jessie mused, giving Buzz a wink and increasing his confusion. "So, this is your own personal fashion shoot." The give and take between the two women was odd, but Buzz sensed no malice in their tone. Perhaps it was normal for girlfriends to banter in such a way, and he suspected that fashion was one of those diverse topics that women never agreed on fully.

Cheryl grinned, wiggling bright red fingernails in front of Jessie. "Fun." She leaned in. "That's what you said. We're here to have fun. I find this. . ." she stroked the skirt of the dress, ". . . .fun." Cheryl's voice was haughty but carried a note of teasing, and they knew she was simply enjoying the attention.

"You say that like some sort of mantra," Buzz laughed. "Is that your life goal?" He looked down at her dress again, bewildered by the way it puffed out.

Cheryl, cocked an eyebrow, a slow smile spreading across her face. "I'll have you know I work very hard." She looked between Jessie and Buzz. "I don't believe God put us on earth to be serious all the time. We do what we need to, and then in our free time we should enjoy life. We can find joy in the everyday things." Cheryl spun, her skirt flared, showing the massive ruffles beneath. "This brings me joy. I really don't care if other people think I'm eccentric or not." She paused, turning to give Jessie a look that spoke volumes. "Real life is in the little things." Cheryl giggled, grabbing her companions each by the arm and marching them toward the door. "Besides, if people are all talking about my outlandish fashion sense, they don't have time to gossip about me."

Buzz scowled, looking over his shoulder as they walked outside. He saw Jessie push the pup back into the house, carefully closing the door, and locking it as Cheryl dragged him toward the car. Turning toward his car, he wondered if Cheryl's clothing choices had as much to do with distraction as the fun she so reverently spoke of. It seemed that so many people always had something to say about others. Giving them a target could be a good diversion.

Buzz opened the back door for Cheryl, then hurried around to the driver's side of the car, turning to watch Jessie skip down the walkway. She smiled, obviously not upset by her friend's good natured ribbing. As Jessie climbed into the car, Buzz slipped behind the wheel, a grin spreading across his face. Fun seemed to be the goal of the day.

Buzz drove down the road along the beach, winding through early morning traffic as the sun continued to rise. The sea on his left was calm, dark waves beginning to shimmer with the first light of day. "Why are we going to the lighthouse so early?" He asked, following the road toward the spit of land that jutted into the Atlantic.

"Oh, didn't I tell you?" Cheryl asked from the backseat. "I got us a private tour."

"No way!" Jessie twisted, her voice filled with excitement. "How? Is that even possible?"

Buzz listened as Cheryl explained, wondering how the girl was able to do so much. Did she have boundless resources as well as energy?

"It is if you know the right academic types." Buzz could see Cheryl's wink in the rearview mirror as he rolled into an empty parking lot. "I talked to my prof at the college in Macon, and he called in a few favors." Cheryl unbuckled her seatbelt and opened the door. "He says I'm the best TA he ever had, and he's happy to help me enjoy my holiday."

Buzz turned to look at Jessie who shrugged and followed Cheryl's lead. A wide grin spread across his face, and he climbed out of the sedan as well, locking it and turning to greet the new day.

"Come on," Cheryl called, hurrying toward the door at the base of the black and white striped lighthouse. "The caretaker is waiting for us."

Buzz glanced over his shoulder, checking on Jessie, but she was already around the car and headed his way. "What do you think?" she asked, falling into step with him. "Will we learn anything here?"

"I don't know." Buzz shoved his hands in the pockets of his khaki shorts, looking at his oversized athletic shoes as he walked. "I know it beats dealing with some of the reprobates I've had to collar lately." He shrugged, not wanting to think of the evil he had seen.

He gazed around the island, noting the neat lawn, brightly painted lighthouse keeper's house, and picket fence. The lighthouse itself rose, a strange octegnal structure painted in black and white. His keen eyes took in the setting. A square block of historical structures sat in the middle of the island with roads surrounding them in a wide rolling rectangle. Houses and apartment buildings could be seen closer to the shore, beach houses for those who wanted to live by the sea.

"Hey," Jessie brushed his arm with her hand. "It will get better. Hang in there."

Buzz nodded, hoping her words were true. He was tired of worrying about his job and how it was affecting him. His lifelong dream had been to become a policeman, but he hadn't realized how much the job would change him.

"Hurry up!" Cheryl yelled, waving to them. Her words banishing his dark thoughts. The sun, a crescent of gold creeping out of the ocean, turned her skirt to flame, and Buzz grinned.

He had a feeling that any time he spent with Cheryl would be interesting.

Buzz looked at Jessie who smiled, breaking into a run. Laughing, he sprinted to catch up.The light run had felt good, and he was pleased to see that Jessie wasn't winded, either, as they stopped next to Cheryl.

"This is Brad," Cheryl introduced a burly man with curly brown hair and dark eyes dressed much like her companions in a shirt and shorts. "He's our tour guide today."

Buzz extended his hand, feeling the other man's firm grip. The guide was in his late twenties or maybe thirty. His smile was bright and he seemed excited about showing them around.

"I don't think I've ever given a private tour before," the man grinned, his square face brightening. "If we hurry, we can see the sun pop into the sky from up there." He pointed upward to the railed observation deck around the top.

Brad turned, opening the door with a heavy key and letting them proceed. Dim lights filled the tower, illuminating a wood spiral staircase on one wall. "Better get a move on." The caretaker hurried toward the stairs, leading them up over one hundred feet to the top. The man trotted up the stairs, obviously used to the workout.

"I thought that lighthouses were round," Jessie said, trotting up the creaking wooden stairs. Buzz grinned, Jessie always had questions.

"Many are," Brad called back. The climb didn't bother the guide at all, and he continued talking as they climbed.

Buzz was surprised that neither of the girls was huffing as they walked up the long staircase. He wondered, not for the first time, if the two friends exercised or worked out.

"This isn't even the original lighthouse," the guide glanced back, still smiling. "The first structure, made of brick and wood, was built in 1732 and completed in 1736, but a storm took that one out. They rebuilt it in 1741 but lost that one, too. Finally, this structure was built of all brick in 1773, and it has managed to survive." They reached the top landing, and Brad pulled his key from his pocket once more, opening a door and letting a cool breeze blow over them. "It didn't even have a light then, just a flagpole and flag that they could use to warn ships of the dangers below."

"There must have been a lot of wrecks back then." Buzz mused.

Still holding the door open, their host ushered them out onto the metal platform of the observation deck. "Most people didn't come this way, if they could avoid it. They kept wide of the shoals as they headed for the bay.

"I read something about that," Cheryl looked out at the glowing water, now swaying in hues of rose and gold. "Wasn't it 1890 or somewhere around then that it became a Federal building, and that's when they fitted the lenses?"

"That's right." Brad stepped out, leaning on the railing and gazing at the sun as it burst out of the sea. "I never get tired of this." His smile was bright, and the others all joined him. The sound of the ocean and birds filled the air, but up here it all seemed far away as if silence had wrapped the old lighthouse in a muffling blanket.

Buzz leaned on the railing, breathing deeply of the fresh air surrounding him. Jessie wrapped her fingers around the railing, holding it tightly. "You aren't afraid of heights, are you?" he asked.

"Not usually." Jessie looked down. "It's just that I can feel the sway of the tower, and it is a little unsettling."

"It's beautiful, though." Buzz smiled, his eyes lingering on her face before turning back to the bright sunshine on the water. A gust of wind blew over them, and Jessie grasped his arm with one hand.

"Can you get seasick on a lighthouse?" she asked, trying to lighten the mood.

Buzz placed a hand over hers, steadying her. "You'll be fine." He looked down at the ground so far below. "Just relax. This place has been here a long time. It's not going anywhere. So, you can trust it to keep you from falling."

Jessie laughed. A nervous titter that seemed to ease some of her tension. "Thanks."

"You must be able to see everything from up here." Cheryl leaned in, talking to Brad. "All of the ships, the skiffs, and small sports craft. I think I'd never want to stop watching." She smiled, turning and batting her eyes. "I bet you can even see that ghost ship when it appears."

Brad stiffened, turning to look at her. "Not that nonsense again," he scoffed. "These tours get more reckless every year."

Buzz stepped close to Jessie, turning to look at their guide. The man's eyes flashed with annoyance, his jaw tightening as he spoke. Brad, unlike Allen yesterday, was stocky, heavily muscled, and dark. There was a presence about their guide. He seemed to emanate knowledge.

"But I saw it." Chery protested. "Big and green and all saily." She lifted her hands wiggling her fingers as she gazed at the sea.

"It's a trick." Brad shook his head, a muscle working in his jaw. "I don't know how they do it, but it has to be a trick. Sure, loads of ships have gone down in this harbor." He nodded toward the rough open water below. "This area has claimed more than you can imagine. Treacherous rocks, shoals, and odd currents make the area dangerous. That's why the lighthouse is so important." He shook his head again, his thick curls bouncing. "We still get those foolish ones who brave it, looking for treasure, though. I can't tell you how many people have been rescued by the coast guard right out there in the past couple of years. If these tours stopped making it sound like there is tons of mysterious treasure right beneath the surface, people wouldn't take these risks."

Buzz scanned the ocean, trying to see what the man was saying. "Have you ever been out there?" Buzz asked, feeling Jessie's hand relax as she turned to look at their guide.

"Sure." Brad grinned. "I grew up around here. I know these waters like the back of my hand, but I'm not foolish enough to believe I can go wandering about out there safely. It's hard to navigate the area on the best of days, and when storms surge. . ." He shivered dramatically. "I'll keep to the safer areas of the bay."

"Do you dive?" Jessie asked. Buzz relaxed, seeing her take an interest in the conversation and forgetting her own fears.

"Dive, sail, surf. I do most everything." Brad braced heavily muscled arms on the railing, his short sleeves falling back to reveal an anchor tattoo with an eel wound around it. "Now, how about the rest of that tour?" The man's white smile flashed as he turned toward another door, this one leading them into the main deck and light mechanics area.

"This is where the magic happens," Brad said, spreading his arms to encompass the equipment. The sun's rays refracted from the vast, octagonal lens, sparkling like multi-colored gems in the room. "The historical society did a major overhaul of the place back in 1999, making the place like new while preserving the history. The color scheme of black and white was researched, taking the structure back to the look it had in 1916." He walked to a widow, patting the sill. "This old girl has been through a lot over the years. I just hope I can weather the test of time as well."

"You love this place, don't you?" Jessie asked, joining him at the window.

"I love the sea, the water, and Savannah." Brad unlatched the window, leaning his elbows on the sill. "It's my home."

"You were in the Coast Guard?" Buzz's question was more a statement, making Brad turn.

"For a time." Brad's coffee-brown eyes flashed.

"I noticed your tattoo," Buzz continued. "It looked familiar." He had learned the various military and law enforcement insignias, often used as tattoos.

"Good men and women doing a dangerous job," Brad said as he lifted his sleeve, showing the tattoo of the anchor. "A friend of mine was killed. We served together." He nodded. "That's when I ended my time." He tapped the eel that wrapped the anchor, smiling at them with a jagged-toothed grin. "Still love the Coast Guard, but that soured it for me."

"I'm sorry." Cheryl stepped up next to the man. "About your friend."

"Thanks." Brad gazed out at the sea. "That's why these crazy ghost ship sightings get me so worked up. It's bad enough having to rescue someone who has mistakenly wandered into dangerous waters, but when these legends convince people it's worth the risk, so they go out there knowing it could lead to ruin." He shook his head. "It's nuts."

"I'm afraid I'm rather obsessed with the ghost ship idea myself, right now." Cheryl dropped her gaze. "I love learning new things, and when Dr. Crumm told us about the AnnaSwift, I kind of fell in love."

"As long as you don't plan on doing any treasure hunting out there, you're all good." Brad offered a bright smile. "History is amazing." He gazed around the lighthouse, then turned back to the door. "It's given me this great job, after all. Now come on, I'll give you the rest of the tour before I have to open for the day."

"That was a great tour, Cheryl," Jessie said as they climbed back into the car and turned the air conditioner on full-blast. "The lighthouse itself was really worth the visit, but what we learned makes me wonder about some other things."

"Like what?" Buzz cracked his window, letting some of the intense Georgia heat escape as he shifted the car into gear and backed out. A few other cars dotted the parking area now, but it still wasn't busy.

"If the fake ghost ship is causing people to go exploring where they shouldn't and putting them in danger, why are the tours allowed to do it? I mean, I know they want tourism here, but you'd think the local government would draw the line when they had to call in the coast guard to rescue treasure hunters."

Cheryl pulled her phone from her red handbag and began searching. "Let me see," she said as they turned toward home, and Jessie looked over at Buzz.

"Buzz, wouldn't local law enforcement voice concerns about this sort of thing? What if it isn't a tour operator making the ghost ship appear?" Buzz scowled, pondering. It was a bit of a jump, but it made sense.

Buzz nodded. "If it's leading to people getting caught in those dangerous areas, I'd think someone would speak up." He pulled into traffic, now busy as people rushed to work or school. "But what purpose would it serve to make a ghost ship appear? Why bother?"

"That's the real question." Jessie sighed, looking out the window as the air conditioning finally cooled the interior of the car.

"There have been fifty-three boats wrecked in the last year out from the lighthouse point," Cheryl interposed. "Over seventy percent of them said they were looking for treasure."

"Wow. That is bad." Jessie sighed. "What happened to the wrecks?"

"Just a sec." Cheryl's phone made soft clicking noises, and Jessie gazed out the windshield. "Most were salvaged, which was super-expensive for the insurance companies or owners." More clicking. "Oh. It looks like some insurance companies refused to pay out for the salvage or damage, so many of the salvage companies simply kept the boats."

"That must add up fast." Buzz drove out of the busy town area and along the road leading back to the beach house. "I'll bet they didn't even bother with the small stuff. It wouldn't be worth the time." He shook his head. "If the insurance companies write off the boats, the normal cost of repairs must be more than the boat is worth."

"We could ask Allen," Jessie said, turning to look at Cheryl who was shaking her phone. "He said he worked in salvage."

"He said that his sailboat was a salvage." Buzz studied the road. "It's very odd."

"I'll give Allen a call when we get home." Cheryl turned her phone again. "Buzz, you're right about the little boats. Most were left to sink. It's estimated that the salvage costs were over three billion dollars over the year. Some of the yachts saved from imminent doom were worth millions on their own."

"So people take their expensive boats out, hoping to find treasure, get in trouble and end up having to be rescued. Then a salvage crew shows up, pulls the damaged boat out and either gets paid by the owner or keeps the boat."

"If they have a good repair crew, they could probably patch up the boats and sell them for way more than the rescue cost." Buzz mused as he rolled down the driveway toward the beach house that shimmered a blinding white in the bright sunlight. Putting the car in park and turning off the engine, he swung an arm over the back of the seat, looking at Jessie then flashing a glance to Cheryl. "If someone is making people think they can find the treasure and ultimately causing them to wreck their boats, this could be a racket."

Jessie blinked at him a moment, thinking it over. "So a salvage company could be using this to entice people to go treasure hunting with tales of wealth and glory, then they collect the boats and money when everything goes wrong." She scowled, thinking about it. "But wouldn't it be dangerous for them as well? What kind of boat could navigate the waters off of lighthouse point safely? What if they got in trouble and lost everything? There has to be some sort of oversight."

"It's still a stretch to me." Buzz turned toward the private beach. "People giving up expensive boats." He shook his head.

"The last boat pulled from the shoals," Cheryl said, waving her phone, was a forty-five foot MSV sail boat worth seven million. Sheets," she huffed. "Some people really do have more money than brains." She winked at Jessie, making Buzz gape.

"Thanks." Jessie said, her voice tight, then she burst out laughing, noting the shock on Buzz's face. "Come on you two. Let's get some lunch and I'll check on the mutt." She opened her car door and headed toward the house. The sound of happy barking made her smile as she approached the front door.

"I thought you put him out back," Buzz said as Jessie unlocked the door.

"I did." She turned looking up at Buzz who scowled. "Maybe the back door didn't latch right." Jessie turned the key, hearing the puppy barking madly as she opened the door. Jessie bent to catch the dog as he bolted through the door, grabbing his collar. Buzz stepped around her, pushing the door wide with his left arm as he stepped through, scanning the house.

"You are such a cop," She laughed, picking up Muttley and holding him as he squirmed with delight. "He just forced the door open." Jessie stopped, looking for Buzz, but he had disappeared up the front stairs. She could hear him moving along the hall between the bedrooms, and she shook her head.

"What's the string bean doing?" Cheryl walked inside, closing the door as Jessie placed Muttley on the floor. Jessie giggled, shaking her head at the appropriate nickname.

"He's worried because this beast somehow opened the back doors and got inside." The sound of Buzz walking down the stairs at the opposite end of the house made Jessie smile, and she headed toward the living room where Buzz stood peering through a curtain at the back yard.

"All clear." He said, turning and raising his brows at Jessie's look. His body was ridged as he slipped into cop mode.

"Seriously?" she asked, placing her hand on a hip. "All clear?"

Buzz shrugged, and she could see his face flush. "I'm a product of my training." He opened the back door, looking into the yard before walking out onto the patio. "Did you lock this when you left?"

"I don't know." Jessie shook her head. "I put the dog out and closed the doors, but I'm not sure if I locked them."

"Make sure you lock up." Buzz turned, dropping his hands to her shoulders while the puppy bounced around his feet. "You can never be too careful."

Jessie opened her mouth, a sarcastic reply on her lips, but she bit it back and nodded. "I promise." She didn't want to worry the man any more than he already was. Buzz had enough to deal with right now. "Come on, Mutt," she called, giving Buzz a bright smile. "Outside."

Buzz followed her out to the back yard, and together they played a game of chase-the-ball with the dog. Muttley hadn't learned fetch, yet. Jessie held her peace as Buzz checked the walls, looking for signs of an intruder. He was a policeman, and as such, he was cautious. His training made him duck in the shadows. A sadness filled Jessie's heart, watching Buzz like this. She missed the quick smile and easy manner he had displayed that fall. Had his job affected him so much?

"He's starting to know his name." Buzz said, finally kneeling with her on the lawn where he rubbed the pup's stomach. "Did you ever get those flyers up?"

"No," Jessie admitted. "Will you help me after lunch?"

"Sure. Pup patrol it is." Buzz chuckled, and now that he knew the house was secure, he seemed to relax.

"I take it I'm making lunch," Cheryl stepped into the frame of the double door, leaning on the jam.

"If you don't mind." Jessie turned, smiling. "Mutt has been alone most of the morning and needs some attention."

Cheryl raised a brow, nodding as she tied an apron around her red dress. "No problem. We have left overs, and I'll cut up some more fruit." She was gone before Jessie could reply, and when she turned back, she was face-to- face with Buzz.

Jessie looked into soft brown eyes, seeing a half-smile tug at her friend's lips. He was quiet, kneeling in front of her. His face was relaxed, his eyes bright, and she could see that playing with Muttley had been fun for him.

For several seconds they sat there, neither saying anything, as they studied each other. Jessie's heart squeezed. She wanted to see his quick smiled. She was glad that Buzz could finally relax. It had been pleasant sitting here watching Buzz roll the ball, and chasing it with the dog.

A soft yip from the forgotten puppy pulled their attention back to the dog, and Buzz chuckled.

"He's getting spoiled."

"Buzz." Jessie stood, brushing off her knees and heading for the table under the wisteria tree. "Do you think this ghost ship really could be a scam?" She let her mind drift back to the issue of the AnnaSwift.

Buzz rubbed the dog's belly, then stood, his long legs unfolding before heading her way. Pulling a chair out, he settled at the table and looked up at the sky. "It's possible." He was quiet for several seconds. "But if the locals aren't saying anything, maybe it's already been checked out."

"Can we find out?" Jessie pushed a lock of hair behind her ear. "I mean, could you talk to someone here?" Her curiosity getting the best of her.

Buzz shook his head slowly. "Not right now." His eyes were serious, worried. "I'd get myself in more trouble."

"Oh, of course." Jessie looked down, catching a glimpse of the puppy sniffing in the flower beds.

"Uncle Paul might be able to help," Buzz said, the smile returning. "He knows so many people in Macon who are connected to stations all over Georgia."

Jessie sat up straighter meeting his gaze. "You think so?" Excitement zipped through her voice. "You don't think he'll mind? I mean, I know it has nothing to do with us, but if people really are getting hurt because someone is running a salvage scam," she shrugged, "Someone should do something."

"I'll give him a call." Buzz stood, pulling his phone from his pocket as Jessie went to see what the puppy was digging for in a bunch of petunias.

***

After lunch, Buzz and Jessie headed for the local police station. Paul had called in a few favors, and they were going to ask some questions.

"Do you really think we'll discover anything, poking around this situation?" Buzz asked. His eyes were on the road but his mind working.

"I don't know," Jessie replied. "The whole thing is rather far-fetched. I mean, with local law enforcement and the coast guard, you would think any sort of scam like this would be uncovered pretty quickly."

Buzz pondered the idea for a moment. "Unless it's all within the norm for this area. Didn't the lighthouse keeper say that boats got into trouble in the area? With so many sportsmen and others buying boats they aren't really able to manage, it might fall into that gray area of plausible happenings. Think about it. If the number of boats is about the same or only slightly higher than usual, who would look?"

From the corner of his eye, Buzz saw Jessie nod.

"Cher's going down to talk to Allen." Jessie looked out the passenger window, flipping a small, shiny disk in her hand and chuckled. "I think she finds him cute.". "She said she'll try to get some more facts about how salvage works from Brad."

Buzz smiled, glancing her way. "Hey, what's that?" the flash of the disk in the sunlight making him look closer. He scowled, returning his eyes to the road.

Jessie held up the thin, golden disk, examining it in the sunlight. "Oh, the puppy found it in the garden. It looks like some old earring or something." She held it between her thumb and forefinger. "At least that is what it looks like to me. It's very thin, like it's been pounded into an oval." She peered at the object closely. "It's probably something my grandmother lost while gardening ages ago. See how tarnished it is?" She extended her hand so he could look at the gold disk.

Buzz glanced at the item, nodding. "I hope Muttley won't tear up the whole garden, now that he's feeling better."

"Me, too." Jessie smiled. "The gardener and caretaker of the place would not be amused."

Jessie glanced over her shoulder at the stack of lost-dog flyers in a box on the backseat. They had stopped at an office supply store to make copies when they left the house and planned on stapling the flyers all along the beach on their way back.

Buzz glanced at the disk in Jessie's hand once more, looking up and meeting her eyes. "Can you check with your mom to see if she's ever seen that?" His eyes were firmly on the road once more as his tone grew serious. "You don't think someone could have dropped it trying to get over the wall?"

"Buzz." Jessie shook her head. "I told you, Muttley dug it up. How could someone have dropped it?"

Buzz shrugged "I'm just thinking. Maybe I'm just getting suspicious of everyone." He let out a breath feeling the deep sorrow in his soul. This was exactly why he was questioning his job choice. Would he forever be looking at everyone as if they were hiding something?

"Well, stop that." Jessie laughed. "We have work to do."

Chapter 7

"Whoo hoo, Allen!" Cheryl waved, trotting down the dock toward the big catamaran. "It's me. Do you have a minute?" She dropped her hand, adjusting her headscarf and straightening her white blouse tied at her midriff over high-waisted denim shorts. She smiled brightly, determined to dig out all the information she could from the handsome sailor. With his salvage knowledge, perhaps he could give her a clue to what questions she needed answers for.

"Cheryl, right?" The man stood and took a step away from where he had been coiling a rope. "What brings you here?." He brushed imaginary dust from his khaki shorts, stretching and rolling muscular shoulders under a thin, white tshirt.

"I hate to bother you." Cheryl smiled, delighted that he remembered her.. "If you aren't busy, could I ask you a few questions about salvage?" She accepted his hand, stepping over the railing and onto the deck of the boat.

"You plannin' on becoming a salvage diver, or do you have a boat that sank?" He asked, his eyes taking in her shapely legs as he chuckled.

"No." Cheryl shook her head, her pony tail swinging as her face flushed. "You know, I'm a little obsessed with that ghost ship. The one that we saw on the ghost tour and then again the other night."

The man shook his head and sighed. "And here I thought it was me you wanted to see."

Cheryl laughed, patting his arm. "That, too." The man was handsome and very fit.The smooth New Zealand accent didn't hurt either.

"I'm taking the boat out to test the waters," Allen said. "Mind coming along? I have a big group coming in for a sunset tour this evening. I want to be sure they won't all be sea sick if the waves pick up."

"Really?" Cheryl hopped, her rope-soled shoes barely making a sound on the wooden deck. Excitement at the prospect of another ride on the big cat with the handsome man was thrilling.

"The old girl needs a run, anyway." Allen flashed her a wide grin. "Cast off, and we'll get underway."

The water was quiet as Allen furled the sails a short time later, setting the boat on auto-pilot while he carried a drink to Cheryl.

"Thanks." Cheryl tipped her head back, enjoying the ocean breeze. She pried an eye open, taking in the sun-bronzed man, swaying lightly with the sail boat.

"Now, what questions do you have?" The man's smile was charming, setting Cheryl at ease.

"First, you don't use this boat for salvage, do you?" She watched as he took a seat. "I wouldn't expect a sailboat is the best for that sort of thing."

Allen chuckled. "No. This is for pleasure cruising only." He waggled his eyebrows suggestively, making Cheryl blush and laugh.

"So, what kind of boat is used for salvage?" Cheryl sipped her drink, soaking in the sun and sea air.

"Most are huge steel vessels with booms and sometimes dive pools," Allen sipped his lemonade. "We use an old tug. She's ugly as sin, but tough and small enough to slip into tight spaces, but with the mother of all engines." He chuckled. He gazed across the waves, beaming with pride.

"I was reading that salvage in this area has been ridiculous this year." Cheryl leaned on her elbow, resting her glass between them.

"It's crazy." Allen shook his head, peering out across the waves as he watched for other boats.

"Have you had a lot of business?" Cheryl lifted her glass, sipping as she studied him. He was handsome. His sandy, sun bleached, surfer boy look was very attractive.

"Not as much as I'd like." Allen sighed, leaning back on his elbows, long legs stretched out before him. "There are a couple of companies that get most of that business in this area. We don't get that much.." He shrugged turning to smile at her. "Between that and this beauty..." he patted the boat, "I manage."

Cheryl ran a finger around her glass, beads of moisture running over her hand. "Do you think this ghost ship thing makes more people try to find treasure?" She looked down, tracing her finger on the lip of the glass as a hint of sound sprang from the rim. She didn't know much about sailing and only what she had read about salvage, but she knew the old saying, l*A boat is a hole in the ocean you pour money into.*" Was Allen really making enough money with his cruises and odd salvage jobs?

"I doubt it." Allen's voice was quiet. "People are crazy, and some of these boat owners have more money than brains." He leaned on one elbow, turning toward her as his eyes looked out to sea.

Cheryl looked up to find the man studying her. "So, you think this would happen even if that green ghost ship didn't appear periodically?" She watched his face, noting the quick smile.

Allen reached out, taking her chin between thumb and forefinger. "I doubt it." He leaned in. "Why worry about it, anyway? It isn't your problem."

Cheryl felt her breath catch in her throat as the handsome man leaned in, his lips brushing hers as all thought of ghost ships and salvage evaporated in the heat of his touch. Her mind spun, and all the questions from earlier disappeared.

For a second she sat dazed by the hot kiss.

The boat bucked, hopping a wave, and Allen broke the kiss. "Sorry," he grinned, not looking sorry a bit. "I need to take the helm."

He rose, walking confidently to the cabin and taking the wheel. Cheryl huffed, out a breath, her heart racing. Shaking off the kiss, she pulled a tube of lipstick from her tiny straw bag and applied a fresh coat. She was supposed to asking the man questions, not letting him kiss her. Cheryl shook her head, trying to put her thoughts back in order, but they couldn't fight the rip-tide of the kiss.

Walking with her hand on the cabin wall to the shade of the salon, Cheryl slipped into a bench-seat, watching as Allen spun the wheel. The sail caught the wind, and the boat heeled slightly, turning on the water. As the boat skipped toward the harbour, Cher tried to clear her muddled thoughts.

"We're having a good day," Allen said, eyes fixed on the green waves. "This evening's sail should be great, especially if we get some good color in the clouds." He looked up, his accent sliding over Cheryl in a delightful shiver.

"Thanks for all of the information," Cheryl said, looking toward the marina that was quickly coming into view. "I'm glad that ghost ship isn't causing you trouble." She giggled when he looked over his shoulder at her. Dropping her eyes to the waves, she road the sweet feeling of the kiss to the dock, thoughts and questions lost to the moment.

Allen reefed the sails, switching to engines as he guided the boat into the harbor and stopped in the slip assigned to his boat. "I'm glad you came out with me." He winked as he offered Cheryl a hand, switching off the engine. He lifted her hand as the engine died, and the boat swayed into the dock, thick bumpers protecting the sides. Allen leaned in, his eyes on hers as he kissed her hand. "Maybe we can do it again sometime." He pouted. "I'm afraid the rest of the day is not mine to waste in sweet companionship."

Cheryl felt the blush heat her cheeks as her breath froze, but she managed to nod as Allen helped her over the side. He waved as she hurried up the dock, still smiling. At the top of the quay she turned, seeing the man tying up the boat, his arms rippling in the morning sun.

Cheryl gave a little skip as she made her way around the path to Jessie's blue and white mini-cooper. Allen had kissed her, and she had liked it. She shook her head, freezing as she clicked the key fob. Hadn't she had other questions to ask the man? Sighing, she slipped into the car, turned the key, and opened a window to let out the hot air as the air conditioning tried to catch up. She shouldn't have let the man distract her. A smile spread across her lips as she turned the radio on and shifted into gear. Maybe she shouldn't have let him distract her, but it had been a lovely distraction. There was no time for a man in her life right now. Still, the fact that someone handsome like Allen would kiss her, completely turned her head.

She smiled, singing along with the tune on the radio, reveling in the warm glow of a kiss.

"So you're Higgins' nephew?" an overweight officer with white hair asked as Buzz approached the front desk, Jessie at his side. "You look like him." The man smiled. "He never calls in favors, so this must be important." The man examined Jessie as she stood at Buzz's shoulder.

"You know my Uncle Paul?" Buzz asked.

The man shrugged. "Paul Higgins helped the department a time or two." He smiled, his eyes still on Jessie. "This your girlfriend?"

"What?" Buzz sputtered, his face going red. "No. We're just friends." He looked down at Jessie, offering an awkward grin.

"Oh. Like that, huh?" The officer grinned, giving Jessie a wink. "I'm Jones." He shook his head at Buzz. "Follow me." He led them down a hall, keys rattling.

"Sorry," Buzz whispered to Jessie, leaning sideways so she could hear. "I hope he didn't embarrass you."

Jessie slipped an arm through his, biting her lip. "Does it really matter?" She chuckled. "After all, we make a cute couple." Jessie giggled, pinching his arm. "Besides, what girl wouldn't want to walk around with a side of beef cake?"

Buzz shook his head, shoulders slumping. "You're killing me."

"In here." Jones called, ending the whispered conversation as he opened a door to a file room. "These dam...darn," he corrected, clearing his throat as he looked at Jessie, ". . . . ghost ship sightings are a menace."

"How so?" Jessie took the seat Jones offered, looking at the stacks of files on the table.

Buzz pulled out a metal chair, cringing at the screeching sound it made on the tile floor.

"We're always getting calls about things like this. Everyone knows it's a hoax, but that doesn't keep them from calling and telling us about hauntings." He shook his head in disgust. "Then there's all those foolish people out hunting for sunken treasure. Anything worth having has been found already. They go out there, barely able to control their boat and get into all sorts of trouble. The paper work alone is a pain in the a.." The older man winked at Jessie this time.

Buzz grimaced. "The bane of our lives," he sighed. Tipping his head, he studied the other officer. "We've heard that salvage operations here have been tallying in the billions," Buzz said, picking up a file.

"That's the insurance companies' problem." Jones hooked his thumbs in the waistband of his uniform, huffing. "It's the Coast Guard that gets the brunt of it. They have enough real emergencies to deal with without having to save simpletons with fancy notions of riches and fame." He let out a breath. "This year has been worse than ever, if you ask me. Not that anyone seems to notice. You go out on a boat, stuff happens."

"How many rescues this year?" Jessie asked, turning to look at Jones.

"I don't know. You'll find most of it in there." He nodded at the files. We get reports. The department likes to keep on good terms with the guard. Sometimes we cross paths with drug smuggling or other criminal activity." He shrugged. "We don't waste our time chasing people who have too much time on their hands. With all of those treasure hunter shows, it seems every glory-hound is out chasing the dream."

Buzz twisted in his chair. "Do you think the ghost ship sightings have anything to do with all of the salvage activity?" His eyes were steady on the other man's. "I mean, if someone with a salvage outfit was enticing folks to make foolish decisions that got them in trouble, wouldn't that be fraud?"

Jones shrugged. "I couldn't say. Maritime law isn't my department." He lifted his head in a half-nod. "Let me know when you kids are done with that mess." He grinned. "You've got some homework there." He stepped back through the door, closing it behind him, leaving Jessie and Buzz staring at each other.

"I guess that gives us an idea how the locals feel about the ghost ship." Buzz grinned, opening a file and starting to read. "Any idea what we're looking for?" He shook his head. "Being a cop isn't what most people think it is." He looked up, meeting Jessie's gaze as he grabbed a file. "It isn't like TV shows or movies. Most of what we do is this." He opened the file. "Digging, trying to put things together. Most stations, especially smaller ones, are overworked and understaffed. I can see why Jones is annoyed by these ghost ship sightings."

"I understand." Jessie was staring at him, studying. "My gut tells me something more is happening here." I'm hoping we'll know it when we see it." Jessie reached into her bag, pulling out two tablets and pens. “Here, take some notes. Maybe we'll see a pattern.” She shook her head. “I hope Cher is doing okay. I don't want anything to happen to her.”

“You think this kind of fraud could turn dangerous?” Buzz sat up, his instincts prickling. “There's a lot of money involved.” He watched Jessie as she gazed toward the ceiling. “That's one motive.” He rested his elbows on the table, the file forgotten. “Do you really think people are this treasure-crazy? I mean who would take their yacht out in dangerous water?

Jessie shrugged. “You know what that man in Macon was willing to do to get his hands on his version of treasure.”

Buzz stuck his nose back into the file, reading through and jotting down information he thought might be relevant. “Yeah, he was downright dangerous and didn't care who he hurt.” His eyes rested on Jessie, thankful she hadn't been seriously injured in that encounter.

“Buzz,” Jessie's tone made him look up again. He was used to paperwork, a rookie cop's most common activity. “I've known people who would drive their Lamborghini at top speed through Atlanta just to get on the news.” She shook her head. “You'd be surprised how easily rich people become bored.”

Buzz raised his brows. The tiny room was warm, a small fan doing nothing to deal with the lack of an air conditioning vent. Shadows filling the corners suddenly became ominous.- There were people who would think nothing of putting others in danger for money. If they viewed the privileged class as deserving what they got, the scam was even more sinister.

It was nearly dark before they closed the last file, and Buzz rubbed the bridge of his nose. “What do you think?” He asked. “Ready to call it a day?” He looked up at an equally tired Jessie.

She had pushed her hair behind her ears and paused to peek up from a file.

"Yes." She sighed, closing the file. "We'll compare notes at my place."

"We've been at this for hours." Buzz agreed. They had worked silently, each taking notes that might be relevant. Now with the notebooks full of scratching, it was time to compare what they'd learned.

Buzz stood, stretching tight muscles before reaching a hand for Jessie and helping her to stand. "How do you get me into these things, anyway?" He chuckled, shaking his head as he opened the door. Since his uncle had asked him to check in on the girl a few months ago, so much had changed for Buzz.

"Find what you were looking for?" Jones looked up from the tall front desk. The station was quiet as the day shift was finishing up.

"I have no idea," Jessie admitted. "We'll let you know if we found anything interesting."

Jones nodded, giving Buzz a half-salute. "I'd think young folks like you would have better things to do on a beautiful day. His smile widened. "Of course, the night is young. You could go out dancing and still have some fun."

"Thanks again," Buzz said, ignoring the man's suggestive tone as he dropped a hand to Jessie's back, escorting her out the door. "We have plenty of fun." He looked over his shoulder smiling at the older officer. "We really appreciate your time."

Jessie stretched, rolling her shoulders as they walked to the car. "He was helpful," she teased.

A warm breeze rolled off the coast as the evening sun blazed, adding to the heat of an already stifling day.

"He's got better things to do than babysit the two of us." Buzz chuckled, opening the door of his sedan for her before hurrying to the driver's side. "Why are we doing this, anyway?" he tipped his head and chuckled, slipping behind the wheel.

"Cheryl is obsessed, and unless we want her to make us crazy, we help." Jessie buckled up, a soft laugh filling the car. "Besides, aren't you curious? The ghost ship could simply be a gimmick, or all of these things could be connected."

Buzz started the car, his eyes focused on Jessie for a few moments as he shifted into gear. "Either way, it's a good distraction until I hear what my fate is going to be back home." Worry fizzed in his stomach, but he pushed it away. At least he had someone to spend his long, empty days with. He smiled. Perhaps not so empty with this little adventure.

He pulled out of the parking area, driving smoothly onto the main road. The car was quiet, and the mood shifted from the light companionship a moment ago.

"Hey, it will all work out." Jessie said, laying her hand on his shoulder. "You'll see. There is a purpose in everything."

Buzz chanced a glance at her, noting the lack of conviction on her face. "Thanks." He wasn't sure what he was thanking her for. Just having her there seemed to help. Maybe just for being a friend who kept him from sitting in his room going crazy with worry.

"The Bible says that all things work for the good of those who believe in the Lord," Jessie said, her voice muffled as she gazed out the window at the last hint of sunset color to the west. "We don't know what comes next in life, but we have to believe." She sighed, and Buzz knew she was clinging to her belief. Like him, she didn't know what came next, and the uncertainty seemed to build a bond.

"You really think so?" Buzz asked, as headlights flickered in his rearview mirror.

"I don't know." Jessie's sigh made him look at her as they rolled over the darkening road. "I mean, I know God is there and that he loves me. . . us." She waved a hand in the air, eyes still fixed outside. "But how does that make a difference in my life, or yours for that matter?" She turned, looking at Buzz. "I believe, but I still don't know where my life is heading. I'd think that if God had a plan for me, I'd know it." She shook her head.

Buzz focused on the road as the traffic picked up, driving carefully as he had been trained. Was it true? Did God have a plan for everyone? He glanced at Jessie, swerving as a car dodged around him, squeezing in front of him. Buzz ground his teeth, repressing the words he wanted to shout at the reckless driver.

"People are crazy," Jessie said, wide eyes turned to him.

Buzz took the turn toward the private beach and beach house, relaxing a little as he followed the far less busy road. "So, you think God has our lives all planned out?" he asked as darkness fell.

Jessie twisted, looking at him again. "Mom likes to quote a verse to all of her children when we're having doubts." She lifted her eyes, looking at the roof as if trying to remember. "Thy word is a lamp unto my feet, and a light unto my path, Psalm 119:105." She smiled, nodding to indicate that she had the words right. "Apparently, I can't see the path, though. Maybe my light has burned out."

Buzz chuckled, turning into the long driveway leading to the house.

"What's so funny?" Jessie crossed her arms, giving him a hard look.

"I'm sorry." Buzz glanced her way, guiding the car into the circular driveway. "I'm not laughing at you." He shook his head, turning the car off and turning to face her. "It's the idea of God having a flashlight."

Jessie chuckled. "Now that's an image."

The mood in the car lifted, and Buzz smiled then grew serious. "The thing about that verse is that when you're on a path and using a lamp or flashlight to find your way, you can't see very far. A few steps is all that is visible, even with a powerful light. The path itself and the destination are still a mystery."

Jessie opened her mouth then closed it again as she stared at him. Her face was illuminated by a garden light outside, but shadows still filled her features, painting her in shades of black and white.

"I've never thought of that," Jessie said. "The question is, can I live with only seeing directly in front of me and trusting God for the rest?"

Buzz shrugged. "It's not much different than me waiting to hear what the men at the top of the department decide for me. I have no control over what happens next."

Offering a sad smile, Buzz opened his car door and climbed out. Pausing to look at the quiet ocean, he breathed deeply of the salt air, hoping it would soothe the bundle of nerves in his stomach. Maybe Jessie was right, and someone up there was guiding them. He closed his eyes, taking in the smell of salt and sea. If that were true, perhaps he could relax a little more.

"There you are!" Cheryl called from the door, light from the windows of the house spilling around her in an odd geometrical shape. "Hurry up, dinner is almost ready."

"I guess we have our orders," Jessie teased as Buzz walked around to her side of the car, and she climbed from the seat, taking the hand he offered.

"She's kind of bossy, isn't she?" Buzz leaned forward, his grin full of teasing. "I'm not complaining," he patted his stomach. "I mean, I can eat."

"She's Cher." Jessie looked up, laughing, her hand lingering in his. "We take her as she is."

"I just hope she's still a good cook." Buzz laughed, his eyes dropped to their joined hands. He squeezed hers gently, then released her.

A black shadow darted out the front door as Muttley raced to greet them, happy yelps and thumping tail keeping them from making their way to the door.

"Mutt," Jessie laughed. "Stop." She bent over, trying to capture the squirming dog.

Buzz chuckled, squatting beside Jessie and ruffling the pup's coat. Wrapping his hands around the dog, he scooped up the puppy who was trying in vain to lick his face. "Someone's excited to see you." He held the dog toward Jessie who stroked his head.

"I think he's happy to see both of us." She leaned back. "No licks," she scolded the dog.

"Any luck on finding the owner of the mutt?" Cheryl asked as they walked through the front door.

Buzz placed the puppy on the floor, grinning as he bounced and wagged. Letting Jessie precede him into the kitchen, he sniffed.

"Don't worry." Cher, busied herself at the stove. "I let him outside and fed him already." She rolled her eyes, but it was obvious that Jessie's friend was warming to the dog.

"We put up flyers all along our route to the station." Buzz said. "Something smells good," he added, trying to see what Cheryl was taking from the oven.

"I put those pictures up on the lost dog websites in the area, as well," Cheryl said, placing a large casserole on the table. "If someone is missing that dog, we'll hear something soon."

"Thanks." Jessie said, looking at the table. "Where are the plates?"

"I thought we could serve ourselves and go out onto the back patio." Cheryl handed them each a plate from the cupboard. "It's too hot in here. The oven has been on for two hours."

"Thanks." Buzz took the plate, following Jessie's lead as she moved to the casserole. "What are we eating?"

"Taco pizza casserole." Cheryl replied. "Don't worry, I didn't make it too hot. Drinks are already outside.

"It looks good." His stomach growled, and he dropped his eyes. "Thanks for cooking. That was thoughtful."

"I like to cook," Cheryl grinned, filling her plate. "I figured a casserole would keep until we all got home." She shrugged. "Not that I planned on waiting much longer on you."

The trio spent the next half-hour enjoying dinner under the stars, Buzz tossing several balls for the puppy with his left hand while he ate with his right. The puppy quickly tired, though, and soon settled at Jessie's feet, chin resting on her toes as he napped.

"So, what did you find?" Cheryl asked, lifting a bite to her mouth. "Anything good?" Her eyes stayed on her fork, and Buzz wondered if she was intentionally avoiding eye contact or possibly trying to hide something from them .

"We have a list of the salvage crews that have been pulling boats off the point." Jessie said, giving her friend an odd look. "Oh, I left my bag in the car." She looked at Buzz, and he grinned, standing and placing his napkin on the table. "I'll get it." He looked between the girls, sure he was missing something but unsure what.

"Be right back." As he stepped through the door, he heard Cheryl's whisper.

"Allen kissed me. That's all I learned." A heavy sigh followed him through the living area. "I'm afraid I got distracted after that." He dashed out to the car, scanning the night for danger as he retrieved Jessie's backpack. Buzz knew he wasn't much good around girls. He had been focused on becoming a cop for so long, and he was kind of gangly and awkward. His eyes scanning the exposed beach, he wondered if Cheryl's being kissed was significant to the case or just her life.

A shadow moved on the beach, a darker silhouette against a flash of white topped waves. A prickle ran down Buzz's spine. This was a private beach. What was the man doing here? He took a step toward the shadow then retreated. He could run after the stranger, leaving the girls on their own or stay with them, offering some level of protection if trouble was brewing. Hurrying up the walkway, he stepped into the house, closing the door and locking it behind him before he joined the girls. Trying to shake off the odd feeling of being watched, Buzz turned toward the open back doors.

Soft voices drifted his way, and Buzz slowed. Was he being paranoid about the man on the beach? He had become far more suspicious of people in the past year. In all likelihood, the visitor was someone who had been out walking and didn't see the posted signs in the dark.

Shaking off his dark thoughts, Buzz plastered a smile on his face and stepped into the garden.

Cheryl looked up, her overly bright smile strained as Buzz joined them. He could tell the girls had been talking about the kiss, but didn't want to pry.

"Come on," Jessie said, reaching for her bag as she pushed her empty plate away. "Let's have a look." Her eyes sparkled as she looked at Buzz. "We'll compare notes." He chuckled, slipping into his chair and remembering a brilliant night when Jessie had written her solution to a fake crime, challenging him to do the same. They had agreed not to peek until the culprit was revealed. The activity had been fun and had given him insight into Jessie's logical and clever mind.

"I'm not seeing any pattern here," Buzz said, running a hand over his face an hour later. "There are dozens of salvage teams that have worked this mess."

Cheryl, surprisingly quiet, had cleared the dishes, returning with coffee and brownies with ice cream for dessert.

"But are any of them related?" Cheryl asked. "Could a larger corporation own some of them?"

"I don't know." Buzz looked between the girls, the image of the dark figure flashed across his mind.

Jessie stretched out a hand taking the tablet from his hand.- "How about some more coffee?" she asked, looking at Cheryl. "Maybe another brownie?"

"Glad you asked." Cher jumped up, collecting plates as a cool breeze ruffled her ponytail. "I'll bring it to the living room." She looked up as clouds skidded overhead, obscuring their view of the stars. "I think we're going to get a storm."

Jessie wiggled her toes, making the puppy huff as he lifted his head. "Come on, Muttley," she said. "We need more light for this, anyway," she added, her eyes meeting Buzz's.

Questions whirled in Buzz's brain, and a strange prickly sensation made his senses tingle. Buzz stood, pushing his chair away and helping Jessie gather the drink glasses. "I think we need to figure this little mystery out soon," he said, following Jessie inside. "I only have a week left here, and you girls need to be careful. If there is some sort of salvage fraud going on, that kind of money can lead people to do risky and dangerous things."

"Make yourself comfortable." Jessie nodded at the living area, taking the items from Buzz and heading for the kitchen. "Maybe keep Mutt out of the way." The puppy looked up at her. He was practically walking on her heels, and though he was cute, he didn't need to be underfoot in the kitchen.

"Sure." Buzz squatted, snapping his fingers. "Come here, boy."' Muttley looked between Jessie and Buzz, torn between where to go.

"Go on," Jessie gave him a gentle push with her foot. "I'll be right back."

While Jessie prepared drinks, Buzz sat with the dog. He wanted to caution the young woman again about doing anything rash. He knew that she tended to act before thinking about the consequences, but the only words he could think of would seem offensive or sound overbearing.

"The caffeine and sugar refill is almost ready," Cheryl shot over her shoulder as Jessie slipped into the kitchen, placing the glasses into the already open dishwasher.

"So, about this kiss," Jessie asked, her tone flat as she filled the soap dispenser and closed the dishwasher.

"It was nothing. Just one of those things. You know, that moment when you're alone with someone and the surrounding is right." Cheryl blushed. "I can't say I didn't enjoy it, though."

"He is rather dashing," Jessie chuckled. "That accent and all."

Cheryl sighed. "You know I'll never see the man again." She looked up. "If I get involved with someone, it has to be a guy you bring home to meet granny." Her smile brightened. "I don't have time for a summer romance." Cher placed clean mugs on a tray, adding a carafe of coffee. "It was a bit disconcerting, though." She lifted the tray filled with coffee items. "I mean, he kissed me then jumped up and took the wheel again. A few minutes later we were back at the dock. My brain is all muddled."

Jessie walked over and hugged her friend. "Life is crazy right now. Do you think it ever gets any better?" She shook her head. "At least you've been kissed," she added under her breath.

"No." Cheryl said. "But at least it isn't boring. Bring the brownies." Cher turned toward the living room. "Come on. Let's dig into this."

Jessie laughed, not sure if Cher was talking about the treats or the mystery.

An hour later, the trio had been through the list of salvage companies listed in the shipwreck files three times.

"Wait." Jessie squealed, waving a page as she sat cross-legged on the sofa. "See?" She pointed at the two pages of notes. "This company is owned by an LLC, and so is this one."

Cheryl leaned close. She had settled on the floor, her laptop propped on the coffee table along with a fresh carafe of dark brew. "Let me check. Emick, Corp." Her fingers flew over the keys, pulling up the company website. "It looks like they are a holding company for a lot of small operators."

"So, they're a conglomerate? Where are they based?" Buzz turned from the cold fireplace where he rested his elbow on the mantle, his tan skin was a warm contrast to the white brick and wood. As they had talked, the tall man had moved restlessly around the room.

"Oh, here!" Cheryl clicked a few more keys. "They're based in Savannah."

"Maybe we should pay them a visit tomorrow?" Jessie looked between her friends.

Buzz walked over to stand behind the sofa, looking over Jessie's shoulder at Cheryl's screen. Jessie looked up, meeting his eyes, her thoughts spinning with excitement.

"We should call Brad," Cheryl looked up, her brown eyes flicking between Buzz and Jessie. "Maybe he knows the company."

"Isn't that a stretch?" Buzz asked. "Why would he be interested in the salvage companies?" The man bent, resting his elbows on the back of the sofa.

"He's the lighthouse keeper," Cheryl looked up, giving Jessie that 'duh' look. "He sees the wrecks, sometimes even as they happen. His job forces him to be interested."

"It's getting late," Jessie said as the puppy nudged her hand with his nose. "After eleven," she added, looking at the large iron and brass clock above the mantle. "He's probably in bed." Behind her, Buzz stretched, and she caught the tired glint in his eyes.

"He's not exactly old, Jess." Cher wrinkled her nose at her friend, pulling her phone from her pocket and dialing. "Hey, Brad? Hi, this is Cheryl. You gave me and my friends a private tour yesterday." She was quiet for a minute, nodding. "We've been wondering about these ghost ship sightings. No, now listen. We aren't going to try to find the AnnaSwift." She flashed a look at Jessie who was about to speak but stopped. "Are you familiar with a company called Emick Corp.? It's an LLC and has a bunch of little salvage companies listed under its umbrella group." She was quiet again for a moment. "Oh, yeah, I thought maybe you would be familiar with them. No, that's okay." Silence again, this time Cheryl's eyes went wide.

"What? You're at the lighthouse now? What would a ship be doing off the point without its running lights on? Isn't the lighthouse on?"

Jessie leaned forward, hearing a note of worry in her friend's voice as Cher shook her head. Jessie stood, moving closer, trying to catch the other side of the conversation. "Oh. If you think they are people who are looking for treasure again, why not call the police or the coast guard? I know there's no law about going in there, but really. . . how stupid can people be? No, I don't think you should go out there to see who they are. Just call someone." Cheryl nodded a few times, her voice filling with frustration. "Okay, I'll keep you posted on what we find. We aren't done digging, yet. Please, be careful. Good night." She paused, and Jessie looked at Buzz.

"He isn't going out there to see who's on the water, is he?" Buzz asked, his voice intense, making the girls stare at him.

"He said he wouldn't." Cheryl said, slipping her phone back into her pocket. "He said he didn't know much about Emick Corp. off hand, but if a group of salvage operators pulled together, they would get better rates and have leverage when dealing with insurance companies. It's like building a reputation. Once the companies know the LLC can deliver, the whole group of operators would get more jobs."

"We're still no closer to understanding this." Buzz ran a hand over weary eyes.

"Tomorrow, let's walk back to the museum and see if Dr. Crumm has any other ideas. He has to know which company sponsors the ghost ship, and I'm sure he would want to stop anyone from letting people wreck their boats." Cheryl looked between Buzz and Jessie as if for agreement.

"Okay." Jessie nodded wearily. They had been over everything several times and only had hints of clues. Perhaps morning would shine a better light on what they knew. "Maybe things will make more sense in the morning."

"Sounds like a plan." Buzz agreed, looking at them and offering a smile. "I want you to both be careful, though. This is all probably nothing, but if we're on to something, there are people who won't want us to know the truth."

"So dramatic." Cheryl laughed, rising and gathering her laptop. "I'm headed up to bed to do some more digging." She grinned. "I'm too young to go to bed at eleven."

Jessie groaned, but bid her friend good night. "How about you?" she asked, turning back to Buzz.

"I think I'll take a walk around outside." He dropped his head, studying his toes. Jessie smiled at the familiar gesture.

"Mind if Mutt and I join you?" Jessie reached down, stroking the puppy.

Buzz smiled again, rolling his shoulders and giving her a sideways glance. "That would be nice." He looked at the dog, who shoved his nose onto Jessie's hand.

"You wanna go outside?" she asked, stroking the dog's head.

The happy yip and prancing feet were all the answer she needed.

The quiet and peaceful walk along the beach with Buzz was just what Jessie needed to relax her mind. The puppy raced ahead, ears flapping as he darted one way and then another. It was midnight before Buzz walked Jessie back to the beach house. She smiled, feeling relaxed. She had good friends, something to keep her mind occupied, and time to figure out what came next in her life.

Pulling in the damp air as a breeze ruffled her hair, Jessie took Buzz's arm. They walked toward the golden lights of the house in companionable silence. Jessie always enjoyed Buzz's company. The man seemed to accept her for who she was. She glanced up, noticing his eyes looking ahead. Maybe he had changed in the past few months, but deep down it was still just Buzz. She smiled, knowing he would caution her to be safe.

She paused, letting the waves find her toes as she watched clouds roll, glowing in the light of a half-moon.

Jessie was content as Buzz walked her to the door.

"Will you do me a favor?" Buzz, stopping at the front door, placed his hands on her shoulders and looked down into her face.

"Sure." Jessie smiled, feeling sleepy and relaxed.

"Lock that front gate when I leave." He turned, looking down the stone walkway to the low wall and cast iron gate, now standing wide in welcome.

"What?" Jessie turned to follow Buzz's gaze. "Why?" She gave him a questioning look. "It's always open when we're here."

"I'm a cop." Buzz shrugged, his eyes intense. "Humor me?" He raised his brows.

"Fine." Jessie pretended to drag her feet, chuckling as she followed him to the gate. "Be safe going home." She appreciated the man's cautious nature, especially considering his job, but she was far more used to taking things as they came.

Buzz stepped through the gates, turning back. "Lock up, and get a good night's sleep. Should I pick you and Cheryl up for the museum tomorrow?"

"We could meet you there?"

Buzz shook his head. "I'm up early, anyway. I like getting to chaufer two lovely ladies." He laughed lightly, but his eyes were serious.

"Good night, Buzz." Jessie, chuckled. "We'll see you in the morning," she added, covering a yawn. The puppy, whined, looking at Buzz before gazing up at her.

Buzz shot her a quick grin and closed the iron gates. "Music," he chuckled, as the lock clicked.

Jessie watched him walk to his car under the security light, waving as he slipped inside and drove away.

"Come on, pup." Jessie scratched the dog's ears then walked back to the house, locking the door behind her as she switched off the lights. It only took a few minutes to close up the house, change into her night clothes, and brush her teeth. Walking to the door leading to her private balcony, she opened it, breathing deeply of the night air. A feeling of contentment washed over her like the breeze. Jessie closed her eyes, soaking in the air.

A roll of thunder far out over the ocean echoed, and Muttley pawed at her. Jessie opened her eyes, scanning the thunderhead rolling toward shore. A flicker of lightning danced in the clouds. Walking out onto the balcony, she settled against the wall, knees tucked up as she stroked the dog. Clouds rolled over the waves, the light from the stars and flashes of lightning outlining the coast.

Muttley wiggled, moving to the balcony wall and barking. Bracing his front paws on the low barrier, he turned, looking at Jessie then continued barking into the dark night again.

"What is it?" Jessie asked, moving on her knees to the wall and looking into the front garden. A shadow slipped over the low wall into the front garden, and Jessie gasped. Fear and anger flashed through Jessie like lightning, and she stood, ready to shout.

The puppy barked again, louder this time as he sensed Jessie's shock. The motion sensor light flashed on, the figure moving toward the house. A sizzle of anger filled her. Lightning flashed and thunder rolled again as Jessie ran to get her phone. She stepped through the door, grabbing her phone from a table by the window and turning to keep her eyes on the intruder. As Muttley continued to bark, the shadow froze, looking up at Jessie. A face, masked in a dark hood, turned. She knew from his posture that he could see her. Hands shaking, rage and fear filling her belly, Jessie dialed.

Another heartbeat. The phone ringing. Muttley barking.The ominous sound of a storm approaching. Jessie shivered.

A second frantic heartbeat, and the figure turned, running and jumping the wall. The motion was smooth and practiced, and Jessie burned as she watched. The intruder disappeared into the night, only the shadows of the closed gate stretching like ethereal fingers after him.

"Hello, Buzz? This is Jessie. Someone just tried to break in." Jessie could hear the squeal of tires over the line, and she knew that Buzz was on his way back. Should she have called the police? Why had her first reaction been to call Buzz? Jessie shook her head. It didn't matter. The burglar was gone now; or at least she hoped he was. Her heart pounded, the fight and flight reaction to fear still warring in her soul.

Chapter 8

Buzz barrelled down the driveway, skidding to a stop in a cloud of gravel and dust. Slamming the car into park, he jumped out, racing toward the house and the locked gate. His heart pounded, fear lending him speed. He had no time to think. No time to feel as instinct and training took over.

"Jessie!" he shouted, looking up at the second floor where a figure slipped from the shadows. "There you are." His voice shook as Jessie appeared, wrapped in a thick blue robe, the puppy clutched in her arms. "Stay there," Buzz waved, stopping at the closed gate. "I'm going to have a look around." Air rushed into his lungs, relief at seeing her safe washing over him like a wave.

"Buzz," Jessie scowled, her features clear in the reflected light of the security lamp. "Be careful. You don't know if he's still out there." Her voice was strong, filling Buzz with confidence.

Buzz grinned, his teeth clenched tight. The harsh light of the security light cast him in shadow, turning cheerful features into a menacing mask. "I'll be careful." He walked backward to his car, his eyes still on Jessie as he opened the passenger door and reached into the glovebox. Reaching behind him, his eyes scanning the area in front of him, he switched off the car, pulled the keys from the ignition, and stood.

The powerful beam of the flashlight illuminated the dark pavement as Buzz looked for traces of the intruder. He moved the light back and forth, methodically searching for clues. His mind whirled with possibilities, but he paused, the verse Jessie had shared with him that day hitting him in the heart. He moved the flashlight, seeing how far it would illuminate his path and sighed. He had been joking when he told Jessie that a lamp can only see so far off a path at one time; and now he stood, surrounded by darkness, his tiny beam the only guide in an ocean of night.

Lightning flashed, then thunder rolled, and the first raindrops fell, splashing on his face. Buzz looked up as the storm reached the beach. A breeze raised goosebumps on his arms, and cold, heavy drops landed in his hair, spattering his shoulders. Buzz broke into a trot, heading back toward the house before the rain washed away any clues.

"He jumped over there." Jessie's voice drifted down to him as the rain began to fall in earnest. He looked up, following her pale, slender arm to where she pointed directly to the far side of the gate. The area on that side of the five foot wall was clear. No bushes, trees, or other obstacles obscured the approach to the wall. The rain pounded as Buzz knelt, trying to find any sign of the intruder. A few turned over pebbles in the border was all he saw as the sky opened, washing away even that tiny sign.

"I'll let you in." Jessie's voice was nearly drowned out by the torrent of wind and rain.

"Don't bother," Buzz shook his head, water spraying from his brown hair which was quickly losing the battle to stay upright. Standing, he placed a hand on the top of the wall, swinging his whole body onto the top, the way a cowboy might mount a running horse. The security light flashed on again, dazzling. Buzz raised a hand, blinded for a second as water trickled over his face. A moment later, his feet squished on the sidewalk, and he ran for the door.

Jessie opened the door as Buzz skidded to a stop under the protection of the balcony above. "You're soaked," she chided as a gust of damp air swirled the hem of her robe, exposing shapely ankles. "Get in here." She stepped away, waving him inside and closed the door, keeping out the rain.

"I'm dripping on your floor," Buzz said, dropping his eyes to the white tile under his feet. The air conditioning raised goosebumps on his skin, and he shivered.

"Don't worry about the floor." Jessie huffed, grabbing his arm and pulling him into the small bathroom beside the entryway. "Here." She grabbed a towel, shoving it into his hands. "You shouldn't have gone looking for that man."

"Thanks," he looked up, studying her face. She was safe. Her lovely face, unmarred by fear, but a glimmer of anger glowed in her eyes.

To his surprise, Buzz chuckled as he dried his face and began rubbing his hair, tussling the once spikey locks into a semblance of bed-head. "You should have called the police." Buzz looked up, meeting Jessie's eyes, his hand still as he pressed the towel onto his hair. "This could have been serious."

Jessie shuffled backward toward the entry, looking at his wet feet. "I thought of you first." She lifted her chin. "Besides, you are the police." She smiled, her eyes sparkling as she stepped out of the bathroom.

Buzz shook his head. Frustration played tug of war with relief in his heart. This was Jessie. This was why he liked her. "Not here I'm not." He rubbed the towel through his hair, his eyes still locked on Jessie's." He tried to keep his face stern, but he suspected he looked pathetic since he was soaked to the skin. "You could still call the police."

"You're soaked." Jessie hedged, grabbing the door and pulling it closed. "I'll get you something to change into." Before he could respond, she was gone.

Buzz sighed, his mind turning over the events of the night, as he unbuttoned his shirt and dried his shoulders and chest. He was happy - and upset - with Jessie for calling him and not the police. If she had called the locals, they might have caught the man who had frightened her. Worry turned his stomach, and Buzz closed his eyes, trying to calm his beating heart.

The soft click of tiny nails on glass made him smile. A moment later, Muttley nosed the bathroom door open, padding across the tile. The pup pranced and slid, thumping into Buzz's legs with a happy yelp.

"Hey, boy." Buzz squatted, rubbing the dog's ears as he sprang and bounced with excitement. "Were you a good boy and scared that bad man away?" He smiled as the dog jumped, trying to lick his face. "None of that now." Buzz pressed the animal back, telling him to sit, and rewarding him with a pat on the head when he did.

"Here you go." Jessie stepped back into the room, holding out a thick teal bathrobe, her eyes on the pup. "I see someone came straight down to see you when I let him out of my room." She smiled, lifting her eyes. "Oh." She froze, staring at him as he stood, towel draped around his neck. Buzz flinched, grabbing the robe as he realized her eyes were fixed on his bare chest.

"Sorry," he said, running the towel over the smattering of dark hair before grabbing the robe. "I'll be right out." Buzz had never been completely comfortable in his overly tall skin. It was only in recent years that he had gained the grace and fluidity of movement that kept him from tripping over his feet.

"Right." Jessie blinked, coming back to her senses. "Come on, Muttley. Let's get this man something hot to drink." She spun on bare feet, the dog springing past her as she closed the door.

Buzz felt the blush on his cheeks as the door clicked. Part of his brain wanted to know what she had felt when she saw him. The other pushed the notion away. Jessie was young, innocent, and perhaps a little naive. Buzz dropped his head, wishing he could forget some of the things he had seen since graduating from the police academy. Jessie had faced true danger, but something in him wanted to shelter and protect her.

A smile tugged at his lips, and Buzz shook his head. "Old-fashioned foolishness," he whispered, slipping into the robe.

Buzz stepped out of the bathroom a few moments later. He had smoothed his hair as best he could and slipped into the fuzzy robe, hanging his shirt and shorts on a hook to dry. "It's a little snug," he mused, as he tightened the belt. The robe barely covered his knees, and the shoulders were so tight that much of his chest remained exposed. He dropped his eyes and shrugged. "At least I'm warm and dry."

The smell of rich, dark coffee hit his nose, and he sighed. "That smells great." he looked up as Jessie sat two huge mugs of cappuccino on the table. "But I still haven't forgotten that you didn't call the police." He studied the young woman's face, seeing her fighting a smile.

"At least I didn't go after him," Jessie said, finally losing her battle with mirth. "You look ridiculous." She laughed softly, her eyes sparkling.

Self-conscious, Buzz pulled the robe tighter. "It's not really my size," he said, shrugging, the robe threatening to burst at the seams. "Or my style."

Jessie nodded, "It was either that or my grandfather's old nightshirt," she teased before growing serious, the light-hearted banter gone as she pushed a mug toward him. She nodded at the opposite chair. The quiet of the house filled the kitchen as the puppy sniffed around the fridge. Buzz watched as Jessie folded her legs under her, her light blue robe slipping enough to reveal an oversized T-shirt and flannel shorts.

Buzz pulled out the chair, holding his robe tight as he took a seat, and reached for the mug. Tucking the thick fabric around his legs, he lifted his mug. "Thanks." He sipped, eyes still on Jessie, as the puppy flopped between them under the table, its tail tickling the man's ankles. Buzz glanced under the table, smiling as the little mutt rested his chin on Jessie's toes.

Silence filled the room for several seconds before Buzz finally spoke. "Where's Cheryl?" He looked at the stairs, expecting her to appear as if by magic.

"Still asleep. I swear a tornado could go through the place, and she would sleep right through it." Jessie shook her head. "She was always like that. If I had a late shift when we were in college, I'd come home, turn on the lights, make all the noise I wanted to, and she wouldn't wake. If. . ." she raised a finger, ". . . .on the other hand, I tried to creep in all quiet like, she'd wake up furious." Jessie shook her head.

Buzz nodded. He knew that they were both avoiding the subject of the prowler until their thoughts settled. His eyes scanned her face, trying to understand her thoughts.

Jessie looked up, a hint of worry in her blue eyes. "Do you think this was an attempted burglary?" She clutched her mug in two hands, an indication that she was concerned.

"Could be." Buzz set his cup on the table, his eyes fixed on hers. "There are a few things that bother me, though."

Jessie tipped her head. "Like what?"

"If this was a thief trying to break in and steal valuables, why did he go to the front wall?" He turned his mug, studying it as he ordered his thoughts.

"It's lower." Jessie's voice was hopeful, but held no conviction.

"Yes, but it also has a motion-detecting light that is sure to go on. Any thief worth his salt would have cased the place for a few days. They would want to establish if there was any pattern to your movements. When you went out. When you went to bed, that sort of thing."

"Maybe it was just an opportunity he couldn't resist. The storm was rolling in. You were gone, and with all the lights off in the place, he must have thought we were asleep."

"But what about the dog?" Buzz peeked under the table at the puppy who lifted his head to look at him, tail thumping. "I'm assuming Muttley barked?"

"He did." Jessie reached down, patting the dog, before lifting her mug once more. "Maybe the burglar didn't know about the dog."

"But he must have heard him bark, before he jumped the wall." Buzz sipped, looking over the rim of his cup. "Where were you?"

"On the balcony, waiting for the storm to break. I like to sit there on the floor and look out at the ocean over the low wall. Muttley barked, and then I saw the man climb over the wall."

"But why there?" Buzz huffed, placing his mug on the table and running his hands through his damp hair. "Why did he still jump the wall when he heard the dog? If I were breaking into this house, I would not approach it from the front gate." He looked up, shaking his head. "He must have known he would be seen. There are at least ten better places to slip through that would keep someone out of the range of that light. All those trees on the far side of the house." He waved vaguely.

"That's the pool area." Jessie scowled, her brows pinching. "It has a light, too, for night swimming."

"That sounds peaceful," Buzz grinned. "A quiet pool with a friend. Swimming under the stars."

He stood, pacing the small kitchen, tugging absent-mindedly at the ill-fitted robe. "It just doesn't feel right." He turned, leaning both hands on the table and looking at Jessie. "What did he do when he got over the wall?"

Jessie blinked, her eyes dropping to his bare chest before flicking back to his face. "He just stood there. He looked right up at me, and I could see him clearly in the light. Well, clearly except that he was wearing a ski mask." She made a tugging motion over her face.

Buzz plopped back into his chair, stretching his legs out and crossing them at the ankles as he adjusted his robe. “So, it wasn’t just chance. He wouldn’t have a mask with him if this hadn’t been planned.” The tall man ran a hand over his face. “I think he wanted you to see him.” He shook his head again. “Otherwise the whole thing makes no sense.”

“You think he wanted me to see him?” Jessie gasped.

Buzz nodded, eyes fixed on his toes as he lifted his mug. “I do. I don’t know why, but I think he was hoping to scare you.” He turned, looking at Jessie and offering a slight smile. “He doesn’t know that you don’t scare easily. Maybe you should just leave.”

Jessie shook her head emphatically. “I’d say he doesn know that one of my best friends is a cop.” Jessie’s smile flashed, and Buzz sat up.

“One of your best friends?” he turned, propping his elbows on the table, and adjusting his feet so he wasn’t stepping on Muttley. Propping his chin on his hands, he grinned. “Do tell.”

“Yeah.” Jessie shrugged. “I know it’s been ages since we hung out in Macon, but it feels like we’re just picking up where we left off. Doesn’t it?” Her eyes were intense, and something fluttered in Buzz’s chest.

“It does.” For several seconds he looked at her, drinking in her lovely face. She wasn’t wearing any makeup, but she was still so pretty it hurt. “Thanks.” He dropped his eyes to his mug as thunder crashed and rain lashed the windows of the house. “I’m going to crash on your couch tonight,” he said, looking up and pinning her with his eyes. “Please don’t argue. Jessie, I think we’ve inadvertently ruffled someone’s feathers.”

Jessie’s eyes went wide. “You are not sleeping on my couch.” She crossed her arms, giving him a stubborn glare.

“Jessie,” he raised a hand in protest.

“You can sleep in one of the spare rooms.” Jessie smiled, already pushing the worries of the night away. “There’s no need for you to be miserable.” She sighed, biting her bottom lip. "I have to agree with you." She met his gaze. "Someone thinks we're poking into things they don't want poked."

Buzz nodded but relaxed, his shoulders easing. "I'll call my folks." He looked down at his attire and cringed.

"I'll toss your wet clothes in the dryer." Jessie rose, heading for the bathroom. "I guess you will need my grandfather's night shirt, after all." She chuckled, and Buzz groaned, it was going to be an interesting end to a long day.

"Do you know what Cher has planned for tomorrow?" Buzz followed Jessie, reaching over her shoulder to take down his wet shirt and shorts from the hook.

Jessie shrugged, turning and leading the way to a tiny laundry room tucked discreetly under the stairs. "I think she wants to talk to Dr. Crumm or maybe head back to the lighthouse."

Buzz followed Jessie, his mind turning over the events of the night. An intruder didn't just hop over a wall and stare at the occupants. "So, what have we done?" he mused. "We've visited the museum." He ticked the first item off one finger. "We've asked around about the ghost ship and AnnaSwift." He looked up, not seeing Jessie as she tossed his clothes in the dryer. "Then we had the lighthouse tour."

"And the sailboat ride," Jessie grinned. "Where Cher got kissed," she added with a grin. "What about the trip to the police station?"

Buzz nodded. "That's a lot of threads to follow." He ran a hand over his face, weary. Nothing added up. Cher and Jessie were just a couple of girls having fun.

Jessie placed her hand on his arm, turning him toward the stairs. "Look, it's late. Let's get a good night's sleep, and see what tomorrow brings."

Buzz smiled. "That's a plan I can live with." His eyes ran over her, and he relaxed. She was safe. The rest would have to wait.

Jessie tossed for what seemed like hours, her mind vibrating with thoughts and questions as the storm blew itself out, drifting inland. When she had seen the intruder, her first instinct was to call Buzz, but he wouldn't always be there. She should have called the police. But she hadn't, and she wondered why. Did Buzz make her feel safe? She knew that no matter how crazy she sounded, the tall man would listen and believe her. Jessie loved her family, but they were more prone to swoop in and take over than let her explore her own skills. Her mother walked a fine line, balancing the elder care home, her three year old, and life as a whole. Jessie's brothers, not intentionally overbearing, viewed her as the baby sister who needed them to save the day.

She tossed again. Giving up on sleep, Jessie rose, walking to the balcony door and opening it. Muttley raced out, placing his paws on the low wall and looking out at the yard. Jessie stood in the doorway, letting the cool, freshly-washed air roll over her. Jessie had put Buzz in the bedroom at the back of the house. It had a balcony overlooking the backyard, but just having him there made her feel more at ease. Now, if she could just get some sleep. A vision flashed through her mind of Buzz, standing shirtless in her bathroom, and Jessie shivered.

"Come in, Mutt." She called the dog, closing the door on the cold breeze and climbing back into bed. Buzz was a conundrum. He was boyish and kind, but tonight she had seen a different side of him. He had been fierce, cold, and deductive. A man had stood before her tonight, his childish grin replaced with determination and a hint of anger.

"What are we going to do, Muttley?" She reached down, rubbing the dog's ears as he laid his head on her comforter. She had finally convinced the little beast that his bed was for sleeping, and hers was off limits. If the animal would indeed be as big as the groomer had indicated, no one needed him getting comfortable with sleeping in their bed. "I don't know what we've done to have someone want to scare us. All we've been trying to do is understand about the ghost ship." She shook her head, flopping back on her pillow. Swirls of color and muddled images raced through her brain. There had to be an explanation, and something they had done had someone worried.

Rolling over, Jessie whispered a childhood prayer, pleading for sleep as the stars crept through the clouds in silence.

Muttley placed his feet on the bed, whimpering. "No." Jessie said. "Go to your bed." She closed her eyes, slipping into a troubled sleep.

"Jessie, wake up." Cheryl's voice intruded on Jessie's sleep as she was rocked back and forth in the comfort of her bed. "Jessie," Cheryl hissed. "Why is Buzz walking around the place in a ragged old night shirt?"

Jessie sat up, blinking the sleep from her eyes as she turned to focus on her friend sitting next to her on the bed. Having Cher shake her awake in the wee hours of the morning was nothing new, but it took a moment to catch up. "Oh." Jessie tucked her knees to her chin, staring at her friend.

"Oh?" Cheryl crossed her arms. "All you have to say is, 'oh'?" She glared at Jessie.

Jessie rubbed her eyes. "I'll explain." She yawned, looking for her dog, but he was gone. "Where's Mutt?"

"He chased your boyfriend down the hall when I opened your door." Cheryl smirked.

"Don't you go down that road," Jessie glared at her friend. "Buzz is a friend. Not my boyfriend." Why did everyone think that if you had a friend of the opposite sex you had to be dating? She blew a wisp of hair from her face. "I don't even know what I would do with a boyfriend." She scowled. "I can't even figure out where I'm going, let alone how a man would fit into my life." She shook her head, grabbing Cheryl by the arms. “We had an attempted break-in last night, and I called Buzz. He insisted on staying the night.”

Cheryl waggled her brows, but Jessie cut her off before she could speak. “Buzz got soaked in the storm last night. He was worried and said he would sleep on the couch. I put him in the back bedroom.” Jessie glared at her oldest friend. “Now be good.”

“It stormed last night?” Cheryl looked out the huge window at the morning sun, bewildered.

“Yes,” Jessie shook her head, throwing off the blankets. “Why did he come back?”

“I called him when someone was snooping around the place.” Jessie shrugged as if it wasn’t a big deal. “He was worried it was a burglar.”

“Oh my!” Cheryl gaped. “Were we in mortal peril?”

“It was probably just someone who thought the place was empty and thought they’d see if they could get in.” Jessie shook her head. “Look, Buzz came back and got soaked. He stayed the night in case the intruder returned. Now, can you get Buzz his clothes while I shower and get dressed? They’re in the dryer.” She looked at Cheryl who was already dressed and had her makeup on. “I need coffee before processing anything else.”

“Will do.” Cheryl sprang from the bed, smoothing her long, apple-green camisole top with spaghetti straps over her white pedal pusher pants. “Now get ready. We have an appointment with Doc Crumm at ten.” She grinned. “I want to stop at the lighthouse first, though. I have questions for Brad.”

Jessie shook her head, smiling as Cheryl swished her way out the door. “Where do you get the energy?” she hissed, closing the bathroom door.

Ten minutes in the hot shower, and Jessie felt like a new woman. The thoughts of the night had blown away, leaving her determined to pull some facts from their visit to the museum and figure out who was feeling threatened by the amateur sleuthing of friends on vacation.

Tossing her blankets over her bed, Jessie walked to the door and almost walked into Buzz. "Sorry," she said, smiling as she took a step back then burst out laughing.

"Thanks." Buzz shook his head. "As if I don't feel silly enough." His face went red as he looked at his unusual attire.

"I'm sorry." Jessie sputtered, looking at his long legs sticking out from under a faded blue and green plaid nightshirt that barely reached his knees. "At least it fits better than the robe." She laughed again.

Buzz looked down at her and grinned. "I have to say, as sleepwear goes, it's rather comfy." He flipped the hem like a little girl in a new dress. "What do you think, can I bring this look back?"

Jessie laughed, noticing that he was holding his regular clothes in his other hand. "I'm going to grab a shower." He lifted his clothes, his cheeks reddening. "I don't suppose you have any hair gel?"

Jessie bit her lip, trying to keep from laughing again. "Vanity, thy name is Theo," she teased. "There's probably some in the bathroom," she nodded to the door across the hall. "Mom keeps the place well-stocked for guests." She glanced up at his wet hair flopping over his forehead in shades of brown.

"Thanks." Buzz turned, casting a glance back at her, and Jessie bit her lip again, laughter spluttering. Dropping his head the tall man groaned. "See you at breakfast."

Jessie followed Buzz to his car, watching as he popped the trunk and dug through a bag. She paused as he pulled his shirt off, slipping a clean t-shirt over his head in one smooth motion.

"Is that normal protocol?" She asked, seeing the ripple of muscles under his shirt. "Do all policemen carry extra clothing in their car?" Sometimes just when she thought she had the man figured out, he surprised her, leaving an odd, unsettled feeling in her stomach.

Buzz shrugged. His hair had been restored to the usual, gravity-defying style, and he looked rested. "I keep workout clothes here and a few Macon County PD t-shirts for other emergencies." He twisted, pointing to the police logo over his left peck.

"I'm ready!" Cheryl called, hurrying down the walkway, white boat shoes scuffing quietly on the stone path. "Mutt seems perfectly happy outside in the back garden," she added, joining them. "Oh, you changed." She smiled at Buzz. "Though that nightshirt was rather fetching." She giggled, and Buzz groaned.

"I'm never going to live this down, am I?" He shook his head, closing the trunk of his car and moving to the driver's door. "Let's just go."

"Nope!" Both girls replied, breaking into peals of laughter.

The sun was already high, the heat intense as Buzz drove them out of the private beach area and toward town. As they approached the museum, the blare of sirens approaching made Buzz pull off the road. They watched as a squad car and ambulance blasted by.

"What happened?" Cheryl leaned over the front seat, staring after the emergency vehicles. "They're headed for the lighthouse."

"You can't know that." Jessie turned, looking at her friend, then back to Buzz.

"There's only one road over there," Buzz said. "Maybe they are headed to the fort."

"Can we see?" Jessie asked, a strange, nagging feeling entering her chest. She felt unsettled, and cold dread filled her.

"Maybe another boat crashed." Cheryl looked between them. "We can at least go see."

"I don't want to get in the way." Buzz stretched his hands before curling them around the steering wheel once more. "I'll ease in that direction, but we are not getting involved."

"I think we should have a look." Jessie placed a hand on his arm. "I can't explain it, but I feel like something important has happened." She pleaded with the man, speaking with her eyes.

Buzz turned, and Jessie met his gaze boldly. "Alright, I'll drive by." He rolled back into traffic, passing the downtown area and heading toward the bridge attaching lighthouse point with the mainland. "I have a bad feeling about this," he said, focused on the road.

A helicopter buzzed overhead, and Jessie tried to catch a glimpse of it. If a boat had run aground, had the Coast guard been called out? Buzz drove down the quieter road, circling the lighthouse and moving closer to the homes built along the beach where the emergency vehicles were gathered.

Jessie twisted her hands, a sour feeling roiling in her stomach. Unfamiliar dread filled her, and she jerked when Cheryl spoke.

"Look," Cheryl gasped, pointing at the coast. "There's a boat."

"It's a rowboat." Buzz scowled. "One of those white, deep-hulled rescue boats."

"Isn't that the boat that Brad showed us the other day?" Jessie covered her heart with her hand. "The one the old lighthouse keepers used to come to the mainland." She looked at her friends. Something bad had happened here. She could feel it in her bones.

Cheryl laid a hand on Jessie's shoulder, her eyes wide as she looked at her friend. "He said someone was out there last night. He wanted to go out and investigate." She shook her head, eyes worried. "Before I hung up, Brad promised he wouldn't go looking."

Jessie's heart skipped a beat as they pulled into a parking area near the lighthouse. Warm sunlight splashed across the water, glinting off the glass dome at the top of the black and white structure, but Jessie's blood ran cold.

"Stay here." Buzz slipped out of the car, striding toward the emergency crews that were pulling the white boat onto the sand.

Jessie crept toward the scene. Sure Buzz had told her to stay in the car but something pulled her forward. She glanced back seeing Cheryl standing by the sedan, holding onto the open door. Keeping an eye on Buzz, Jessie shivered. She knew something terrible had happened. She didn't know how, but she had to see it for herself.

"Stay back, please." A stocky policeman stretched out an arm. "No looky-loos."

"Jones?" Buzz asked, making the man turn around and look. "It's me, Theo Benzelly. Paul Higgins' nephew."

"Oh." The man flicked his eyes back to the water. "What are you doing here?"

"We were coming to talk to the lighthouse keeper." Buzz rolled his shoulders as if a heavy weight rested there.

Jones turned, giving Buzz a hard look. "I don't think he's going to be talking to anyone." He nodded toward the boat where two younger officers were lifting Brad's lifeless body from the polished wood of the boat.

"Oh no."

Buzz wheeled, seeing Jessie a step behind him. "You shouldn't be here." He hissed. "You don't need to see this."

Jessie looked up, her eyes filling with tears. "I was worried." She looked at Jones, her hands trembling as she lifted them to her face. "What happened?" Her eyes strayed to the boat were two officers were taking photos and dusting for prints.

"We don't know." The older man looked between her and Buzz. Buzz wrapped a protective arm around Jessie, offering some comfort. "I think you had better come down to the station and tell us what you wanted to see the man about." His eyes glinted. "It seems you kids are poking around in things that don't concern you." The man's dark eyes were hard as he looked between them. "That can be dangerous."

"How did he die?" Buzz asked as Jessie buried her face in his chest, hiding from the grizzly scene when two men lifted a black body bag onto a stretcher.

"Looks like he was shot." Jones hooked his thumbs in his belt. "And that's all you'll get from me. Now get out of here. "I'll see you at the station in half an hour." He nodded again. "And that is a favor to a fellow officer."

Jessie slipped her arm around Buzz's waist as he turned, leading her back to the car. Cheryl was standing outside the vehicle, trying to see what was happening, and Jessie wondered if they should leave the mystery of the ghost ship in the past. She shivered. So much was happening. Her emotions swirled. The intruder last night, the strange sightings on the coast, and now this. Brad had been a wealth of knowledge, and now all that was lost.

"What happened?" Cheryl looked at the two of them, her eyes flicking between Jessie and Buzz as Buzz guided her back to the car.

"Brad is dead." Jessie's words were flat, but her heart pinched.

"Oh, no." Cheryl's eyes instantly filled with tears. "I liked him. I knew he shouldn't have gone out to see who was in the water. Did he capsize?" Her hands fluttered, and Jessie twisted, catching one in hers.

"It looks like he was shot." Buzz spoke, and Jessie looked up, seeing a hard glint in his eyes. A scowl marred his usually cheerful face, muscles rippling in his jaw.

"We have to go to the station to tell the police what we know." He shook. "Or what we think we know."

Cheryl swallowed hard, her eyes sad as she reached out and clung to Jessie's wrist. "We'll do what we can to help." She darted a look between her companions, tears rolling down her cheeks.

Buzz walked Jessie around the car, helping her into the passenger seat. She felt numb, confused, and shock made her shiver. There was something much bigger going on in the quiet harbor of Savannah. Something dark and sinister had cost one man his life. No matter what the police report read about Brad's death, something told her he had been murdered.

"Do you think the man who tried to break into the house last night has anything to do with our little campaign?" She turned to Buzz, catching Cheryl's startled gasp.

"I think it's possible." Buzz started the car and pulled out onto the street, heading back up the beach to the police station. "Maybe we should all go home." He glanced at Cheryl in the mirror, then at Jessie. "I mean, back to Macon."

Jessie stared out the window for several seconds as they crossed the bridge, her mind racing.

"No." She shook her head. "I think we know something, but we don't yet know we know it." She rubbed her temples, racking her brain. "There is something hidden in all of the information we've gathered." She looked up, studying Buzz's serious face, then back at Cheryl, who wept quietly. "We'll tell the police everything we know."

Buzz raised a brow, and Cheryl patted Jessie's shoulder, but neither spoke. Shock, doubt and worry overwhelmed their speech.

Jessie studied both of her friends, weighing her words carefully before she continued. "I know this was a fun adventure, chasing a silly ghost ship story, but there is something darker going on here. "We have to keep digging. We owe it to Brad."

Chapter 9

Something akin to anger vibrated through Jessie as she sipped iced tea on the pool deck of the beach house.- She, Buzz, and Cheryl had driven to the local police station and given an account of how they had met Brad. The officer had been polite and especially attentive to Buzz, but had taken their statements with little enthusiasm.

"I don't think what we told the police made enough sense for them to look into it," Jessie's voice carried over the stone deck. "We have a lot of facts pulled together. We know that there have been an increase in ship wrecks and salvage lately. We know Brad saw someone off the point. We even know that the tour operators are not the ones creating the ghost ship." She shook here head. "It all seems logical to me."

Buzz had been doing laps in the infinity pool. Strong, smooth strokes carried him from one end of the crystal water to the other. He paused, swimming to the side of the pool and propping his arms on the edge. The infinity pool shimmered, the aquamarine water rippling as he came to a stop.

"What's that?" Buzz looked up, his eyes running over Jessie's one-piece red suit.

"Jess, we're supposed to be relaxing." Cheryl chided from a curved deck chair built into the far end of the pool. She had buried herself in a book, and Jessie knew she was trying to push the horror of the morning away. "She doesn't think, the cops are taking us seriously." Cher added, winking at Buzz.

"You can't really blame them," Buzz sighed. "To them we're overimagintive kids."

"I know." Jessie sat up, putting her glass on a teak table. "I can't stop thinking about this, though. I really believe we're onto something. Otherwise, why did this happen to Brad?." She raised her hands in exasperation. "Why did someone try to break into the house?" She looked at Buzz. "Are you guys taking this seriously?" Jessie scowled at her friends. For a moment Jessie wondered if she was imagining the connections, but if she had, what about Brad? Why had he died? No, deep down she knew something was very wrong in the shipping lanes of Savannah.

"Hey," Buzz spoke up, his voice gentle. "This isn't your fault. Brad was already at the lighthouse when he saw that boat. He would have gone out there anyway." He flicked his eyes to Cheryl at the far end of the pool. "Cher even tried to stop him."

"Jess, it isn't that we aren't taking this seriously," Cheryl sighed, leaning her head back on her lounger. "Some one is dead." She shook her head, eyes closed. "But we need time to process it. We need to find some normal in our day until we can come to terms with what's going on." She sniffed. "I liked Brad. A lot."

Jessie fidgeted with a fingernail, then pushed her hands onto the chair. "I know." She watched as Buzz pulled himself from the pool, his lean, well-muscled body sparkling with water as he grabbed a towel.

Cheryl turned, pulling her dark glasses down her nose and adjusting the hat on her head. "Jessie, this was supposed to be fun," she called, swinging her legs around and placing her feet in the water. Scooting forward on the lounger, Cheryl adjusted her two-piece, forest green swimsuit. The bottom twisted, covering above her belly button, and she pulled the skirt-like garment straight before tugging on the babydoll top. "This isn't fun anymore."

"I know." Jessie closed her eyes as Buzz flopped into the chair next to her, still drying his hair.

"Hey." He turned, looking at Jessie, his hands wrapped around his head. "We're taking this afternoon off." His smile was half-hearted as he shook his head. "Look, Nancy Drew, I know you're stuck on the topic, but try to relax."

"I can't." Jessie unfolded her legs, turning to look at Buzz. "If this continues, Brad will not be the only casualty." She sighed, placing her feet on the deck and meeting his dark eyes. "If this is connected to a salvage scam, people could die in a shipwreck."

Buzz looked down at the stone deck, resting his elbows on his bare legs. "Hey," he looked up. "I'm taking this seriously, but right now we have nothing. No proof." His eyes flicked to Cheryl. "We are all upset about Brad, and I believe others could be in danger, but until we have some proof we need to unwind." He half-grinned, his dark hair flopping into his eyes. "I did get a message from Uncle Paul. He thinks we're on to something, and he is in touch with his friends here in Savannah." Buzz sighed and shook his head. "He said the police report on Brad declared it an accident. It looks like Brad was skin diving, and somehow a spear gun must have seized or missfired or something." He looked up. "I don't know how Paul gets this info, but I can't agree with that verdict."

"Are you saying Brad was killed with a spear gun?" Jessie felt a wave of shock roll through her, her mind struggling to make sense of this news.

"What?" Cheryl yelled, jumping up and splashing through the small sundeck. "I talked to Brad. He was going to investigate a boat, not going spear fishing in the middle of the night." She rested her hands on her hips. "This is ridiculous."

Stopping at the edge of the sunshade, she pulled her glasses down, glaring at Buzz. "I thought I had talked him out of going out there. Now look what's happened."

Jessie nodded. "Something isn't right." Jessie stood and began pacing then flopped back in her chair. "Maybe I'm crazy, but I can't agree with any of this." She shook her head. "Buzz, what if the police are involved? I know it isn't likely, but there are things we don't know."

"We won't give up." Buzz looked up, eyes troubled, but he smiled. "Right now, though, try to rest. Jumping to conclusions will muddle things further." He smiled and Jessie returned it, trying to switch off the nagging questions in her brain. She wasn't even sure why she had been convinced that something fishy was happening in Savannah, but with Brad's death it had solidified her belief.

"Buzz is right." Cheryl huffed. "It's not that I don't think we should keep digging, I'm totally in for that, but we need to take a break. Step away from this, and let the facts filter through our brain." She sat on the corner of Jessie's lounge chair, looking at Buzz. "You could be right, Jess. Maybe someone in the police force is trying to cover this up." She shook her head and looked at Jessie. "But we don't know that. We can't jump to conclusions or think negatively about people. We'll take today off and dig into the mystery in the morning." She smiled again. "Or maybe later tonight."

Buzz looked up,but before he could speak, a blur of black fur raced around the corner as the puppy hurried toward them.

"There you are," Jessie laughed. She had left the gate to the backyard open, and the pup had been exploring the garden and pool area. She reached down, petting the puppy, her eyes locked on Buzz as she tried to silently beg him to let go of Cheryl's statement.

Muttley flopped at her feet, tongue lolling, as he thumped Buzz on the legs with his tail.

Buzz slumped, giving her a slight nod as he stroked the dog. Jessie was sure that Buzz didn't like her or Cheryl's suggestion about the police being involved in this scam, but they needed to look at every angle.

"I guess we can all just chill for a while longer." Jessie stroked the puppy's head, her hand grazing Buzz's fingers. "We've worried over this enough for now and at the moment there is nothing we can do."

Cheryl sighed wearily. Standing, she turned and headed back to the sundeck chair and her book. "Can we go out for dinner tonight? I don't think I can cook." She glanced over her shoulder at Jessie, eyes imploring. "Besides, we need a break. We need to get out and see things from a different angle."

Jessie smiled. "I'd love that. We haven't been out for a few nights." Jessie watched as Cheryl ambled back to her chair. "Besides, you're both right. We need some down time to gain perspective." The thoughts and doubts still spun, a malstrom in her brain, but Jessie pushed them aside, determined to have fun with her friends. Nothing in this life was guaranteed, but with faith, and hope, she would carry on, remembering to be thankful for the quiet moments in her day. She turned, looking at Buzz. "Will you come along?" Her eyes held his, the connection between them strong after the day's events.

Buzz leaned back against the wooden lounger, closing his eyes. "I think I'd better." A worried grin tugged at his lips, and he tucked his hands behind his head. "I'll probably need to keep the two of you out of trouble."

Jessie laughed, a sense of relief hitting her in the chest. It was good to have Buzz with her in this mess. Perhaps, if they were lucky the police would be right and nothing illegal or deadly was happening here. Looking down the long rectangular pool, she saw Cheryl working on her phone. "I think our friend over there has more planned than just dinner."

Buzz looked toward the other end of the pool, using his six-pack to lift him halfway up. "That's what I was worried about." Buzz relaxed back in the chair again and closed his eyes. "I still can't believe you've been hiding this from me." Jessie grinned, knowing he was distracting her. "This pool is amazing." A soft breeze ruffled his hair, and Jessie smiled, mirroring his pose as she tried to relax. "The pool at my parents' condo is wall-to-wall children."

Jessie peeked at him, and he grinned, giving her a dramatic shiver. "That's why I swim in the ocean."

Jessie laughed, leaning back into the shade of an oversized umbrella. "You're welcome to swim here anytime." She tipped her head looking at the lush trees and wall surrounding the pool area. At first glance no one would suspect this of being a pool area. It looked more like an overgrown garden, the trees shading and shielding the area from prying eyes. Jessie leaned back in her chair feeling the warm sun on her legs. It was always nice having Buzz around. She was comfortable with him and felt safe. She knew that he was struggling with his own issues right now and wanted to make him feel welcome. Over the past few months she had missed his presence and now, with another mystery at hand, she was thankful he was at her side. Good friends were hard to comeby, especially once what didn't think you were crazy.

The puppy yipped as if in agreement, and Buzz grinned. "Be careful what you say. I might take you up on that offer." Buzz chuckled. "I do enjoy swimming in the ocean, but sometimes a place like this would be nice too."

Jessie, forced her mind to relax as she lounged in the sun. The soft ripple of water blended with the waves on the beach several yards away. A variety of trees bordered the surrounding fence, offering shade while the pool deck soaked up the rays of the hot sun. She was still troubled by the events of the morning, but Jessie was determined to relax until Cheryl was ready to reveal what she was up to.

Buzz was reluctant to leave the beach house and the two girls he had grown so fond of. It had been a quiet day of chatting, eating, swimming and enjoying the pool area. He was surprised that he had fallen asleep in the shade of a big striped umbrella, while Jessie read. The sun soaked into his bones, hot and soothing, and he sighed. But as the sun inched closer to the western horizon he knew he needed to leave.

Unfolding his lean frame from the lounge chair, he stood, pulling his shirt over his head. "I'd better get back to the condo," he said, making Jessie look up. "I'll grab a shower and change." he looked down at his knee length swim trunks and rumpled shirt. "Then I'll come back and pick you up." He smiled, trying to let Jessie know he enjoyed being here and hanging out with her and Cheryl. Perhaps it wasn't the vacation he had expected but the questions they had about shipwrecks and salvage had kept him from worrying over his own case.

"Don't take long," Cheryl waved at him, hopping from her own chair and trotting along the pool. "We have to stop at the museum before dinner."

"What?" Jessie sat up, turning her face toward the sun.

"I have a couple of things I want to ask Dr. Crumm. I promise it won't take long."

Buzz raised his brows, looking at Jessie who shrugged. "So, now we're back on the case?"

"We were never off it." Cheryl shook her head. "We just needed time to rest and recoup our energy." Her smile was bright, and Buzz suppressed a chuckle. Cheryl seemed to have boundless energy and he was sure she had spent more time searching on her phone than relaxing throughout the day.

"I'll be back in an hour." He looked between the girls. "Will that work?"

Cheryl checked her phone, nodding. "Oh, and no fancy dinners tonight. There's a little cafe downtown that I want to check out." She glanced up at Buzz. "Casual wear accepted."

Buzz nodded giving Jessie a knowing glance. He didn't mind letting the girls make plans at this point. He just hoped that they would listen to him when the time came. "See you soon." He turned toward the hidden gate at the front of the pool area. "Be good." The puppy whined as he let himself out, but he was careful not to let the little mutt escape.

The drive home gave the young officer time to think, and he turned the events of the past few days over in his mind. He knew that Jessie was right and that what had happened to Brad was no accident. The man may have been killed by a fishing spear, but the odds of it being a misfire were astronomical.

Jessie's instincts were right. There was something fishy going on. He bounced through the door of the condo, expecting his parents, but the small space was quiet. Trotting to the kitchen, he spotted a note indicating that his folks were out with friends and that he should sort out his own dinner. Buzz chuckled. Perhaps the reasons for this vacation were not ideal, but his folks were certainly enjoying the change of pace.

Moving back to the tiny bedroom where he slept, he grabbed his things and headed for the shower. Buzz chuckled to himself, wondering what his parents would think about Jessie's family beach house.

For that matter, he wondered what his folks would think of Jessie. They had met her mother on many occasions when visiting Paul at the Estonia, but Jessie was something else.

He shook his head, turning the tap. The last thing he needed right now with so much uncertainty in his life was his parents assuming that he and Jessie were dating.

The hot water pounded on his head as he stepped into the tub, and Buzz turned the cold up. A day in the sun had left him overly warm, and the cool water was welcome. Mindful of the time, Buzz kept the shower short and was soon dressed in his best shirt and shorts, his hair restored to its usual gravity-defying coif. With less than a week left of his unplanned-vacation, he needed to help Jessie wrap up this odd mystery. He couldn't leave, even to discover his fate, knowing she was still seeking answers that could prove to be dangerous.

"Hi there!" Cheryl waved,trotting down the sidewalk as Buzz pulled into the drive. "Come on, Jess." The young woman shouted over her shoulder. She was wearing some sort of one piece short and tank top in coral orange.

"Sorry if you've been waiting." Buzz slipped from the car, resting his arm on the top of the door.

"No." Cheryl shook her head, her ponytail swaying. She looked more casual than he had seen her this whole time. "Jessie is putting the dog out back, and we didn't want him barking before we left."

Buzz grinned as Jessie stepped out of the house, turning and locking the door. She was wearing jeans and a white t-shirt, but she looked great. A breeze off the ocean lifted her hair, and she turned, smiling. The young man couldn't help but compare the two women. Jessie, though wealthy seemed to have simple taste in attire while Cheryl dressed in way the displayed her exuberant personality. Both girls were lovely, but Buzz felt something flutter in his heart as Jessie hurried toward him.

"I guess we're ready," Jessie hurried toward them, giving him a wink. "Cheryl has everything organized for us."

"Oh, good. I love nights where I don't have to think." Cheryl scowled at him, and Buzz laughed, rolling his eyes. He was only half joking. So often there was tremendous responsibility on him and not having to plan his meals, or organize what was happening each night was rather fun. Most of his recent days had been spent worrying about his suspension or going over cases that needed his attention. It was hard switching off and having someone else take the reins was rather fun, at least in something like where to eat or where to go on vacation.

Buzz was starting to realize that Cheryl wasn't truly bossy or overbearing, she simply ran a speed others couldn't match.

A minute later, they were rolling toward the museum and hopefully, answers.

"Does she know what she's doing?" Buzz asked as Cheryl walked into the museum ahead of them.

Jessie shrugged. "I don't know, but I have a few questions for the good professor, too."

"Like what?" Buzz dropped his eyes as they walked, his tone suddenly serious. He had seen how Jessie tended to jump into things and he didn't want her getting in over her head. Maybe it was old-fashioned to feel protective of Jessie and even Cheryl, but he had been raised to be a southern gentleman and his heart was in the right place.

"Cher and I were looking at a map, and from what we could find about the legend of the AnnaSwift, a few things don't add up. "First, the ship came down the Savannah River toward the sea. It didn't launch from the bay. Second, that night was chaotic as the city was sacked. Sherman marched straight through to the coast. The reports of the ship leaving were mixed and confused. Some say the AnnaSwift sailed straight for the open water. Others claim she was driven toward the harbor by northern ships. Others say she never made it out of the river."

Buzz swerved around a model ship, turning in the direction Cheryl had gone. A familiar painting appeared, and they moved to the area where the display of the ship was open for viewing.

"Oh, hello." Dr. Crumm approached, a jaunty smile on his face. "You're back."

"Dr. Crumm." Cheryl waved, standing on tiptoes. "I was hoping I'd see you here." Her smile was bright as the man approached. "I'm afraid a friend of ours had an accident." She turned, giving Jessie and Buzz an odd look. " I have some questions about the AnnaSwift. We think it might all be related."

"I'm sorry about your friend. I hope everything will be alright." He looked around at the group, his eyes resting for a moment on each one.

"Thank you. Well, uh, about the ship. . ." Cheryl directed the conversation while Jessie and Buzz watched. "We've ready many conflicting statements about what happened to it." She brushed her hair over her shoulder. "I mean you said you thought it was captured further out to see. Others think it went down in deep water, and others think it never really left the area. We aren't interested in the treasure aspect just the mystery of what happened to the ship. The real history, so to speak."

The man chuckled, moving closer and grinned. "It's nice to see people interested in the legend for reasons other than the treasure. People are crazy when they hear the word treasure. In my opinion it isn't even worth going after anymore. Whatever you find has to be split up between so many factions." He ran a hand over his thinning hair, smoothing it down. "The history, that's the thing." The man smiled. "Besides," he looked around the group again. "Treasures of the past belong in a place like this." He waved a hand around indicating the museum. "The past belongs to all of us."

Jessie looked at Buzz, wondering where Cheryl was going next. What questions did she have. Crumm obviously was more interested in the past than the present. Would he give them any insight at all?

"Oh, treasure is totally overrated." Cher grinned. She wiggled her pink nails, gazing at the displays. "I am curious about the mixed reports on the disappearance and how it might relate to salvage scams."

"Salvage! What can that have to do with the AnnaSwift?" The man's brows rose above his glasses. "Sailing or any maritime endeavor is filled with risk." He shook his head. "No. I can't see what you mean."

Cheryl shook her head. "That 's not what I'm talking about." She smiled at the man. She seemed to be working hard to wrap him around her finger, and Buzz could see why she did so well as a teaching assistant while she worked toward her Masters.

Buzz stepped forward, worrying about what Cheryl was about to say. Was she going to tell the man what they believed the motivation of the legend of the AnnaSwift was really about? Suspicions like these were mere conjecture without proof.

"I've been studying a bit, and there are at least three different accounts of the disappearance of the ship."Cher smiled. "I was wondering where you think she actually went down." The young woman wagged a finger. "Don't tell me she made it to sea. Nothing indicates that."

Dr. Crumm looked between the three guests, removed his glasses, and rubbed them with a cloth from the breast pocket of his tweed jacket. "You don't plan on going looking, do you?" The man looked up, replacing his specs.

"No." Cheryl waved the notion away. "Jessie doesn't need the money, and I'm too busy to add treasure hunting to my resume." She smiled. "Now spill."

Crumm shuffled a rope soled deck shoe on the tile floor. "If you aren't interested in the treasure, what's your interest?"

Buzz waited to see what Cheryl was thinking. Did Crumm know more than he was telling? Would he take the information they gave him and use it to find the treasure himself? The man seemed transparent. An academic, interested in the history of shipwrecks not the reality of emerging danger.

"I'm curious." Cheryl looked at her nails. "I don't like things to be unfinished." She smiled again. "Call it the academic in me. It's just who I am." He eyes were bright as she looked up expectantly.

"It's true," Jessie laughed. "Cher gets a bee in her bonnet, and you'll never hear the end of it until she gets the answers she wants." She shook her head. "She researches everything to death."

Buzz flinched at Jessie's final word. One man was already dead, not to mention the many souls lost to the sea over the ages. His eyes flicked between his three companions and he wondered if Dr. Crumm would answer. The man was supposed to be an expert in his field and Cheryl was not only asking him questions she was telling him she didn't believe his original theory about the AnnaSwift. His eyes fell on Crumm who smiled. He didn't seem offended by Cheryl's questions or tone. Perhaps she knew something about dealing with professors that Buzz never would.

"I see why your professor back in Macon is so fond of you." Crumm chuckled, his glasses glinting under the lights. "In my opinion, the AnnaSwift made it to the blockade before it was blasted to bits." He sighed.

"Thank you." Cheryl patted his arm as if he were a very old man. "What proof do you have? You see, this ghost ship sighting is a disturbing occurrence. It comes from the area of the Tybee Lighthouse and disappears on open water."

"Follow me." Crumm gestured toward the display, and he pointed at a faded log book. "This is from one of the other ships at port that night. It claims that the AnnaSwift rounded the point off Tybee and headed for open water. Of course, no one knew anything about the ship at the time. If they had known it was laden with treasure, perhaps it would have been stopped and not destroyed."

Buzz studied, the book. It seemed like no matter where they looked, there were

"Thank you." Cheryl grinned. "I've been digging up info on this ship, and it sets my mind at ease to see this." She paused, scowling. "I suppose if she was sunk in deeper water, people would be foolish if they were looking for her near the island, then?"

"Yes," Dr. Crumm nodded. "But many still do. They are convinced they'll be the ones who find her and all of that gold." He looked up, his eyes hidden behind the glare of his lenses. "Gold makes people do foolish things. We've had several accidents off the coast with people trying to be the first to claim the hidden secret of the AnnaSwift." He smiled. "I'm glad you kids aren't foolish enough for that. The ship is gone. Unless some geographical studies of the trench off the coast find something, she and her contingent of lost souls will never be found."

"Thank you." Jessie offered, smiling at Dr. Crumm. "You've been very kind, giving us your time." She turned to Cheryl. "Come on, roomie, it's time to eat." She slipped her arm through Buzz's, giving it a squeeze as she gestured for Cheryl to hurry. Buzz looked down. Jessie seemed more relaxed again, but he knew her mind was working on everything she had heard. He reached over placing his hand over hers. "That was smooth," he whispered, drawing a smile.

"Thanks again, Dr. Crumm." Cheryl said, walking toward Jessie. "I guess that puts everything to rest." She waved, he face open, innocent, then took Jessie's other arm. "Now about that dinner."

Buzz pondered the odd discussion as he walked back to the car. Opening it absently, he let the girls get in then slipped behind the wheel. Something didn't add up. The reports were so contorted that it seemed they were all blinds trying to hide the truth.

"Well," Cheryl huffed as he started the engine. "What do you think of that?"

"I don't know." Jessie twisted in her seat. "What are we supposed to think?" Her voice was flat, a change from the often teasing tone she took with her friend.

"I think that someone knows where that ship is, and they have told so many versions of the story, everyone is chasing their tail trying to find it." Chery shook her head. "I also think Crumm isn't telling the whole truth."

"Why?" Buzz glanced in the rearview mirror.

"I know these academic types." Cheryl blew out a breath. "They think everything should belong to them. Not to own but because it is there area of expertise. I doubt that even if he knew where the treasure was he would tell us."

"So, where do you think the AnnSwift is?" Buzz asked.

Cheryl sagged, and he could see the defeat on her face as he glanced at the woman in his rearview mirror. "I don't know."

"Cher," Jessie looked straight ahead as Buzz drove toward the restaurant Cheryl had picked for him. "Where was the last reliable sighting?" Buzz shot Jessie a glance. "In the end, I'm not sure knowing where the ship went down is as important as finding out who would use these sightings to their advantage."

"More like who is the last reliable witness." Cheryl lifted her phone,nodding. The screen glowed lighting her face as night fell. "The lighthouse was closed at the time, you see. The lenses had been removed to protect them during the war. The harbor master wrote in his log that the ship was last seen at the mouth of the river." She looked up. "Other reports agree that she sailed down the Savannah, but after that, nothing ever matches up."

From the corner of his eye, Buzz saw Jessie nod. She was thinking, but he couldn't read her expression. The clues and information was all so convoluted. Maybe they were just imagining a conspiracy. The ship was a legend it might not have anything to do with the troubles here in Savanna. Additionally, the coast line was known for its hazards. His mind rolled over all they knew coming to stop at one fact. Brad was dead. Why would they need to kill him if none of this was related?

"Are we almost at the restaurant?" Jessie spoke again after several moments of silence, startling everyone.

"GPS says two minutes." Buzz chanced a glance in her direction. He wondered if she had been thinking the same things he had.

"Good." Jessie grinned. "I'm starved. I guess lazing by the pool all day is hungry work."

Buzz could tell that this time Jessie was distracting the trio and was thankful. A body could lose their mind going over all of the seemingly disconnected information.

Putting the discussion on hold the trio slipped into a brightly painted eatery andchatted over a simple meal of authentic Mexican fare. The meal was delicious and filling but before he knew it, Buzz was driving the girls home. They still didn't have the answers they sought, but several things had fallen into place. None of the people they had spoken to about the AnnaSwift were telling everything they knew. He shook his head as he pulled into the driveway.

"What's up?" Jessie asked as Cheryl, still gazing at her phone, climbed out of the car and headed up the walk.

"Either no one knows the facts about the lost ship, and ghost ship sightings, or they are not telling us the truth." He twisted in his seat, facing Jessie. "It feels like if we just had one or two facts, we'd know what was really going on."

"Who do you mean by 'they'?" Jessie asked. "There are so many factors in play."

Buzz turned, looking at her. Her soft features and pretty face were illuminated by the light of the security lamp, and the blue of her eyes seemed as dark as the ocean at night.

"Everyone we've spoken with. Crumm is all about the history but has no more info than Cher can find on her phone. Allen, all but blew Cher off and the police don't see any connection between the ghost ship, salvage operations, or treasure. The only person who really told us anything is dead. Brad belilved that the ghost ship sightings were causing maritime trouble, and now he's gone." Buzz shook his head. "But is any of it real? Maybe we're just looking for something to keep us busy."

"Hey," Jessie said, offering a sad smile. "You don't believe that. Like you said, Brad is dead, and we know for a fact he had spotted a boat off the point." She paused, studying his face. "So, you think Crumm is lying?" Jessie squinted, marring her smooth skin.

"Or ignorant. It's hard to tell." Buzz huffed out a sigh of frustration. "Most of the ships that admitted looking for the treasure were salvaged off the lighthouse point. A place that is dangerous at the best of times."

"Right." Jessie nodded. "When Cheryl was on the phone with Brad, he saw a boat out there with its lights off. Why would you put your boat at risk like that? Even on a clear night, you wouldn't be able to see what's under the surface of the waves."

"But where exactly?" Buzz ran a hand down his face. "Were they far out, away from the dangerous shoals, or were they among them? If they were close, how did they navigate the area at night without running up on something?"

"Sonar?" Jessie quipped. "Of course, I don't imagine Brad would have been worried about them if they were far enough out. Besides, he must have rowed out to them, so how far could it be?"

Buzz chuckled, shaking his head. "Maybe we're just crazy."

"Buzz, I really think all of this is tied together." Jessie turned, meeting his gaze. The air conditioning was cool and prickled on his skin as he gazed at her. "I think someone knows where the treasure is and instead of pulling people to it with the ghost ship, they are using it to mislead divers and treasure hunters and are actually taking them further away from it."

"Which gets them into trouble." Buzz looked at Jessie, getting her point.

"Exactly." Jessie nodded. "If not for what happened to Brad, maybe I could let this go. It's none of our business, but his death has already been written off as an accident and that isn't right. We both know it."

Buzz nodded. He couldn't disagree . For several minutes they sat, silent, before Buzz spoke again. "Hey, it's late. It's been an emotional day. Get some sleep, and we'll really dig into this tomorrow." His eyes scanned her face, hoping she would listen. Jessie seemed so young some how. Her impetuous nature, and seeming innocence a contrast to her keen mind.

Jessie nodded. "Thanks." She reached out, patting his hand. "And thanks for being here."

Buzz twisted his hand, capturing hers in his fingers. "You'll be careful, right? I mean, maybe that was just a burglar the other night, but maybe we're stepping on toes. Don't do anything rash." His eyes held hers for long moments. Perhaps they couldn't pinpoint what was happening with the ghost ship, but he knew he needed Jessie to be safe.

"Me?" Jessie laughed, patting her chest. "I'd never. Besides, I'm just going to bed. Maybe after a good night's sleep, I'll be able to fit some of these pieces of the puzzle together."

"Jessie, you already had one attempted break in, or whatever that was. And you almost got brained last time someone was snooping around your house back in Macon," Buzz growled. "I know how it is." he squeezed her hand, holding her in place. "When something happens, you get mad. It's how you're made. Your first instinct is to investigate, but it isn't safe." He shook his head again. "If something bad is happening here, the people behind it are capable of anything. Remember what happened to Brad."

Jessie smiled, squeezing his hand and sending warmth up his arm, all the way to his shoulder. "How about we compromise? I won't do anything impulsive without calling you."

Buzz groaned. "That's as good as I'm going to get, isn't it?"

"Probably." Jessie released his hand and turned to open the door. "Good night, Buzz." Her eyes were bright, and he could see that all of the information they had talked about was still swirling in her brain. She closed the door, leaning over to wave at him before turning toward the house, her silhouette outlined by the security light.

Buzz closed his eyes, rolling his hand into a fist. Jessie was put together in a way he couldn't explain. She was smart, fun, caring, and couldn't leave an unanswered question alone. It made him worry, but he knew he wouldn't have her any other way.

Jessie was restless. No matter how hard she tried to put the thoughts of the ghost ship from her mind, it turned and twisted like a river through marshland.

"Come on, Mutt," she smiled, calling the puppy. "Let's go for a walk."

Cheryl had gone to bed early, and the house was quiet.

Clipping the leash on the dog, Jessie walked out onto the dunes. Seagrass waved in a light breeze, and the stars twinkled above. A shiver of apprehension washed over her, but Jessie pushed it away, refusing to be intimidated by the prowler from the night before.

Tonight, the quiet of the ocean was soothing, but instead of moving to the shore, Jessie turned into the open dunes of the area, her feet sinking into the sand. She looked up at the bright, star-strewn sky. There wasn't any cloud cover to hide someone's approach.

The puppy tugged on the leash, making her laugh as he sniffed at every lump and roll in the sand. He was excited to be outside, and Jessie wondered what she would do when she had to give the dog up. So far, they had not received a single phone call or message about a lost dog. It had been three days with no response and the longer she kept him, the harder she knew it would be to let go of little Muttley. The little beast truly must be a stray.

With no real destination in mind, Jessie walked over the dunes, gazing into the marshy areas where the wetlands ran to the sea. It was a beautiful area, wild and seemingly unchanged by time. She paused, listening, but her eyes had adjusted to the darkness, and she could see no one in the area. The puppy yipped, and she looked down at the mutt.

"Sh," she chided. "We'll go home." She turned, walking toward the house which, from this distance, was merely a pale gray shadow on the horizon. The day had been warm, but the evening had cooled, and Jessie breathed deeply of the sea air.

The dog barked again, tugging harder on the leash, and Jessie trotted to give Muttley a chance to stretch his legs. She was less than a hundred yards from the house when a shadow moved in the distance. Muttley growled and barked loudly as she broke into a run.

Jessie spotted a dark shape on a rise overlooking the house. The wind shifted, and the puppy barked, tugging at the leash. A shiver raced down her spine as she slipped below the rise of the dunes, momentarily unable to see the house.

As she once again reached the crest of a dune, the shadow raced up the hill as Jessie skidded to a stop, her heart pounding. The roar of an engine filled the night, and headlights illuminated the darkness.

Tugging on Muttley's leash, Jessie raced to the house, climbing into her car. The dog bounded into the passenger seat as Jessie dropped the keys from the visor and started the engine. In moments she was racing out of the driveway. Making the turn onto the main road, Jessie saw a vehicle drop down over the dunes of the private beach area, merging with traffic.

Pressing the button on her steering wheel, Jessie dialed Buzz's number, eyes glued to the car only a few lengths ahead.

CHAPTER 10

Jessie switched off her headlights, coasting down the dark road and rolling onto a sandy track. The car ahead of her moved confidently, turning and twisting between large oaks draped with Spanish moss. Shadows spanned the intermittent moonlight, flickering over her windshield like spectral hands. Each turn held her at bay as she kept her distance from the car before her. The headlights flickered in and out of the sheltering trees.

"Hello." A sleepy voice replied as her car phone dialed through.

"Buzz," Jessie whispered, peering through her windshield. "Someone was at my place again. They took off when Mutt barked but got in a big SUV. I'm following them."

"Jessie," Buzz all but yelled. "Go home."

"I can't." she shook her head, looking at the pup who sat up straight, staring at her from the other seat. "Buzz, this has something to do with Brad, and the boat wrecks. I know it." Anger fluttered in her gut. The lack of justice for the innocent spurred her on.

"Jessie, these people are dangerous. If they're boat-wreckers, their salvage operation alone is earning billions; and if you're right about them being linked to Brad, that means they may be murderers. That's nothing to mess with." She could hear the fear in his voice.

"Look." Jessie pressed her lips tight. She knew that Buzz was right, but white-hot anger pumped through her veins. People like this needed to be caught. "I'm only going to hide out and see if I can get a peek at what they're doing. I'm on a back road. It looks like we're headed for back water along the river."

"Jessie, please." Buzz's voice was full of anguish, and Jessie could hear him getting dressed. "Just go home, or call the police."

"I can't." Jessie shook her head, and the pup yipped. "They didn't listen to us before. The department is already overworked; or worse, someone is on the take in that department." Her eyes scanned the road. "I won't get close. I'll just scout it out, and you can tell Paul. He'll know who can be trusted."

Cold silence met Jessie's ear, and she looked down at the display screen on her dash to be sure the call hadn't dropped. "Buzz?"

"I'm on my way. Tag me on your GPS tracker. Now!" Jessie had never heard that tone in the man's voice. She flinched, but she complied. "Okay. Get here as soon as you can." She set the tracker for her phone and switched off the line. The car she'd been following had come to a stop, it's headlights glimmering over dark water. Reeds glowed green in the lights on the other side of the deep river.

Jessie stopped, pulling in under an old growth of southern pines, and switched off the engine. Leaning forward, she tried to make out what was happening.

"What do you think, Mutt?" She stroked the dog's head, squinting as fast moving clouds scudded above, revealing a half-moon. A boardwalk or wooden quay reached out into a slow rolling river. "I can't see." She huffed. Patting the dog again, she looked at him, pointing a finger. "You stay." She patted the dog. He had been the first one to see the man on the dunes. If she hadn't taken him out, she never would have seen this stealthy figure.

Muttley tipped his head, ears flopping, and she half-smiled.

Slipping out of the car, the windows cracked to allow a breeze for the dog, she crept toward the dock. Stooping low, Jessie crept along the road, holding close to the tall swamp grasses and trees.

Voices caught her ear, and she slipped into heavy undergrowth, listening. As the moon peeked out again, she could see a fat, squat boat, bobbing at the end of the dock. Standing a bit taller, she peeked over the grass. Two men were loading diving gear into the black tugboat.

Wind whispered through the reeds, hissing a song of southern nights and stealthy seamen.

Jessie crept closer, ducking behind a bush as the powerful beam of a flashlight flickered her way.

"What was that?" one of the men asked, his voice muffled by a hood.

"Just the wind," another voice echoed, and Jessie's heart raced as a light accent reached her ears. Leaning forward, she tried to hear more of the men's conversation.

A hand wrapped around her face, covering her mouth and filling her head with cobwebs as the world went black.

Buzz felt his heartbeat in his ears as he followed the tracker from Jessie's phone. Why did she do it? Why couldn't she stay home and call the police? He shook his head, gripping the steering wheel until his knuckles were white. "Because she's Jessie." He answered his own question with a sardonic smile tugging at his lips. "She needs a permanent reminder."

The tires of the old sedan rolled from the pavement onto sand, and his pulse quickened. Jessie's lighter car would manage well enough on this terrain, but his big, heavy, powerful vehicle could easily get stuck.

Clouds scudded above, revealing a beam of moonlight, and Buzz turned off his headlights. If Jessie had found the salvage operators, rolling up on them with his lights on would only endanger her. His chest nearly pressing against the steering wheel, Buzz traced the road, his tires gripping - then slipping - in the sand.

A dip in the road slowed the young man's progress, and his police training kicked in as he eased into the deep rut, then gunned the engine, bouncing out of the dip with a spray of sand.

"Jessie," Buzz whispered. "Be okay. Please, be okay."

The road evened out, and Buzz could feel the change in traction as his tires bit into hard packed Georgia clay. He sighed, stretching further when the outline of Jessie's car came into sight. He huffed out a breath, filling his lungs after what seemed like hours. The moonlight reflected off the white roof of the Mini Cooper, and Buzz turned off his engine, coasting the last few yards.

Creeping from his car, he bent nearly double as he walked up on the car. A sharp bark made him flinch, then he saw Muttley, pawing at the partially open window. "Jessie?" Buzz walked to the driver's side, but the girl wasn't there. A shiver of fear raced down his spine as icy dread filled his stomach.

"Come on, Mutt." Buzz opened the door and grabbed the leash, whispering to the dog. The mutt whined softly, wiggling as he nosed the man in the stomach. "Shhh." Buzz pressed a finger to his lips, grabbing the dog and placing him on the ground. Squatting, he stroked the dog's head, trying to remain calm. Closing his eyes, the tall man sighed. "Okay, Mutt. Where did she go?" The puppy bounced, but seemed to understand the need for silence as he tugged on the leash, rushing toward the tall reeds along the road.

Buzz stood, holding tight to the leash as the dog led him. Hopefully they were headed in the direction Jessie had gone.

The grass was nearly waist high, but Buzz stooped, walking bent over to stay out of sight. The roar of an engine filled the air, and he stopped, popping up to see a tiny running light come on in the wheelhouse of a squat tugboat.

Water churned, and Buzz froze. A lean figure in a black scuba suit tossed something heavy over into the boat and threw off the tie lines. The boat slipped into the narrow passage, headed for the river.

"Jessie!" Buzz yelled, seeing a familiar red tennis shoe peeking over the bumpers. "Jessie!" Buzz sprinted, the sand and stone slipping under his feet as sharp reeds slapped at his bare legs. A gunshot echoed in the night, and he ducked, the puppy racing ahead.

A sharp yelp and heavy thud filled the night as the engines revved, and the boat left the dock behind.

Anger surged through Buzz, his heart beating as he dashed forward. His shoes pounded like sledge hammers on the rickety dock, but the boat turned, disappearing into the night. "No." Buzz felt the tears on his face as the last thing he saw was the tail and back legs of the little mutt scrambling over the edge of the boat.

Something wet brushed against Jessie's cheek, and she rolled her head away. The wet rasp of a tongue and hot breath of Muttley pulled her from a troubled sleep. Her head felt like it was stuffed with cotton wool, but she blinked, fighting the sensation as she tried to push the mutt away.

Something sharp bit into her wrists, and adrenaline surged. Jessie's eyes snapped open, and she looked down at her hands and feet bound by cable ties. What a fool she had been. She had thought that she was safely hidden in the reeds, but someone she hadn't seen had spotted her.

Struggling to sit up, Jessie turned her back to the side of the boat, the puppy slipping his head under her arm.

"What do we do with the girl?" A man's voice drifted from the wheelhouse of the boat. It was muffled but distinct. "We'll pitch her over when we get to the site."

"No," another voice snapped.

Jessie's head was fuzzy, but the puppy pressing against her side gave her some hope. If Buzz had found her car and let the dog out, perhaps he was following. She shook her head. He couldn't follow. They were on a boat.

Fear clutched at Jessie's heart, and she squeezed her arms as the puppy climbed into her lap. *God, please help me. I didn't mean to be foolish. I was trying to help.* She closed her eyes, snapping them open again and looking at the little dog, as a tear rolled down her cheek.

"Look. . ." Another voice, deep and gruff, drifted her way. ". . . .I didn't bargain on anyone getting hurt when we started this. "You already killed that lighthouse keeper. We don't need to do anything else like that. She hasn't seen us. She can't identify us. We'll put her in a life raft at the site. She'll drift back to shore, and we'll leave."

"I'm not leaving a scrap of gold behind." The man with the accent growled. "And how do you know she can't identify us?"

"She's just a kid." A man in a black dive suit stuck his head around the corner, his hood and mask hiding his identity.- "We'll dump her and go. We have enough."

"We don't have enough." Anger tinged the first man's words. "What's one more soul among the dead? You've seen the remains on that wreck. She'll be a runaway, or some missing kid. They'll barely look for her."

The door of the wheelhouse slammed, and Jessie couldn't hear the words anymore, but loud voices and shouted anger echoed.

Muttley wiggled close, looking up at her and whining as if he understood the danger.

"Get off," she said, tipping her head to the side. "Get off, Muttley," she hissed. The dog looked to the side, then hopped from her lap as she braced her back against the bulkhead and started to shimmy upright.

Perhaps she could drop over the side of the boat and somehow swim to safety. Jessie looked down at her hands and feet, still firmly bound, and she knew it was useless. She was stuck. All she could do was bide her time and pray.

Buzz raced to his car, slipping on the sand as he grabbed the door and wrenched it open. His heart was pounding and fear gave him speed.

Starting the car, he shoved it in reverse, jerking the heavy sedan into a slide that turned him in the direction he wanted to go.

Pressing a button on his phone, he waited, pleading for the call to be picked up.

"Hello."

"Paul." Buzz was terse as he hit the gas racing down the road. "You need to call someone you trust here in Savannah. They have Jessie."

"What?"

"Don't argue." Buzz shouted. "Just get someone moving. I think I know where they're taking her. Send them to the lighthouse. Do it."

The phone went dead, and Buzz was sure that his uncle was already calling in favors. Not knowing who to trust, he couldn't risk alerting someone on the police force who might be involved.

"Please," he pleaded again, unsure if he was praying or simply pouring out his heart. "Please let her be alright."

The car bounced and slid over the loose sand, and Buzz held tight to the wheel, using all of his defensive driving training to keep the car moving and on the dirt track. When his tires hit the pavement of the country road, the car lurched, metal screeching as his undercarriage dragged over the transition. Buzz pushed the pedal to the floor, swerving along the road as he raced to the only place he believed the boat could be going.

Anger and fear warred in his chest as he thought of Jessie's carelessness. Would the woman never learn to be cautious? Perhaps that was part of her charm, but right now, fear for her life overshadowed his appeal for the woman's nature.

The car skidded onto the main road, the big engine roaring as Buzz pushed the car to its limits. The roads of Savannah were nearly empty at this time of night. Even the bars were closed, and he sped past a few early delivery trucks, focused on his destination.

By the time he hit the bridge leading to the lighthouse, his hands were sweating with dread. Slamming the car into park, he opened the door and raced for the lighthouse dock. Tearing through the police tape, Buzz untied the line of the old rowboat and pushed it into the dark waves of the Atlantic. Stepping into the deep ribs of the skiff, he grabbed the oars, pulling hard against the breakers barring his way.

Buzz pulled, glancing over his shoulder as muscles flexed and strained. Down the coast he could see a tiny light, a glint on the water as a boat floated out of the mouth of the river past darkened docks and slips. Gritting his teeth, Buzz pulled, a wave breaking over the bow and soaking him as he reached the calmer waters. His eyes flickered between the dark shadow of the boat, and the rough, treacherous waters of the point. Ignoring the danger to himself, Buzz continued to row, matching his path to the one of the tugboat.

The sound of the powerful engine, muted by thick cowlings, reached Buzz's ears over the crashing of waves on rocks. His heart skipped as he tried to make out what was happening on the dark boat.

The sharp bark of a pistol stopped his heart, and Buzz froze. "No. No." Tears pricked at his eyes, and his whole body shook. "Jessie."

****

"Sit down." A man stepped from the wheelhouse, pointing a gun at Jessie. His tight scuba suit and black hood obscuring his features.

Muttley stepped in front of her, barking as fiercely as a puppy could. The man pointed the firearm at the dog, the tiny light of the wheelhouse glinting off the pistol.

"No!" Jessie screamed as the man pointed at the menacing puppy. Pushing off the railing of the boat, she lunged, slamming into the man and knocking him off his feet. The pistol fired, and Jessie fell, rolling over the deck as the dog lunged, biting the man's hand with razor sharp teeth.

"Get off," the man yelled as someone else stepped from the wheelhouse, kicking the puppy and sending him rolling.

"You idiot." The second man grabbed the shooter by the neck. "You want to bring the cops?"

Jessie scooted to the puppy, grabbing his collar and slipping behind a bundle of diving gear.

"She has a dog. It attacked me." The first man struggled to his feet. "How'd she get a dog?"

"Who cares? Leave them be. We'll figure out what to do with her and the dog once we have the treasure."

Jessie's eyes filled with tears as Muttly shivered next to her, whimpering. She looked back at the two men arguing, her eyes trying to find some weakness. She knew if she couldn't find a way out of this, she would soon be dead. Biting her lip, Jessie held back her shock as her glance fell on a pair of rope-soled deck shoes. She looked up, trying to judge the size and shape of the second man. Mr. Burly with the gun seemed to be a total stranger, but recognition soon dawned. She knew two of her assailants, but how would she convince them she was ignorant of their identity? The only chance she had of getting out of this alive was by assuring them she didn't know who they were and that they could get away with all of their ill-gotten gains.

Jessie gathered the puppy close, soothing him and checking him for injuries. “Shhh,” she whispered. Twisting her bound hands, she grasped the puppy’s leash. Slowly, she pushed herself to her feet using the side of the boat for support, teetering with the sway as it rocked on the waves.

“Look.” She swallowed when the two scuba swathed men on the deck looked at her. “I have money. Lots of it. My family will pay for my ransom. You don’t need to do anything rash.”

“Shut up.” the burly man spat.

“Isn’t this about money?” Jessie tried to force confidence into her tone. “I’m not a danger to you. I can’t even see who you are under your suits and masks. You can put me in a skiff, and let me and the dog drift back to shore. We can set up a drop, and I’ll get you the money.” Jessie’s heart raced and she pleaded silently that the men would take her offer.

The engines slowed, and the tiny guide light flickered off as the third man slipped from the wheelhouse. “Money. You can’t imagine what kind of money we’re talking about here.” his voice drifted on the night, soft, with a lilting tone. “We’ve made millions with the salvage operation, but what’s below...” he shook his head... “the gold we’ve been pulling from this site is worth more than you can imagine.” He pushed his two companions aside, stepping close. “We don’t need to turn any of it over to the government. Once this gold is melted down, it will be untraceable, and we can all live like kings.”

Jessie cringed at the tone of the man’s voice. Once, it had been soothing, a nice contrast to the sun and waves, but now the note of menace made her blood run cold.

“I’m still no threat to you.” Her fingers curled in the leash, keeping Muttly close.

“I’m not going to be run off this wreck by some nosey girl who doesn’t know her place.” The man took a step closer, and Mutt growled. “I have plans, and if taking you out gets me what I want, what’s one more death?” He reached out, shoving

Jessie who fell to the deck, landing painfully on her shoulder. Muttley barked, but the man stepped forward aiming a kick that the dog dodged.

"Shhh." Jessie pulled Mutt close. "I won't be any trouble."

"Get moving." the man stepped back, turning to his companions. "We're already late, and we have a long night."

Jessie cowered against the stern of the boat, her cheek resting against the steel bulkhead as she held Muttley close.

The men all moved, grabbing the dive gear, nets, and baskets. The man in the rope-soled shoes turned, looking at Jessie, a dark shadow in the blackness of night.

She opened her mouth, wanting to call out to him to try to convince him, but he disappeared around the front of the wheelhouse as the other two went over the side. The sound of a winch being lowered growled softly over the waves.

Buzz twisted, seeing the tugboat stop and drop anchor. He was too close to shore to make out what was happening to the boat. With nearly a quarter mile between him in his goal, Buzz felt his heart race. Clouds filled the night, obscuring the stars, plunging him into darkness until the turn of the lighthouse lamp flickered out over the water. The lens was focused further out to sea, and his skiff floated dark and silent on the waves. Something surged in the man, and he turned the rowboat toward the dark silhouette of the boat. If Jessie was dead, they hadn't tossed her body over the side, yet. A glimmer of hope filled his heart as he rowed toward the boat. Approaching from behind, he wouldn't be seen. The sound of a winch spinning and the splash of divers made him turn, watching as two inky figures switched on underwater lamps and began to descend.

"Jessie." His heart pounded as he moved the skiff toward the dark tug. If two divers were overboard that meant that only one criminal remained aboard.

Rowing toward the back of the black tugboat, Buzz moved far enough away that his skiff might not be noticed. A shadow moved at the front of the boat, managing the winch lines, and Buzz breathed. His deduction had been correct, only one person was left manning the winch. Pulling his shirt over his head, Buzz slipped out of his shoes and took a deep breath. Leaning to one side, Buzz let the rowboat tip as he slipped into the black, endless depths of the ocean. The cool waves engulfed him, and he gasped as his head broke above the water. Reaching down, he looped the rowboat's line around his ankle and began to swim.

Slow, even strokes brought him to the tugboat, and Buzz pulled the rope from his ankle, tying the little skiff to the big, flat-bottomed workhorse. Waves dashed him as he struggled for a hold on the bigger boat. His fingers gripping the seam of the metal plates, Buzz began pulling himself up the side of the boat. Fingernails snapped, but he didn't feel the pain, as an arm finally fell over the thick rubber bumper, and he pulled himself up and over the side.

A whimper caught his ear as he slithered onto the deck, gasping.

"Jessie," he whispered, rolling to his stomach and pushing himself upright. Bent nearly double, he scanned the black deck."Jessie."

Something wet poked at his ankle, and Buzz bent, rubbing Muttley's ears. "Jessie."

"Here." Her voice was barely audible over the noise from the winch.

She was alive. Buzz sagged with relief, moving quickly in the direction of her voice, the puppy crowding him.

The puppy bounced, and Buzz looked down, following the mutt to where Jessie lay on the deck, a darker shadow in the night.

"Are you hurt?" His hands ran up her ankles and over her body, stopping at her face.

"No." Jessie shook her head. "I'm tied with cable ties."

"Be still." Buzz rummaged in the pocket of his shorts, pulling out a knife then moving his hands until he found her wrist.

"Buzz." Jessie sounded chagrined. "It's Crumm. Crumm and Allen. I don't know who the other guy is."

"Shh." Buzz hushed her. "Let's get out of here."

"But they killed Brad." Jessie sniffed. "They found the treasure, and all the rest of this is a way of hiding their activities. I think the salvage scam was a sideline."

"Jessie. Keep your voice down. We can talk about this later. The police are on their way. We need to get out of here, and let them figure it out."

Buzz stood a little taller as flashing lights appeared on the island. "Come on."

The sound of the winch spooling caught his ear, and he looked forward.

A helicopter buzzed overhead, and a light shimmered onto the deck.

The man at the front rushed to the wheelhouse. The clunk of an anchor chain screeched, lifting the heavy hook as he started the engine and pushed the throttle.

"He's running." Buzz shouted over the roar of the engine, jerking the knife through the strap on Jessie's ankles. "We need to go."

"No. Stop him." Jessie squinted as the helicopter lowered, and sprays of water lashed the boat.

Buzz helped her to her feet, trying to lead her over the swells, but she broke loose, rushing for the wheelhouse.

Buzz jumped up, racing after her, the puppy on his heels.

"Crumm, stop." Jessie shouted, grabbing the door frame as the boat hit a wave head on. "You can't get away."

Buzz skidded to a stop, water from the rotor blades dousing him.

"Stop!" He shouted, watching the man wheel.

"You can't get away." Jessie yelled. "Give yourself up."

"It wasn't supposed to be like this." the man yanked his scuba hood off, wheeling and exposing the face of their trusted museum guide. "No one was supposed to get hurt."

The boat rocked and swayed, bashing over breakers.

"I'm sure if you turn yourself in it will be easier for you," Jessie spoke. "Please, no one else needs to get hurt."

A loudspeaker blared from above. "Stop." Chopper blades beat the air as the boat shuddered. "Stop." The unseen speaker shouted again as the tug rose high on a wave, slamming down with a screech of steel.

Buzz grabbed Jessie, snatching the puppy from the deck as the boat heeled hard to port.

"Turn it off!" he yelled over screeching metal. "We've run aground."

The tug listed further, engines roaring as the propellers broke from the water.

"Help!" Crumm screamed as he tipped, sliding into the side of the wheelhouse.

"Jump," Buzz yelled, dragging Jessie and the puppy with him as the dark water swallowed them.

The engines sputtered as Buzz swam, using one arm to hold Mutt as he struggled toward the back of the boats. The water was illuminated as the chopper flashed powerful spotlights on the wreck.

Jessie swam hard at his side, and Buzz focused on getting to the skiff. The little boat, battered by the breakers, slipped around the side of the tugboat. Buzz tossed Muttley into the rowboat, then grabbed Jessie's arm, pushing her up as his head slipped beneath the waves. Sharp rocks bit into his arms as he surfaced, a wave slamming him into the side of the skiff.

"Here." Jessie reached over the side, grasping his arms and pulling.

Buzz looked up, brown eyes intense as his hands grasped the wooden rim of the skiff and hauled himself over.

Breathing hard, he collapsed onto the deck. "Get the rope," he huffed.

Fingers straining, Jessie untied the knot at the bow of the row boat that was holding them to the doomed tugboat.

Buzz waved the chopper off, squinting into the glaring light as he pointed at the tug.

Lines dropped from the helicopter, and two divers dropped into the sea, swimming hard toward the tug.

Buzz sat up, taking a seat in the boat and grabbing the oars as the little boat bobbed and teetered in the waves. The back of the rowboat pitched, turning toward the side of the tugboat, and Buzz pulled. Fear gripped his heart as he strained against the waves and the shoals that tried to crash his skiff into the ruined tug.

Gritting his teeth, he pulled with all his might until the boat inched away.

"They've got Crumm!" Jessie shouted over the roar of the waves and the churn of the chopper.

Buzz glanced up, still pulling at the oars as he broke from the swirl of the shoal into smoother water. One of the Coast Guard divers hooked a line to the limp form of Crumm, waiting until he was hefted into the chopper before turning to look at Buzz.

"Wave them off." Buzz said wearily, his arms working rhythmically as he skimmed the waves.

Jessie raised her arms, waving them frantically and then giving a thumbs up.

The divers grasped a line, clipping on as the helicopter turned, heading back to shore as they lifted the rescue crew from the water.

Buzz watched as Jessie flopped crossed legged on the hard bench seat of the old boat. His arms were numb with effort, but he continued to pull the skiff, drifting over the waves. He finally caught a wave that lifted it, driving it toward the beach.

"You okay?" he huffed.

"I am now." Jessie gripped the seat as they rose, riding the wave. Buzz pulled hard, and the bottom of the boat caught sand, slowing and cutting into the beach. Before he could release the oars, Jessie hopped over the side, slogging through the waves and pulling the boat out of the water.

Buzz sagged, his arms feeling like rubber. Rising, he grabbed the puppy, now trying to leap overboard as well. Cradling Muttley in numb arms, he staggered to the beach, collapsing in the sand.

Chapter 11

Lights flashed red and blue as the lighthouse blasted a gold beam on the water. Jessie collapsed beside Buzz. Muttley crowded between them, and she let the tears fall. “Thank you, God.” She sighed. “Thank you.”

A hand, wet and shaking, reached over and took hers as she and Buzz tried to fill their lungs with air. Something warm trickled over her hand, and Buzz flinched. “Your hands?” She looked up, shocked at his battered fingers.

“I’m all right.” Buzz nodded toward the water, and they turned to watch the action over the Atlantic.

Over the water, the chopper turned, spotlights searching.

“They’ll be waiting when the other two surface,” Buzz huffed.

“Won’t they just swim away?” Jessie looked at her friend.

“They have to surface when they run out of air.” Buzz dropped an arm over her shoulders.

“How did you get the police here so fast?” Jessie closed her eyes, clinging to his hand. A feeling of safety and well-being filled her heart.

“I called Paul.” A ragged chuckle rolled from her friend.

"Are you two always this much trouble?" A familiar voice called, and Jessie struggled to sit up.

"Good to hear ya, Jones." Buzz didn't move, the wet sand sinking around him.

A blanket fell over Jessie's shoulders, and she pulled it tight with one hand, tugging on Buzz with the other.

"Yes, they're always this much trouble." a craggy voice mingled with the crash of waves.

"Higgie?" Officer Jones turned, dropping a blanket on Buzz's chest.

Jessie got to her knees, tugging on the hand in hers and making Buzz sit up. "Paul?" she said, struggling to her feet as Buzz groaned.

Jessie tugged again, and Buzz managed to stand, the puppy whining as they turned to face the newcomer.

"I can tell this lot belongs to you." Jones, reaching out to shake Paul's hand as he trudged down to the beach.

"My nephew and his friend seem to have a knack for finding trouble" Paul Higgins slouched to the officer shaking his hand. "Been a while, Jones."

Jessie looked between the two men. Paul Higgins, Buzz's uncle and a retired police detective from Macon, Georgia, grinned. His white hair, ruffled and windswept, was back-lit by police lights.

Paul, nearly as tall as Buzz, tugged the blanket from him and draped it around his younger counterpart's shoulders. "I called in some other favors." He jabbed his thumb behind him, indicating the small bell-chopper sitting on a patch of grass. He patted Buzz on the shoulder, glancing at the soggy dog. "Yours?"

Buzz shook his head, shooting a grin at Jessie.

"Mine." She sagged, shaking her head. "I can't let him go now."

Paul draped an arm around her shoulders. "Come on. Let's get you checked out."

Jones glanced back at the water, and Jessie cringed when she caught a glimpse of the once-rugged tugboat getting battered by the waves.

The radio on Jones' shoulder crackled, and the muffled voice made Jessie strain to listen."

"Albatros one has contact." the radio crackled, but the words were not clear.

"Looks like your divers are up." Jones grinned.

Together, everyone walked to an ambulance, the EMTs forcing Jessie and Buzz to take a seat on the bumper in the pool of warm lights.

"You two look like a couple of drowned ship rats." Jones teased. "Are you up to giving a statement?"

An EMT gave the tall man a hard look, examining Buzz. "I'm alright," the young officer sighed, waving the short woman away.

"No, you aren't." The woman looked at his blood and sand encrusted legs then his ruined fingernails. "You both need to get to a hospital."

"Not yet." Buzz said, he glanced at Jessie, and she nodded.

The woman shook her head and reached for a bottle of saline, starting to clean the sand away.

"We'll see about getting a statement," Jones nodded, pulling a notepad from his pocket.

Another officer walked over, joining the gathering as Coast Guard boats converged on a spot of water illuminated by the chopper.

"You young folks sure got in a pickle now didn't ya?" An older man approached, wearing a faded ZZ Top t-shirt and shorts. "Paul."

Paul turned, shaking hands. "This is Jim Rivers." He turned back to Jessie. "He's a good man. We need to know everything."

Buzz leaned against Jessie as the EMT addressed his injuries and began to tell the whole tale.

***

Jessie leaned back on the lounge chair, the first rays of the sun washing over her as a new day dawned.

Beside her, the puppy sighed, sprawled on a beach towel in deep sleep.

"Are you sure you're all right?" she asked, turning to look at her companion.

"The doc fixed me up." Buzz looked at his legs, drawing Jessie's gaze.

She cringed, seeing the scrapes covered in antibiotic salve. One deeper cut had been glued back together and covered with a white bandage. His fingers were wrapped, but he seemed to not feel much pain.

"I'm glad you went to the hospital after everything last night." Jessie smirked.

"I don't think either of us had a choice once the detective was done with us." Buzz grinned. "Uncle Paul would have hog-tied both of us and dragged us to the ER." He chuckled then shook his head. "I still can't believe Crumm was involved in this mess," Buzz said, resting his head against the chair.

"The sound of footsteps behind them made them turn, and Jessie smiled at Cheryl who walked across the sand, carrying a tray of drinks and snacks.

"You two look like you need this." She gave Jessie a sad look. "I'm glad you're okay." She settled the tray on a small table, then plopped into a chair, pouring coffee. Her smile was tired, but her eyes were full of relief.

"I didn't plan on running off like that," Jessie dropped her gaze. "It kinda just happened."

Cheryl handed Buzz a mug, then grasped Jessie's hand. "It all worked out." She poured another cup of coffee, adding sugar and cream and handing it to Jessie. "Now spill."

Over breakfast, Buzz and Jessie recounted the events of the night. Jessie shivered at the close call. She hadn't been seeking danger, but finding answers seemed to be a risky business.

"But who was the third man?" Cheryl scowled, shaking her head. "I can't believe that rat, Allen kissed me." She sat up, fixing plates of fruit and handing them around.

"That's right, he kissed you.' Buzz sipped from his mug, watching the girls.

Cheryl blushed, shoving a bowl of fruit and yogurt into his hands.

"I'm sorry, Cher." Jessie took the bowl her friend handed her. "I think he did that to stop you from asking questions."

"Well, yeah." Cheryl squirmed, her yellow capris and dandelion top brightening as the sun rose. "I liked Brad better, anyway." She slouched. "I'm afraid where men are concerned, I have no luck."

"Be patient, Cher." Jessie's words were kind. "You're always telling me you don't have time for a relationship, anyway."

Cheryl turned, smiling at her friend. "So right. Now who was criminal number three?"

Buzz sipped his coffee, setting it back on the table. "He was a part of the salvage crew." He shook his head. "Apparently, the legit salvage operation led to all of this. Allen was working with a crew, pulling boats out of trouble and number three, as you put it, was the one fixing them. When Allen was diving on a storm-wrecked salvage off the point, he found the AnnaSwift. He didn't know what it was at first, but he figured it out when he came back."

Jessie turned, looking at Buzz. "How did you get all of this info?" She raised a brow, smiling. "Paul?"

"You know it." Buzz shook his head. "He's still at the station. Rivers made him a special liaison since I'm still..." he shrugged. "You know."

"Okay." Cheryl drew their attention back to her questions. "So, Allen found the wreck. Then what?"

"He approached Crumm who put two and two together and demanded full partnership."

"But what about the ghost ship?" Cheryl shook her head, her blonde hair swishing in the breeze as the sky turned gold.

"Since number three was the one fixing boats for them. " Buzz smiled, and Jessie watched him closely. "Allen and Crumm wanted to keep any focus from falling on what they were doing; so they rigged the tugboat with a projector that looked like the ghost of the AnnaSwift."

"That's morbid," Cher sighed. "I mean, people died in that wreck."

"So, they used the ghost ship as a ruse. It was supposed to be a distraction, nothing more." Jessie spoke, shaking her head in disgust.

"The hitch was that with the ship making appearances, more treasure seekers and glory-hounds started showing up." Buzz looked at Jessie. "When big, expensive boats started getting wrecked, and the insurance either wrote them off as totaled or wouldn't pay, claiming owner-fault, the salvage crew would bring in the boats and get the money from what they fixed."

"It paid for their treasure hunt." Jessie added, looking at her friend.

"Pretty slick." Cheryl looked at Buzz and Jessie. "Devious."

"They had already made millions on the salvage." Buzz said. "That's why they killed Brad. The night he rowed out to their dive sight, he either figured out they had found the AnnaSwift or that they were creating the salvage problem."

"I think he figured out the salvage scam, too." Cheryl looked sad. "I got a delayed email from him yesterday. Boy, did that freak me out." She shook her head. "It was an article about the 'Wreckers' in Key West. The gist is that a crew of salvage operators set up false markers causing ships to wreck. They'd then swoop in and either raid the ship or salvage it, claiming most of the profit from the action."

"Oh!" Jessie's eyes went wide. "That's terrible."

"People died." Cheryl said, looking at her nearly-empty bowl.

Jessie turned to look at Buzz. "I hate to say it, but I was starting to suspect the police here. I don't want to be skeptical, but they didn't seem to take us seriously."

" I get it." Buzz turned his eyes sad. "To them, we're some crazy kids with vivid imaginations. I'm a police officer on admin leave, and you two are 'hysterical girls'." He shrugged.

"That's how they'd see it. Ships wreck. Savannah has a history, and foolish people get into trouble. Why would that be suspicious?"

Jessie nodded. "I see what you mean." She settled back into her chair as the sun rose, shimmering like a gold coin on the water. The soft ripple of the waves on the sand was a soothing song as a new day glowed into being, bringing with it new hope, light, and grace.

***

Buzz sat on his bed, pulling his laptop onto his knees, and flinching when he bumped a deep scratch.

His eyes were tired, and his body ached from the effort of the night before. He rolled his shoulders, feeling the pain ripple down his arms as the laptop booted up.

Sunlight poured through the window of his room, a warm glow of morning as his parents began to rise.

Paul had sent him a text saying he'd stop by later and would be riding home to Macon with them.

Buzz looked up at the sun on the water. The day was warming, but he was thankful that he and his friends had survived to see this day dawn. He was glad the condo bedrooms were off the side of the main area so that he could see the sea.

The screen flashed to life, and Buzz clicked on a file. A picture flashed on the screen, and a sad smile tugged at his lips. An image of Jessie dressed in a peach satin dress filled the computer. She had turned, looking over her shoulder at him, a bright smile on her lips as he'd snapped the shot. The young woman was elegant, beautiful, and sophisticated in this shot. She looked older here, with the odd 1930's hairstyle framing her face. This picture had been his private torment, and as he gazed at it again, he knew that when he'd been avoiding seeing Jessie over the past year, it hadn't cured what ailed him.

It was that night nearly a year ago that Buzz had lost his heart to a girl stepping into womanhood. He had tried to bury the love that had bloomed in his soul, but no matter how long he stayed away, the girl tugged at his heart and his mind.

Jessie was everything he could ever ask for, but at twenty-one, she didn't know what her life was about, let alone her own heart. She was too young.

Buzz chuckled, he was only two years older than she was, but he felt much older. His time at the police academy, and the darker side of his job were taking a toll on him. He couldn't expect Jessie to have feelings for him. He wasn't in a place to even consider a relationship.

Closing the computer, he dropped it on the nightstand and collapsed into bed, the warmth of the sun caressing his skin. Jessie had told him she missed him, and the thought gave life to a tiny blossom of hope. Could he be her friend? Could he keep his heart in check while building that friendship? Sleep overwhelmed him, his weary body surrendering as his heart surged toward the girl that had stolen it. Only time would tell if a friendship could be more. If all she had to give him was friendship, Buzz would take it. She was too special to leave behind.

***

Macon seemed empty as Buzz jogged through his neighborhood that weekend. He was returning to work on Monday, with no black mark on his record. He had shoved much of his anger and discontent down deep, his feet pounding the pavement as sweat rolled down his bare chest. His phone vibrated, and he twisted it on his arm, smiling when he saw Jessie's name flash.

"Hey." He stopped, pulling a damp cloth from his neck and mopping his face, breathing hard.

"Hey." Jessie's voice was cheerful. "When are your next few days off?"

"Off?" Buzz gaped. "I start back to work on Monday." He wiped his head, still unsure if he was relieved by the verdict.

"So you have Friday through Sunday off?" Jessie giggled.

"Yes." A hint of suspicion slipped into his tone.

"We're diving on the AnnaSwift on Saturday."

Buzz listened to the silence on the end of the line.

"Wow." he breathed.

"Can you come?" Jessie's voice seemed serious.

"Yeah. I can't believe they're letting you do that already."

"We're the first." Jessie said. Cher and I did our diving course, and our instructor will dive with us."

"Jessie, I'm not certified." He didn't think he could dive without training, though he had some knowledge of the activity.

"Get back over here to Savannah. We'll get it done, and you can join us."

Buzz blew out a breath. What would it be like to dive the wreck that had caused so much grief? He nodded. It would be nice to wrap up this mystery by seeing the cause of much of it. He smiled, and he would get to see Jessie again.

"Yeah. Okay. I'll see you tonight."

"Are you okay staying with me and Cher?" Jessie asked, waiting.

"It's only for a couple of days, so sure." Something fluttered in his chest. Cheryl would be a good chaperone and they could all catch up.

"Don't worry." Jessie chuckled. "We have a chaperone."

"Who?"

"You'll see." Jessie laughed. "See you tonight."

Dive

Jessie tipped backward over the side of the boat, her air tanks splashing and dragging her down as she held her nose. She popped back up, bobbing by the dive boat, giving the O.K. sign.

Beside her, Cheryl bobbed, pushing her hair out of her face as Buzz popped up, shaking his head and splashing them.

"All good?" their guide asked.

Jessie nodded, noting when her friends placed hands over heads in the dive sign for good.

"Okay." The man adjusted his mask, turning to Cheryl. "You're with me," he grinned, placing his respirator in his mouth.

Cheryl nodded, and he turned, pointing two fingers between Jessie and Buzz.

With another okay sign, the guide turned and dove, Cheryl following.

Buzz looked at Jessie, reaching out and taking her hand as they dove deeper into the ocean.

The water closed over them and Jessie kicked, grateful for Buzz's grip on her wrist, as his more powerful stroke would outpace her. Sun sparkled through the water, and a few silverfish darted by. The crackle of creel and other plankton filled her ears, as she continued, following the bubbles of Cheryl and the guide.

They paused, holding a dive rope for several moments as they headed into deeper water. Jessie blew out her ears as she bobbed, keeping an eye on her companions as the water grew murky and dark.

Resuming the dive, they slipped through the water, the blue light of the sun, turning the water a deep green as visibility diminished. Jessie squeezed her dive-buddy's hand, kicking along the dive line. She knew that police and salvage divers had been to the site, but the wreck hadn't been opened to dive operators, yet.

Silence engulfed her as Buzz squeezed back, and the light fluttered, casting shadows. A shark darted away, turning a white belly and smooth jaw, tail thrashing.

Jessie shivered, continuing into the depths, here breathing the only sound in her ears. A shadow began to emerge.-A sharp, corral encrusted bow, broken, and dark, like a sleeping behemoth formed in front of them. Jessie paused, pulling back, suspended in the water, Buzz at her side. The outline of the ship, though broken, was clear. It lay half-way upright in the silt at the bottom of the ocean. A few fish darted around the sides, and Jessie felt the weight of it on her heart.

Buzz squeezed her hand, and they started forward again, only the sound of their breathing heard above the silence of the deep. The guide turned, following the edge of the ship's rail. The hull nearly buried in the dust of time, rose only a few feet above the bottom. The sand had been disturbed in several places where whatever treasures remained had been retrieved for preservation. The men who had tried to raid this timeless tomb would stand trial for their crimes.

Dark rocks held the ship where she lay, gripping it like the teeth of some underwater beast. Motion caught Jessie's eye, and she turned to follow the guide's pointing finger.

The small group dove, edging closer to the murky ocean floor, careful not to disturb the layer of silt and obscure visibility.

Jessie tipped her head toward the mound of smooth dark rocks, her feet up and head down. Buzz moved a little closer pulling her down as he waved his hand over the smooth rounded stones. As the silt of decades floated away, the first ghastly grin of a skull appeared. Jessie's hand tightened on her buddy's, feeling strength from Buzz.

Though long dead, the empty eyes implored. Perhaps now, after all this time, the silent souls who had gone down with this ship could finally rest in peace.

Floating in the silence of the sea, Jessie thought of the injustices in life. Her heart turned, her eyes seeking the light from the sun as she realized her calling and offered a prayer for strength from above.

The End.

few feet above the bottom. The sand had been disturbed in [illegible]

[illegible]

www.ingramcontent.com/pod-product-compliance
Lightning Source LLC
LaVergne TN
LVHW050540160826
845677LV00011B/2109

* 9 7 9 8 8 0 6 2 5 4 3 6 9 *